the House at Number 10

Two of Dorothy Johnston's novels — *One For The Master* and *Ruth* – have been shortlisted for the Miles Franklin Award, and her award-winning crime novels *The Trojan Dog* and *The White Tower* are being published in North America by St Martins Press. She lives in Canberra with her husband and two children.

By the same author

Tunnel Vision
Ruth
Maralinga My Love
One For The Master
The Trojan Dog
The White Tower

the House at Number 10

Dorothy Johnston

Wakefield
Press

Wakefield Press
1 The Parade West
Kent Town
South Australia 5067
www.wakefieldpress.com.au

First published, 2005

Designed by Liz Nicholson, designBITE
Typeset by Ryan Paine, Wakefield Press
Printed and bound by Hyde Park Press

National Library of Australia
Cataloguing-in-publication entry

Johnston, Dorothy, 1948–   .
The house at number 10.

ISBN 1 86254 683 5.

I. Title.

A823.3

Publication of this book was assisted by the
Commonwealth Government through the
Australia Council, its arts funding and advisory body.

For my daughter Helen

'The garden is a personal gathering of nature,
and the room is the beginning of architecture.'
Louis Kahn

Introduction to the Side Room

He was taking an age to come.

Sophie could move her legs and hips, did move them, knees balanced on the large bed, propped up at one corner with a wedge of newspaper. But he was taking an age to come.

She had her back to him. It was a hot night. There was a fan in a corner, but it was still hot – a close, sticky heat, unusual for Canberra. Soon they would have airconditioning in all the rooms. Sophie could hear voices, faintly, through the wall between the room she was in and the next, not loud enough to hear what was being said. She wondered if the renovations would make the walls thicker.

The balance and position – it was important to get these right. Sophie felt her thigh muscles tighten as she knelt symmetrically on the bed, hands wide for balance, fingers splayed, arms straight but not stiff. Locked elbows made it harder to change position. She could move better with the spring, the possibility of give still there, in joints as well as muscles.

It had taken a while to find the best position, and then manoeuvre into, or insist on it. It was a matter of small professional pride to Sophie that she'd done so. The one she favoured was known as doggy. She had at first found the word and what it conjured up distasteful, but talking to Kirsten, listening to Kirsten, was making her think differently.

She liked to face the wall and closed curtains of the side room, but not to be too close to them. This, also, was important.

The walls and ceiling needed painting. Watermarks from years of leaks travelled down and out across them. In the glow from the lamp, on the table by the bed, these marks sprang towards her. She stared at their lines and colours, some dark, some faded almost into disappearing. She moulded them into shapes that she could recognise, liking the way the marks changed depending on the light, the way their contours altered with the evening.

He came at last and pulled away. Sophie felt her buttocks shrink, not quite able to believe in their good fortune. He was panting, his breath slowing. Sometimes they overdid themselves, especially on summer nights. Once Kirsten, in a fit of rage, had thrown water over one and soaked the bed. Marshall had been furious.

Sophie knew her face was blank. Sometimes clients, when she turned to face them, willing them to get up off the bed, get dressed, had a look of apology, sometimes they even apologised in words, and this she could not bear. The ones who became quickly, simply, self-sufficient, wanting *nothing more from her ever* now the agreed exchange had been completed – these ones Sophie recognised, though she did not respect them. They answered her desire for clean lines of division, endings that were neat.

She took the condom from the client and dropped it in a small metal bin, plastic-lined, beside the bed. She stood up, reached for her sarong, and wished him goodnight.

It was not yet ten-thirty. Quickly and efficiently, Sophie knotted her sarong under her left armpit, shut the side room door behind her, and walked to the kitchen at the back of the house. In a little while, she would return to change the sheets and tidy the room, but she'd earnt a few minutes' relaxation first.

Relieved to find the kitchen empty, she opened the oven door of an old, but carefully cleaned stove, and deposited the money from the sweaty client in a wooden box that already held a satisfying pile of notes. Then she fetched a glass of water from the fridge and settled herself into an armchair that faced large windows, looking out onto a quiet Canberra night.

The First Day and the Second Day

Sophie pressed her right forefinger on the doorbell, then waited a few moments, hearing only silence on the other side of a door which had once been painted red. Most of the paint had peeled off, leaving brown and grey wood that she felt might crumble under determined fingers, riddled, as it was, with grooves and dusty hollows. Yet the lock was new and sturdy, and the bell, though it seemed silent and had not brought footsteps, new as well.

She frowned at the door, which remained determinedly opaque, and when, after a few more moments, nobody had come to open it, she made her right hand into a fist and knocked.

The woman who answered Sophie's knock looked about sixteen, and wore black tights under a long, pale-green men's shirt. The shirt was far too big in the shoulders, yet she wore it comfortably, with the sleeves rolled up. Her face was oval, smooth. She had good skin. Resigned to a camouflage of freckles, an inability to tan, good skin was a feature Sophie noticed. Blonde hair in a ponytail swung behind the young woman. The smile she offered was distracted, and Sophie's first thought was that she'd forgotten all about the phone call.

They'd exchanged names on the phone. Elise repeated hers now and said, 'Come in.'

She shut the door carefully behind Sophie, and led the way down a dim corridor to the back of the house. Tracy Chapman sang behind another door, which Elise pushed open to reveal a room full of late afternoon light.

Sophie blinked. Disoriented and half blinded, she stood just inside the doorway. Windows, which had been cleaned so thoroughly that they seemed themselves to be a source of light, faced west.

Elise raised her voice against the singer's and said, 'Kirsten. This is Sophie.'

Sophie looked for the owner of the name, and found her half hidden in an oversized armchair, nodding her head in time to the music, which Elise, moving swiftly to a CD player, switched off.

As Sophie's eyes continued to adjust, she noted that a large, bare wooden table took up a good third of the room, that the armchair facing the window was covered with a tartan rug, and that a foam mat was laid out on the floor.

Elise began rolling up the mat. The woman called Kirsten was smoking in the armchair. She had dark hair above tanned shoulders. Smoke circled the chair's back and made its way, with the lethargy of midsummer, out the window. The woman turned around, but slowly, slowly, as if there never would be any need to hurry. Her expression, which was veiled but curious, suggested that all the rest of the afternoon remained to be enjoyed – the window and the armchair, and the music and the cigarette.

'Put that fag out, Kirst,' Elise said, standing the mat up behind the door, 'and come over here.'

Kirsten did as she was bidden, and they sat around the table, which suddenly seemed much too big for the room. Sophie smiled at the two women facing her. They were the real thing, weren't they? She was a little surprised that it didn't show. Elise was older than she'd first appeared. Her clear blue gaze met Sophie's directly. Kirsten looked as though she might be pushing thirty, with smudged, shadowy rings around brown eyes that studied Sophie, who looked away.

She went on smiling, but began to feel nervous. She reminded herself that this was her adventure – coming across the ad under positions vacant, no name, just a phone number. Putting it aside, then coming back to it a few days later – telling herself not to be stupid, that she couldn't possibly. But then she'd given in – to curiosity, to seeing for herself, to the enticement of making some fast money behind her ex-husband's back. And now, sitting opposite Elise and Kirsten, whose fingers moved while the rest of her body remained quite still, Sophie congratulated herself on having got this far. What harm was there in asking questions? None.

She opened her mouth. 'How much would you make, on an average night?'

Kirsten's lips parted. She exchanged the swiftest of glances with Elise.

Elise spoke levelly, but there was a hint of laughter in her voice. 'That depends,' she said. 'There's pay weeks and there's off-pay weeks.' She raised a pale, plucked eyebrow. 'Pay week – Friday, Saturday – you might take home five or six hundred.'

'Each of you?' asked Sophie.

Elise nodded. Blonde hair moved against a shirt whose softness and colour were soothing to the eye.

'And the other nights?'

'Off-pay week, half that.'

'It's swings and roundabouts,' said Kirsten, with another lightning glance at Elise, who began explaining, 'Once we can advertise properly, once the law's been changed – '

Sophie interrupted to ask, 'Have you had any trouble with the police?'

'None,' Elise said. 'They're waiting to see which way the vote goes.'

'Which way do you think it will?'

'Oh, for sure it will be legal. That's what Marshall says.'

Elise answered Sophie's next question before she could ask it.

'Marshall owns the house.' There was an undercurrent of disquiet in her voice.

'You need him for protection?'

'Yeah. Maybe.' Kirsten laughed. 'His own.'

'Shut up Kirst,' Elise said comfortably. 'It's early days,' she went on, with another look at Sophie. 'We've only been open for a bit over a month, and we've had to rely on word of mouth.'

'Did you start the business together?'

Elise nodded, but Sophie sensed the displeasure, or disquiet, again. She felt the ground shift subtly and rearrange itself beneath her, though the table, when she pressed her left hand down on it, was solid as could be.

Kirsten said, 'I'd get rid of that ring, if I were you.'

'Excuse me?'

'Customers don't like it. Reminds them of their wives.'

'Oh,' said Sophie. She wasn't sure why she kept on wearing her wedding ring, since she and Andrew had been separated for three months.

Elise asked, 'Would you like some juice?'

'Give the girl a Cooper's.'

'Cooper's Lite for Kirsten,' Elise said, 'but she's giving up booze and fags tomorrow.'

'Any day now,' Kirsten replied with an easy lilt, reaching for her cigarettes.

Sophie said thank you to juice.

Elise straightened from the fridge holding two bottles, then turned back for glasses. All her movements were athletic, suggesting reserves of energy which no-one had yet tapped.

Sophie realised that she was thirsty. She avoided looking in Kirsten's direction while she drank.

'Where have you worked before?' Elise asked.

Sophie began to talk about her job with the public service, before Tamsin was born, wrenching herself with an effort back to the single woman she'd once been, then realising this was not what Elise meant.

'Nowhere,' she said abruptly. Kirsten laughed again. She began ripping the cellophane from her cigarette packet into slivers, using a long, shapely thumbnail that was somehow at odds with the rest of her appearance.

Elise asked Sophie where she lived, and the question of experience, which Sophie lacked, which surely they had noted at first glance, was left to dissolve into the air between them, a light veil rather than a hurdle or impediment, a veil which needed only a modest kiss of wind to lift aside.

'We should tell you a few things about ourselves,' Elise said. 'We don't do line-ups, for one thing.'

'Line-ups?' Sophie asked.

Kirsten explained. 'It's when you parade, and the punter picks one.'

'What do you do instead?'

'Take it in turns with the newcomers. You have your regulars, those who ask for you.'

There was a slight emphasis on 'you', which Sophie felt suddenly to be the most ambiguous of pronouns.

'If I didn't like the look of him, could I get you, or Elise?'

'If you like,' said Kirsten. 'We might be busy though.'

'What does Marshall do?'

'We've got rules. Five of them,' Kirsten said, as though this was the only reasonable answer. She told Sophie what they were, adding her own emphasis to the condom rule. 'Break it, and we'll strangle you with one.'

Sophie laughed. Kirsten and Elise did not.

'Tell her more about Marshall,' Kirsten said, flicking her lighter, and narrowing her eyes in the direction of the armchair.

Marshall was Elise's boyfriend. Neither woman wasted words in expanding on the house's owner, but offered them to Sophie in an oblique and teasing way, tossing details between themselves, and watching to see which ones she caught.

Aware that their assessment of her had moved into a new phase, the moment fast approaching when one of them would say yes, or no,

Sophie half absorbed the information. Marshall had big plans for the house. It would be remodelled inside out, after the laws were changed, and prostitution legal. Marshall was busy in Civic today, but would be there tomorrow. The balance of judgment shifted to make way for his opinion. Sophie's heart beat faster.

They asked her more questions about herself, and she described her marriage break-up, her four-year-old daughter Tamsin, how she'd found a nice place for the two of them to live, but not the job to pay for it. How she'd seen the ad.

'I have Tamsin for half the week. Whatever work I do would have to be fitted in round that.'

Kirsten smoked and listened. Elise nodded and said that flexible hours wouldn't be a problem. 'If you want to try out, that's cool with us,' she said.

Sophie swallowed the tremor in her throat.

'Did you bring anything to wear?' asked Kirsten.

'What now? Today?'

'Why not? You haven't got your daughter, have you?'

'No.'

'We open at six,' Elise said, putting Sophie on the spot and watching to see if, and how, she wriggled off it.

Sophie said, 'I could buy something to wear, I guess.' She paused. 'I'd like to see the bedrooms.'

Kirsten showed her, lighting one smoke from another, and hitching up the faded sarong that left her shoulders bare.

Kirsten stood in doorways, first of the front, and then the two side rooms, blowing smoke into the corridor, making no apology for tatty floral carpet, walls in need of paint, watermarks that mapped the ceilings. All of it, if Marshall had his way, would go.

'What's wrong with the bell?' asked Sophie.

'Overuse,' said Kirsten with a lazy smile. 'Marshall's getting a new one from Magnet-mart.' Out of Elise's hearing, she said his name with carefully controlled contempt.

'So.' She turned to Sophie with a raised, dark eyebrow. 'I can go over the prices with you, if you like.'

Sophie and Kirsten sat on the back step. This time, Sophie joined Kirsten in a beer. 'I'll never remember all of that,' she said.

'Of course you will.'

Kirsten smoked and stared out over a backyard that had been let go something dreadful. Tall dead grass, stooping heavily with seeds, obscured a path to a hills hoist, a single white garment rotating slowly on it in the breeze. Sophie watched it, framing a question that she decided not to ask just then. There were no trees or bushes in the yard, no plants that had been deliberately cultivated.

Sophie wondered what Kirsten had been looking at when Sophie walked into the kitchen and caught sight of her behind that drenching light.

There were prices to memorise, 'the spiel', Kirsten called it in a mocking voice.

'A G-string massage is fifty-eight,' Sophie repeated.

'They hear the fifty, not the eight. They think it's cheaper than it is.'

'What do they get for that, then?'

Kirsten told her.

'What if they want more, try to take more?'

'Say no,' Kirsten said. 'Listen, Sophie – the customer is always right? Forget it. Be sure they understand, then give them what they've paid for, not a pinch more.'

'What if they want me to spell it out?'

'Don't. It's against the law for them as well as you. Marshall sweet-talks the first-timers. Or he thinks he does. There aren't that many. Most know the ropes by the time they get to us. Go through the prices again if they want you to, but don't feel obliged to explain.'

'Doesn't Marshall take the money?'

'When he's here, and it's a regular who knows what he wants. Sometimes, with first-timers, he leaves it up to us, hoping we'll persuade them to pay more.'

Kirsten explained that, once the negotiations were completed, and the money handed over – 'Make sure you get it *before* he has his shower' – Sophie would need to concentrate on when, and how, to draw the line, and then make sure he was finished within half an hour.

'What do I do with the money?'

'Keep it in the room with you, if you like. Or bring it out to the kitchen while he's in the shower.'

'Where will I put it?'

'In the stove,' said Kirsten, as if this small fact was self-evident.

'What about change?'

'There's a jar of shrapnel, and some small notes. I should be here, if you get in a muddle.'

Sophie repeated the five rules under her breath. Showers obligatory. No drugs. No line-ups, and no clients in the kitchen. And condoms a must.

Elise finished talking on the phone and came and stood behind Kirsten.

'However much the prick might offer you,' she said, 'however much you might be tempted. Don't.'

Of course, condoms could break. There could be accidents. Of course there were bastards and Sophie was bound to come across them. But for themselves, Elise made it clear, insofar as they were able to make rules, to dictate, the prohibition was absolute.

The phone rang again. Kirsten said, 'I'll get the next one.'

Here was another task – to entice custom, rather than wait for it to appear.

'One thing,' Sophie said. 'If I'll be using that small room on the side, I might just go in and open a window.'

Kirsten helped Sophie through her nervousness over the next few hours. She lent Sophie a sarong, and went with her to the Kingston shops to buy lingerie. But Kirsten could not possibly have known what would help Sophie most through her first night.

Sophie did not forget the prices, as, in some part of her mind not affected by stagefright, she'd been confident she wouldn't. She drew them forth and reproduced them perfectly, like a nursery rhyme learnt in infancy.

She showed her first customer into the side room and told him, 'A complete massage is a hundred dollars.'

The client nodded. He looked her up and down.

She had opened the front door to him and led him to the side room, wrinkling her nose at the stale smell that a few hours of open window hadn't quite dispelled. She tried not to let him see that she was scared. She guessed that it was far from his first time.

She had not stopped to take in much of him, outside. No potential customer wanted to stand on that porch and be scrutinised.

Understanding was swift, and Sophie thanked her lucky stars that she did not need to go through the price list. He knew what 'complete massage' meant. He had two fifties folded, ready, in the pocket of his jeans.

'You have to have a shower first,' she said.

He nodded, paying no attention to the room, while Sophie straightened clean sheets on the bed.

She suspected that this man knew the house's set-up and its rules, perhaps had been with both Elise and Kirsten. But he had not rejected her, had not asked for either of them.

She handed him a towel. He bent over to take it. Outside, the sun had set behind Black Mountain, but some fugitive ray of it glanced downwards on his hair.

Sophie sucked her breath in. It was Andrew's, her ex-husband's, colour, cowlick at the front, gentle waving at the nape.

'What did you say your name was?'

'I didn't, but it's Ian.'

'Mine's Sophie,' she said, feeling a strange, new possession of her name as she did so.

At the same time she thought, If he scarcely registers who I am, and where I might have come from, why should I care, after all?

He returned, easy and relaxed, the white towel wrapped around his middle.

'Do you want the lamp on?'

He said he didn't mind.

The neat sarong – clever Kirsten to have spare ones – slipped down without a fanfare. The sheets made a space wide as an undiscovered continent. Sophie lay in the middle of the bed and felt it rock unevenly, and thought, I will have to do something about that.

With her two strong hands she took the blond hair that the customer called Ian shared with her ex-husband and held it tight, for a long moment, while she stared at him. The hair was all there was by way of resemblance, but it was enough.

She handed him a condom and he rolled it expertly. Now, she thought, now, as grief at her failed marriage made barriers transparent, each one constructed of material so thin she could burst through it at will. Anger welled up, and resentment and self-pity. Blame struck out and swam through the lamplight towards this stranger who wore Andrew's hair.

He sweated on the sheets, and sighed with textbook satisfaction. He even thanked her, after he had put his jeans back on. He took out a small hand mirror and combed his yellow hair.

Narcissus, Sophie thought, smiling from the centre of the bed.

Leaving the glow of evening behind her in the side room, she walked with a light step back to the kitchen, to Kirsten smoking in the arm-chair, feeling, on her skin, the aftertaste of her first customer, already in his car and driving along Andover Street, away towards a night of his own.

Without turning around, Kirsten asked, 'How was it?'

And Sophie, not thinking about her reply, not knowing what words she would use until she heard them, but laughing with the rightness of them when she did, said, 'Piece of cake.'

Kirsten went on smoking, smiling to herself, offering no word of encouragement or praise, and no further questions either. And Sophie, hesitating, then walking over to the fridge where Elise had told her to help herself to juice and bottled water, felt the perfect rightness of this also.

The following afternoon, Sophie parked her car and walked to 10 Andover Street, a still-young woman, small and thin, with light-brown hair and freckles she did nothing to disguise, a woman passers-by would not turn to look at in the street. She carried a large shoulder bag that contained her purchase of the morning. Dust and resin from the dry summer rushed to meet her. Tree roots made the footpath buckle. She looked down and saw, with absolute, unnatural clarity, four ants carrying a huge desiccated leaf, and wondered at the effort and the teamwork. She looked up, and there was Marshall.

He stood on Number 10's front porch, waiting for her with an expression that suggested haste of any kind was not only unnecessary, but inelegant, and – she saw this from a distance, and it made a strong impression on her – with an enterprising watchfulness entirely his own. He was not a tall man, yet appeared tall to Sophie at that moment.

'Come on in,' he said.

Sophie climbed the crooked concrete steps, and followed Marshall into the house. She felt that her right to entry had been stamped from yesterday, but was aware, suddenly, indelibly, that she would also need to impress this man who turned to her, over his left shoulder, with a smile of ambiguous welcome.

He cleared magazines from a low coffee table to one side of the hallway, and indicated three plain chairs around it. This narrow space, these items of furniture, Sophie had barely taken in the day before.

He sat down next to her, spreading his legs in tight black jeans, so that Sophie noted just how tight they were. His black hair was spiked, and complemented by his body piercings.

He smiled as he told her his full name – Marshall Hegarty.

Sophie sat with her legs close together, thinking of the blue and brown sarong she had bought that morning. The small folds of material secreted in her bag were a comfort to her, as she braced herself to answer Marshall's questions.

He looked her up and down, and asked how old she was.

His eyelids flickered when she told him twenty-eight. She could give him – what? Four, five years? But Kirsten was older than she was, and Kirsten held her place in the house. She wondered if Elise and Kirsten were in the kitchen, or whether the house, behind their backs, was empty.

She kept her legs together, picturing the kitchen, and the side room where she'd spent much of the night before. Would Kirsten be sorry if Marshall sent her on her way? Would Elise argue with him? Sophie did not want to be dismissed by this pierced, olive-skinned, politely probing man.

She smiled and told him that the work would suit her. The hours were manageable, the pay attractive. She was sure she would get on well with Kirsten and Elise.

She was sure, watching Marshall respond to her smile with an expression that was courteous, but with a hint of mischief – it made his lip ring wiggle – that nothing she told him was news.

He said in a different, harder voice, 'You don't look the part. I told Elise – '

He chose to leave the sentence hanging. He held out a ringed hand, more a gesture of command, it seemed to Sophie, than one of meeting her halfway.

'What part is that?' she asked him.

Marshall frowned, as though her question had been designed to confuse.

But Sophie stood her shaky ground, and did not apologise for her looks, or promise to augment them. Rather, she uncrossed her legs, hidden beneath old, comfortable jeans. Mentally, she fingered the smooth cotton of her new sarong, though, now she'd met Marshall for herself, she wasn't sure he would approve.

She smiled again, opening her legs a fraction further, catching her breath, conscious that she was inviting the crossing of a boundary that might prove to be more hazardous than the front door.

Marshall looked and blinked. He had thick lids, Sophie noted, where the pigment was less dark, but more opaque.

'I can learn,' she said. 'I'd like to.'

Marshall blinked again. His eyes cleared. How could he turn such willingness aside?

He leant forward with an expansive gesture. 'I've got plans. All this will have to go.'

A wide sweep of his rings – the stones were reddish, golden brown – took in the shabby hallway, the ceiling cracks and water stains, down at heel furniture and dog-eared magazines.

'Fix the rooms up, make them nice, add a fourth one, get another girl. There's heaps of wasted space in this old tub.'

Marshall clenched his buttocks in their close-fitting jeans.

'I'm finding my way around this town. There's not much to it. A good architect, one with a bit of originality, you know? I've been given a few names.'

'I know an architect,' said Sophie. 'She might be interested. I could ask her.'

'A woman? Is she any good?'

'The best,' said Sophie loyally.

'Why not?' Marshall grinned. 'Tell her what I've got in mind. If she wants to, she can give me a call.'

He stood up and held out his hand again, to shake Sophie's this time. She took it, conscious of the impressions his rings made on her bare fingers. His skin felt warm and young. His handshake suggested that they would have plenty of time to get to know each other. She saw his actions as impulsive, reviewing each one of them swiftly. Each impulse held an element of danger, which she'd moved towards.

Standing, he was not much taller than she was. He repeated the no drugs rule, looking pleased with himself as he did so, as if drugs were one area where, with this new girl no longer a girl, he need have no doubts.

He offered Sophie another smile then, not of welcome with a sting in it, or of egotism, but of openness towards the future and what it might bring. He was young, so was his business. Predicted changes to the law were in his favour. He was poised to take advantage of them. There was no shortage of girls to hire, and fire. Sophie was older than he would have liked, and did not look the part, but her potential, now hidden underneath the surface, might prove all the more lucrative for that.

The bell rang. Marshall lifted his chin in the direction of the kitchen.

Sophie hurried. She pushed the kitchen door firmly shut behind her, breathing hard with apprehension, excitement, and relief.

Much later, after the night's work had settled into a routine, and Sophie was enjoying a lull and Kirsten's company, while Elise was busy in the front room, she asked how often Marshall spent his evenings at the house.

'He likes to greet the customers,' was Kirsten's answer, her sarcasm light but unmistakable.

'And after that?'

'Watch him,' Kirsten said.

Sophie nodded, glad Kirsten had given her the warning. She saw again those stretched, tight thighs, her own foolhardy response, and, strangely, the four ants carrying the leaf, and how her observation of them had been interrupted by a lithe and seeming tall man on a porch. But mostly she was pleased because of Kirsten's thoughtfulness, the comforting idea that Kirsten might be looking out for her.

A Raft of Girls

Sophie sat with Andrew, and their daughter, under a crab-apple tree. They watched Sophie's landlady walk towards them, holding a tray of lemonade.

Tamsin ran forward, calling out, 'Let *me* help!'

Mrs B bent over with her tray and gave Tamsin one end of it to carry, carefully and slowly, so the liquid did not spill.

Andrew, who had his back turned, looked over his shoulder at the old woman who had made friends with his child. Mrs B smiled, her wiry hair caught back in a bun, her brown eyes offering homemade lemonade on a wooden tray.

Sophie knew that her landlady was curious about her ex-husband, who, for his part, was wary, yet prepared to be won over. Mrs B was interested in finding out what kind of man this was, who'd left her tenant, not for another woman, but a floating, open-ended freedom.

A Polish Jewish widow who was into gardening. This was what Sophie had told Andrew when she said she'd found a place to live. She added later, after she moved in, that B was short for Biberstein, which Tamsin couldn't say.

They walked towards the shade of the crab-apple, across the grass, a woman in her seventies, a small barefoot girl. 'Here,' said Sophie, brushing leaves. Carefully, they put the tray down. Ice and slices of freshly cut lemon floated in pale yellow liquid. Sugar crusted a glass jug, four empty glasses standing to attention round it.

Tamsin hugged Mrs B around the thighs, and, though there was a chair for each, asked if she could sit on her knee.

Mrs B let her hold the jug, one hand each side. Sophie tasted, complimented. Tamsin sipped, screwed up her face. Her father smiled.

Mrs B's shrewd, kindly eyes took in the scene, ex-husband and wife enjoying the refreshment she provided underneath her tree. She left after Sophie had promised to come up to the house later for an egg salad and, to tempt Tamsin, homemade ice-cream.

Sophie knew she would not probe or pry. There was trust, which she offered, went on offering. Sophie wondered if it would be withdrawn, and when. Would the withdrawal, when it came, be her fault? She thought, I don't want this. Not a debt, another one. There was the flat, the garden, hospitality. There was an old woman's curiosity about young people, what they talked about, their laughter, what they smelt like. Sophie had seen this curiosity flash across Mrs B's face before she realised that her timing was wrong, that Sophie and Andrew were in the middle of something that could not include her.

With a small gesture of relief, Andrew reached into his pocket and brought out some pamphlets. He explained that they were course outlines from the Institute and University.

Between the top of his sunglasses and his pale, bright hair was an expanse of forehead which Sophie longed to touch. She pictured herself grabbing blond hair near the roots, while, with the expansiveness of Saturday morning, Andrew said, 'You should go back to study.'

Soon it would be too hot to sit comfortably out of doors. Sophie thought of the deep green dimness of her bedroom with the curtains pulled, of pampering herself, indulging the delayed soreness of her Friday night. She did not take the pamphlets. 'Why?' she asked.

'Well – ' to Andrew it was self-evident.

Are you okay? Sophie would have liked to ask him.

Too soon for such a question, though maybe not that much too soon, maybe they were getting round to it. To soften the question she would add, 'It takes courage,' meaning courage was something they both had, though neither might choose to recognise the form it was taking, at present, for the other. She would ask a question, pay a compliment, barbed, but all their exchanges had thorns of one kind or another. It was a matter of degree. Suddenly, and this awareness was better than a cool drink, she thought she could see a way forward with Andrew, a way of speaking minds – though not all of what was in them, of course. Neither wanted that.

Lines existed through their daughter. Sophie saw these lines clearly under the apple tree. At the same time, she saw Andrew spreading himself across his raft of girls. For some reason, she pictured the raft in a backyard swimming pool, and Andrew lying across it, wearing a pair of speedos and his sunglasses.

She smiled, feeling an affection for him. She no longer quite knew who he was behind his glasses, or what his girlfriends saw. At least he didn't boast about them directly. There was still the possibility of tact between the two of them, the tactful giving or withholding of a piece of information.

Through the open window, they could hear Tamsin singing in her room. She sang as she put away her clothes and toys, a tidy child. Nothing distressed her more than leaving behind a favourite toy at one parent's or the other's.

Andrew waved a hand at the pamphlets, taking in what they had to offer, together with Sophie's indifference. 'I thought you'd be pleased.'

'That you're taking an interest in my education?' Sophie blushed. 'I am,' she said. 'I mean, I will be. I'll read them later. Thank you.'

'Waitressing,' said Andrew.

'It pays the rent.'

'You know I'd never quibble over money.'

'Of course not. I mean, of course I know you wouldn't.'

Andrew was generous with money. What was the way he'd put it?

How had the sentence gone? *I'll help out with money while you're getting back on your feet.*

Sophie wriggled her toes in the grass and repeated, 'It pays my rent. And Tamsin's.'

Mention of the flat gave Andrew pause. There was an undertow of disbelief that she could afford it. Sophie referred vaguely to good tips. This was at the basis, she thought, of Andrew's wariness with Mrs B. He suspected female collusion, though ignorant of the precise form it was taking, or what might be behind it.

When they'd separated, Andrew had offered Sophie the house. She'd said no, certain that she didn't want it. She didn't even want to visit it, though she smiled sometimes, thinking of him floating through those rooms designed for a family on his raft of girls.

Andrew took his glasses off. Sophie glanced up, curious. His brown eyes were blank, his desire satisfied in quite other directions. His gaze, uncovered, had the power to thrust a knife between her ribs. She lowered her own eyes quickly. He's bored with me, she realised, yet he still wants to give advice.

'Have you given any thought to my suggestion?'

'Of course I've thought about it,' Sophie said. 'I like having Tamsin half the week.'

'She'd still come and stay with you. But I'm the one with the secure income, and the house. And switching every three days is disruptive.'

'I'm her mother. And being with me is less disruptive than going to a babysitter after preschool.'

'Mrs Jaireth is very kind and helpful,' Andrew said.

'I'm sure she is,' said Sophie, going red, imagining, right then and there, a full confession. Just for a second, for the second after she finished speaking, before Andrew's roar of rage, they would be facing the same thing.

'I want you to leave now,' she told him.

Tamsin and Sophie considered one another, with the awareness that, for the last three days, Tamsin had been living in her father's house. Sophie reflected that, if three days was a long time in the life of a four-year-old, it was also a long time in the life of a separated parent.

Until that morning, Sophie had believed that Andrew preferred having Tamsin for half of every week. He'd once asked her the name of the restaurant where she was working. She'd said the first one that came into her head.

The question of money floated, settling now there, now here, around the garden flat. Sophie watched Tamsin carefully, respecting her quick, alert ear for what wasn't being said, for what might make trouble, go on making trouble for her parents, whom she still, sometimes, spoke of as though they lived under the one roof.

A few days later, Andrew rang as Sophie was getting ready to leave for work. There was Schubert in the background, her favourite piano trio.

'What's wrong?' she asked. 'Is Tamsin okay?'

'Fine. I went to a concert last night, that chamber music one.'

'Oh,' said Sophie, 'was it good?'

'At University House, in the Great Hall. All that bloody Leonard French. But actually, it was marvellous.'

Sophie did not want to mention work, the restaurant, but she wanted Andrew to know that she was on her way somewhere. She waited for him to tell her who he'd taken to the concert, to let her know, by name or voice inflection, that her place at his side, at concerts, had been filled.

He said, 'Smetana and Beethoven both fantastic. And a work I'd never heard before by Rebecca Clarke.'

Sophie said, 'I have to go.'

'I'm sorry about the other day. I don't want to push you.'

'We can work something out.'

'It's just what's best for Tamsin, what's in her best interests,' Andrew said.

Sophie took a deep breath. 'I really have to go.'

She put the phone down and had two thoughts about music. While she no longer believed she could reclaim her marriage, she wished to spirit herself, for one evening, to a concert with Andrew. She wanted to sit by his side, listen to his breath quicken, the movement of his blood. And before this, before they'd got dressed up and the babysitter had arrived, listen to him practise the piano with Tamsin's high voice in the background.

Her second thought was about melody, played in a major, then a minor key, what that shift might mean. What if the rhythm stayed the same? Ta-tum, ta-tum, it might be.

All that was left of her six years of marriage were sudden shafts of memory, vertical lines running downwards, parallel and fast. The music ones were best, the concert ones, the sensuality in them deeper, more satisfying in recollection, than her memories of sex.

A Working Night

'A lot has been written about prostitution in recent months,' began the letter to the *Canberra Times*.

> *Prostitution has always been with us. Abolition doesn't work. It should be legal, so the health of 'sex workers' can be monitored, so that they and the brothel owners pay their share of taxes. We do not necessarily disagree with these opinions. But for the last few months, we have had the experience of living opposite a brothel. Once these establishments are legal, and able to advertise freely, it's reasonable to assume their custom will increase. Do we really want to import the problems of Kings Cross and St Kilda – curb crawling, constant late night traffic? Do we want our daughters to be molested on the way home from school?*
>
> AG and CF Bellamy
> 13 Andover St
> Kingston

'Constant late night traffic – ' Elise was reading aloud, Kirsten and Sophie looking over her shoulder.

Kirsten said, 'It's not a description of what actually occurs. More a fantasy projection.'

Elise giggled. 'I like that. Our clients are as quiet as lambs.'

Kirsten sat down and took out her cigarettes. 'That's a crap movie,' she said. '*Silence of the Lambs.*'

Sophie wondered if the Bellamys had daughters. 'A daughter,' she told the other two, 'would make a difference.'

They stared at her with identical expressions, in which curiosity about her life outside the house was mixed with a complete lack of interest in the difference daughters made.

Sophie held their gaze for a long moment. The phone rang, and Elise moved to pick it up.

10 Andover Street was built on what Sophie thought of as the flat-lands of Kingston, though they were no flatter than most other lakeside areas. Many people knew Kingston only for its railway station and its markets, others for old houses where the rent was cheap. Though the suburb touched the lake, it was not a posh one, yet. These were the flatlands and housing prices were depressed, which was why, Kirsten told Sophie, Marshall had been able to pick up Number 10 as cheaply as he had. There was the old bus depot, with its car parks of rutted asphalt, thistles growing in the cracks. In Spring, Salvation Jane burst out along the gutters, in the vacant block next door, seeded down from mountains called Ainslie, Majura, Black. Purple flowers in November, terrible weed of a thing flourishing.

The houses on the other side of the street were all in better nick, and, not too far away, attractive new apartments were going up around the shopping centre.

The house across the street, Number 13, had gained a personality. Or its owners had.

'Fat cow,' Kirsten said.

'How do you know she's fat?'

'Stupid old fat cow.'

'What about him then?' This was Elise, who claimed to have seen both Bellamys, to be in possession, as she sometimes did, of superior knowledge.

'Stupid old fat bull.'

Elise giggled again.

'What if he's been here?' asked Sophie.

Kirsten said, 'A bull we might remember.'

This was safe ground. They often compared clients as to how this or that one was hung.

Their laughter drew Marshall from the front of the house.

He'd read the letter earlier. Now he challenged one of them to answer it, standing, legs apart, arms folded on his chest, just outside the kitchen.

Elise said, 'Why don't you?'

Sophie wished Elise had not suggested this, because he might. There was that in Marshall which liked to fan a flame.

She understood, as well, why Elise spoke to Marshall in a particular voice, one she kept for certain times. It was to resist his right to cross the line that separated the kitchen from the remainder of the house.

Marshall came right inside and sat down at the table. He felt the teapot, though from the empty mugs he must have known that it was cold.

Kirsten took the newspaper and folded herself into the armchair.

The phone rang again. Elise put her hand over one ear, and crooned into the receiver.

Marshall smiled. 'Hey, Soph,' he said, keeping his voice low. 'How's your architect friend coming along with her drawings?'

'Oh, very well,' said Sophie.

There was an edge to Marshall's voice now he'd made his point, was sitting with them, one of the girls. Sophie's friend, Ann, had reported their conversation, how Marshall had asked her to make some sketches.

'How long have you two known each other?' he asked now.

'A long time.'

Elise ran her hand lightly across the back of Marshall's neck.

'On his way then, is he?'

'Yes.'

'That's good,' said Marshall, as though the work of persuasion had been his.

Sophie was aware of both pairs of eyes on her, Marshall's and Elise's, was aware, more than anything at that moment, of how alike they were, in their desire to make a lot of money, the way they both enjoyed playing to an audience, and the sex they had, that everybody knew about. It made them attractive. People seeing them as they were just now would say, What a striking couple.

Kirsten sighed and flicked the newspaper to another page. At the back of her mind, Sophie registered that Marshall had been quick to drop the subject of Ann's drawings.

Small details could become enormous in the winking of an eye. Sophie pictured a *Canberra Times* photographer arriving outside Number 10. The local TV station might send a camera crew, a young presenter with blonde hair in a ponytail, tight pale summer suit, high heels for marching up and down the footpath till one of them – Sophie, Kirsten, or Elise – was caught by steely words, the camera's unforgiving eye. A photographer might wait till 3am to catch her leaving in one of those pictures they took of street workers at Kings Cross. The street workers in those pictures wore short skirts and high, high heels.

Sophie counted off the people who would be angry, shocked, were she to appear in the glare of Number 10 – the preschool teacher, Andrew, Mrs B. She had a daughter to consider, a helpful landlady, an ex-husband with definite ideas. She did not disagree with the letter-writers' sentiments, yet there was something both foolish and alarming about finding herself the subject of them.

She thought, If we were across the road, we'd be Number 13, since the houses on the other side did not correspond exactly. In her defence, and Kirsten's and Elise's, she might have pointed out to the owners of Number 13 that they'd never had a problem with curb crawling or excessive late-night traffic. Kingston was not a red-light district. Canberra had no such thing, though the collection of brothels in Fyshwick and Mitchell, a growing collection, in anticipation of changes to the law, might in time create one.

It was the idea of Number 10 being used as a brothel that the owners of Number 13 and their supporters objected to. Its consequences were still, so far as Sophie could see, underneath the surface, shielded from the public eye. Sometimes, when she read one of these letters, she had the notion – she knew it was ridiculous – of inviting the owners of Number 13 *inside* Number 10. She knew this would be as futile as attempting to defend the idea that the owners of Number 13 were opposing. And yet. She argued with herself, having no wish to defend prostitution, but retaining a fantasy of showing her neighbours around. The most important part of this was a feeling about the house – her house, Kirsten's and Elise's – a feeling that the house was, not haunted – haunted suggested too definite a presence of the supernatural – but that it pulled you in. Somehow, if their neighbours were brought closer, people who, after all, were spending a fair amount of time thinking about what sat opposite them, they must feel this pull, could not be immune to it.

They weren't legal, not yet. But they weren't being treated as illegal either. The police were staying away. Nobody was being prosecuted. Health standards were left, in this holding-your-breath time, up to them.

Marshall called Sophie to the front of the house.

'So, Soph.' He patted the chair next to him, and asked her about Ann, what kind of person she was, how long she'd been an architect.

Sophie answered easily enough.

Once there was no need to hide behind a suburban façade – 'Not that it fools our nosy neighbours' – Marshall wanted his house to stand out, to be a true original.

Sophie praised her friend, proud of her talent, sure she would prove equal to the task. She crossed her legs. There were many questions she would have liked to put to Marshall.

How he felt about Elise working was one, for Sophie was fascinated by relationships that seemed to have shut the door on jealousy. How did he feel about the clients? was another. Sophie wondered what went through his mind, as he welcomed them into his dingy foyer, made first-timers feel at home, or so he claimed, in the face of Kirsten's light, but steady mockery.

She'd been at the house long enough to understand that Elise would just as soon have managed the customers, from their moment of arrival, without Marshall's help. When she could, Elise invented errands for him, and could be irritable on days when he showed up before six o'clock.

Kirsten had told Sophie that Elise and Marshall lived together, in such a way that suggested the arrangement was more to Marshall's advantage than Elise's.

Sophie opened her mouth to ask about the clients, but Marshall was quicker with his question. 'Where's that sarong of yours?'

'In the kitchen,' Sophie said. Surely he had seen it, hanging up behind the door?

'It suits you,' Marshall said, spreading his tight thighs. His lip ring was suggestive, silver-tongued.

'Thank you,' Sophie said.

'You're doing well,' he told her.

'Why wouldn't I?'

'Well, Soph, you're not exactly – I don't mind. I think you're cute, in that sarong of yours.'

Marshall reached across and ran his hand from her knee upwards to her groin, slowly, pressing down. Sophie's skin shrank.

The bell rang, not the first time it had released her.

'Get changed then, sweetheart,' Marshall said.

One thing you could say for him, thought Sophie as she hurried down the corridor, he did stick to the no line-ups rule.

In the kitchen later, when Elise was busy, and Marshall reading magazines up the front while he waited for the bell to ring again, Sophie picked up that day's *Canberra Times*.

She asked Kirsten, 'Why do they always put "sex workers" in inverted commas?'

'I prefer whore myself,' Kirsten answered from the depths of the armchair.

She told Sophie she gave that, or prostitute, as her occupation when she filled in forms. Smoking, staring out at the high, bland, summer sky, Kirsten told the story of how once, on her way to an AIDS conference in Manila, she'd been held up for five hours at the airport, having written prostitute on her entry card, while officials argued over whether or not she should be allowed in.

'However you say "sex worker",' she concluded, 'it will always be in inverted commas.'

'Oh, I don't know.' Sophie smiled at Kirsten's tone of voice, the way her smoke caressed the armchair's back. 'Things change. Expressions change. One day it will be accepted.'

'Like partner,' Kirsten said.

Sophie laughed, while Kirsten said, 'Partner's chalk in the mouth.'

'Still and all, I wouldn't mind one.'

Kirsten turned around to stare. The shadows underneath her eyes were black. 'But you're sentimental,' she told Sophie.

Sophie groaned, 'Not *that* again,' but this time Kirsten's teasing had no bite.

Her story was interesting, and Sophie wanted to hear more. She opened her mouth to ask a question, but Kirsten was too quick for her.

'How's Marshall Matt?'

'Okay, I guess.'

'What did he want?'

'To talk about the renovations. How do you handle him?'

'I piss him off,' said Kirsten.

Sophie nodded, wanting to ask for details and a plan of action, but unsure of herself, and unwilling to admit details of her own.

'We knew each other in Sydney,' was all Elise had said of her association with Kirsten. Elise had also told her, 'You can't just work with anybody,' and Sophie had taken this as a reminder that she was on probation. It was all Elise had said of Marshall too – no long association spoken of, or hinted at. 'Sydney', and 'knew each other', had been left to speak for themselves.

As though to set itself against this, the early evening light, making its way through the kitchen window, had a great solidity. It sat four-square with the armchair, an invited guest, immensely solid and sustaining, though Sophie knew that it would soon be gone.

The kitchen table was heavy, comfortable, necessary. When Elise had bought it at the old bus depot market, she'd asked about previous owners, but the second-hand dealer had not been able to enlighten her. Sanded back and varnished, the table's deep burn rings spoke of an injury too great to have been made by pot or pan. It was strengthened by disfigurement.

All of this, the buying of the table, the sanding back and staining, had taken place before Sophie had arrived at Number 10. She knew the story of the armchair too – bought not from the market this time, but a shop in Elroy Street. It had been sitting on the footpath in front of the shop. The sun had been shining down on it, the way sun did in Canberra, flat, clean, with a greedy kind of clarity. Sophie provided these words for herself, but the suggestions were there in the way Kirsten and Elise had spoken about the morning, the kind of day it had been. Number 10 had been a novelty then, yet still there was pleasure and relief in getting out, shopping for furniture, pleasure in the story and its repetition.

Both Kirsten and Elise had stopped to look – a lumping great ugly 1950s armchair, springs all over the place, upholstery threadbare. They'd turned to one another, smiled, knowing it was right, was perfect.

Kirsten had fixed the springs, or modified their sharper points. She hadn't considered herself skilled enough to mend the upholstery, so the chair was covered with a tartan rug, itself faded, by no means new or glamorous, a rug that fitted itself into the chair's deep cracks, folding and re-folding, having to be smoothed or straightened out. The colours of the tartan, dark green, navy, black, drank the light and made the chair too warm. But that was okay, that was fine. Crumbs collected, and were brushed off. All three women liked to eat in it. Elise read magazines. Kirsten listened to CDs.

Kirsten stood up to get herself a drink. Sophie took her turn in the chair. The sun was going down. She raised her head to stare out at neglect, then fences, her mind's eye taking over.

Elise came in. The phone rang. She picked it up and said, 'Number 10?' running the words together with a rising inflection, as though she was in a hurry, a great rush, customers lined up. Kirsten used her cigarette voice on the phone, a dark voice to go with her looks, a swarthiness that reminded Sophie, now and then, of Ann. But in Kirsten it was careless, or it seemed to be, just as Kirsten seemed careless of herself in some ways, though serious in others, in the way she chose to call herself a whore.

Resting in the armchair, Sophie pictured the potential customer on the other end, the rush dark and cheap, immediate. But no, not always. Elise had a way of bringing them to the house. Kirsten did as well. Sophie was perfecting a telephone voice. The two of them were coaching her. It was a handicap to picture the man on the other end. More than once, Sophie had walked into the side room on the heels of a question.

'Was that you on the phone just now?' the new customer would ask, his voice aggressive but uncertain, because Sophie did not look the part.

Sophie would smile and invite whoever it was inside.

The telephone voice she aimed for was neutral, a receptionist's voice, perfectly adequate, she said, putting on a huff when Kirsten teased her. But it was probably true, thought Sophie on probation. She probably was sentimental. Underneath, at bottom, she suspected she had the heart, the capacities, ambition, of a wife who worked as a receptionist.

She watched Elise unroll her yoga mat. The prospect of contorting her body into so many different shapes appealed, yet made her feel tired before the night's work was well underway.

In addition to her yoga, Elise went to the gym most mornings, only partly as a result of Marshall's encouragement, his belief in keeping fit.

As Marshall would have it, sex work was a branch of gymnastics. Slack, unhealthy bodies were abhorrent to him. He would never, he declared with venom, employ a fat girl.

Kirsten made fun of him in Elise's presence, testing to see how far she could go. She mimicked Marshall's upstanding blue-black hair, the way his right nostril flared, setting off the thin silver ring beneath it, through his upper lip. She stuck her tits out, tweaking her nipples through her brown sarong, talked about Marshall's nipple rings, putting on *his* put-on voice, asking Elise, What about his cock?

Elise laughed good-naturedly from the middle of her mat. 'Shut up, Kirst,' she said, willing to give way to Kirsten in all these small mockeries that didn't count.

Summer evenings, Kirsten favoured a sarong. She had her store of lingerie, of course. Following Kirsten's example, Sophie wore her blue and brown sarong night after night, and could not be persuaded to adopt more fashionable attire. A sarong was easy to slip out of, no falseness about undressing when all that was required was to undo a knot under her left armpit, no teasing on her part or the customer's, though there were clients who would make a game of anything. But then Sophie would decline, politely, the invitation to striptease, at the beginning of her exchange with this, or that one. She liked untying the knot herself, from just above her breasts, folding the length of material, placing it on the chair.

She sometimes felt afraid of Kirsten, sensing that, however light the banter, antipathy ran deep with her, was both instant and long-lasting.

Sophie's first regular of the evening wore a copper bracelet, talisman against arthritis. It did not enhance his freckled, wrinkled skin. He always wore it on his left wrist and it looked too tight. His grey eyes had a steely glitter. He looked straight up at the ceiling, and only ever paid for hand relief.

She knelt over him in the side room, in the middle of the bed. The window of what she now regarded as her room was right up against the fence, but she seldom saw the fence, or the block next door, since both blinds and curtains had to be drawn to protect the client's privacy.

The ceiling's watermarks were still visible in masses, some khaki brown, some, in the corners, darker. Dirty clouds they looked like, clouds that were absent from the high, thin sky outside.

'You're nearly there,' she told the bracelet man under her breath, eye-balled suddenly by a rose in the centre of the carpet, close-up and stifling, as though she was lying flat out, flush against it.

It was hard to balance evenly this way. For one thing, she had only one hand to stretch out, a single arm. Accessories were disconcerting. It was hard to stare, keep staring, at a watermark. The copper shone strangely, and there were the roses to consider, the sheet rucked up when she preferred it smooth, and, if this wasn't enough, an old man's unreliable erection.

She wondered if his visits to her were how he spent his pension money, parcelling it out. Conscious of the need to save, she would have liked to ask about his super payments. Then the larger question – was he afraid to come inside her?

He wore a wedding ring. Perhaps his wife was in the habit of checking their bank balance, and he had to pretend he'd lost money at the races. He didn't look afraid or nervous, merely absorbed by the effort he was making. At the same time, it seemed to Sophie that he'd worked out his approach in advance, and the unfolding of this approach, the execution of it, suited him.

She leant over and counted just under her breath.

Oomph, the next one said behind her. The bed in the side room rocked. It shook. Surely the wedge of paper had come loose.

Sophie thought fondly, romantically, of turning numb. Oomph, he said again, and she thought, not long now, he's nearly there. She opened her legs wider, which usually helped.

She tested her thigh muscles, tested and then measured them against tendons and connective tissue. Her spine clicked into place. Her arms were straight, but not stiff. The sheet stretched out like a large, flat continent on either side of them.

She hoped this one would not try, as some did, to push her flat, face-down. If he did, she would resist. She was discovering her own small hierarchy of rules, and methods of enforcing them.

She began to count. Her mind moved across wall and ceiling marks to the idea of matching her indifference against any man's, against her ex-husband's. For what could it be but a deep indifference that had brought the man behind her here, to an exchange of skin and lubricants for cash?

She had believed, at first, that sensation must be all that mattered, a swift, uncomplicated orgasm. Or a cure for complications. But now she wanted, in this probationary time, to keep an open mind. And had already thrown away too many boxes of chocolates and bunches of roses not to be left wondering about what sidestepped at the edges of indifference.

Vaseline worked when her body's juices rebelled, vaseline on her fingers and the outside of the condom. There was an ache in the small of her back. She was developing whore's back – though not from lying on it – a kind of crunch at the base of her spine, even with the position she favoured. Doggy, it was called, Kirsten called it, with blunt good humour, making the name her own.

Sophie projected herself into a future with a ceiling interest, a future where she didn't mind lying on her back. She thought a bell might be a good idea, the kind used for debating teams. This one seemed to be getting nowhere. But there was no-one to complain to, call a halt, except the man behind her, to whom she did not wish to speak, to whom she wished to remain her silent, anonymous self. She thought about the pile of notes she would take home that night, her pot of gold, her wheel of fortune spinning.

He removed himself from her.

She took the condom and dropped it in the bin.

'That was nice,' he said.

'I'm glad you enjoyed it,' Sophie answered. 'See you next time then.'

She complained to Kirsten in the kitchen.

Kirsten said, 'You're an idiot. Pull him out when the half hour is up and get off the bed.'

'But if he's nearly there?'

'*Nearly*,' Kirsten said.

'If he complains to Marshall?'

'What?' Kirsten was on her high horse now. 'You think Elise and I put up with shit like that?' She shook her head. 'You're such a baby, Sophie.'

Her next customer, a doctor, looked at her speculatively, professionally.

He looked her up and down and said, 'Young woman, are you aware that one of your legs is shorter than the other?'

Sophie looked at her two legs next to one another, below where her sarong had just now fitted snugly, unsure whether or not she'd heard him correctly.

'Your right leg, here, is shorter than the left.'

She could not tell by looking down, so she raised her eyes to the doctor's, unwilling to admit ignorance about her own anatomy.

'See here,' he said, touching her lightly on the kneecap. 'One is fractionally higher.'

He smiled, pleased with himself, then brought his soft fingers into contact with her back. 'The curve you have here, the S curve,' he explained, 'is caused by that.'

Sophie turned lightly, under the doctor's light hands turning her, as a dressmaker might, to check a dipping hem. She asked, 'What kind of doctor are you?'

He had introduced himself as Doctor Tate. She'd registered the crisp sound of it. A neat name for a neat man, she'd thought, watching him undress. He had not asked for her name. It was now that he was curious.

Hand resting on the base of her spine, he said, 'I could show you if we had a full length mirror.'

'I'm glad we don't. Are you a gynaecologist?'

'What? Oh no. Forty years a GP.'

The doctor's erection wasn't firm enough to support a condom, a herbal tea erection Kirsten would have called it, Kirsten with her names, her categories. She preferred the double whisky, not because of the manliness it promised – manliness being neither here nor there to Kirsten – but for the ease it made of getting on the condom.

Sophie stroked and pulled and nothing happened.

But then, suddenly decisive, as though he'd been arguing with himself, in his head or at the base of his straight spine, and had reached the energetic moment in the argument, though not its resolution, the doctor took charge of things himself. He inserted his herbal tea in the lubricated rubber and, hand beneath the small of Sophie's back, tested her lower vertebrae. With the strength of long experience, he supported her like that.

'Let's try a pillow,' he said, 'underneath the hips.' He kept his hand on her back after she had manoeuvred the pillow into place. His hand, the pillow, sheeted bed with its one leg shorter than the other, its hidden wedge of newsprint, all were layered, ready. He held her high, with her short leg – a flaw only a professional such as he was had observed, a flaw that Andrew, through six years of marriage, hadn't. The curve of her spine felt sticky, though it was not so hot tonight. His hand applied considerable pressure. His breath quickened, then he sighed.

Sophie looked across at her sarong folded on the chair, at the doctor's suit on a matching chair beside it. He'd tucked his black socks well inside his shoes. He had an air about him of a man who was accustomed to commercial sex. Nothing about it was likely to surprise him, his expression said. He saved his curiosity, at this stage of his life – for surely he must be well over seventy – for small chipped bones of fact, the decision in the womb, within the foetus, or in egg or sperm, which decreed that one leg would emerge shorter than the other.

A little later, while he was dressing slowly, and Sophie was praying he would not be one of those who felt he was entitled to use up every minute of the half hour, he said, not looking at her, looking down at his black socks, 'At my age, a man can come and not even know.'

Sophie would have held up the condom then, fetched it from the bin, as proof of her, and his, underlying practicality. She contented herself with assuring him that he had come, indeed. And thought also, the thought a comfort to her, that marriage might end, but rejection did not have to be complete.

She showed the young first-timer into the front room. It was an occasion for her to be using the front room, since both Kirsten and Elise preferred it. She'd left them arguing with each other in the kitchen.

It was an occasion also for the young man. He was getting married on Saturday.

He came straight out with it. 'I'm getting married.'

His mates had paid for him to visit a brothel. They'd clubbed together, passed the hat around. They were waiting in the car. He lifted his chin towards the window, and Sophie noted that he and Elise had the same chin, small and pointed. She pictured the car the young man and his friends had driven over, parked outside – the bravado in this, simply, three or four young men waiting with lifted chins, kidding one another.

He knew about Number 13 and the letter. He teased Sophie in an offhand way. It was daring for a young man, getting married, to be standing there and joking with her.

Sophie felt motherly, felt like warning him. 'Marriage – ' she might begin.

Marshall had been over the services and prices. The young man was handsomely provided for and needed no further explanation.

He bent to unlace his running shoes. His fair hair opened on a childish part. He looked up suddenly, and Sophie saw herself through his eyes, at once and completely, the way she'd just pictured the car, saw herself small and thin and freckled, how the young man, with his childish part, his buck's night treat, had looked forward to something different.

There was Elise in the kitchen, answering another call perhaps. Elise and – he said his name was Alan – would make a handsome pair. But no, she wouldn't call Elise. She would not offer up Alan to Elise, or vice versa, and Alan, for his part, did not ask to see another girl, though, whatever Marshall might have told him, Sophie felt this question at the back of his eyes. She watched him unbuttoning his shirt, physically readjusting. She already had some experience of this.

When he came back from the shower, he was ready. He might have turned nasty from disappointment, the mismatch between desire and what was, *who* was, but found reserves of courtesy, even of gentleness, and got it over quickly.

Notes grew. They multiplied in the kitchen, in the stove's black belly, as the night wore on. At night's end, the sweet pile was divided, Sophie's share given into her hand and then her handbag. The fifties, twenties, now and then a hundred, sat in their fat paper splendour on the seat beside her as she drove home through the greying, blue and copper, aching end of night. She saw strange flowers on the trees, filling empty streets, stretching from an old man's prophylactic bracelet, to these that were peculiarly her own, these splendid banknotes, to keep, or give in turn.

She remembered walking up to the house the first time, raising her fist to the crumbling door. There'd been no cars outside, no sign of life, curtains and blinds drawn close. She remembered Kirsten in the armchair, Elise's yoga mat, her questions that had amused them, and their enjoyment in putting her on the spot.

Two images stood out in her recollection – her first customer's blond hair, Andrew's hair, and, flushed with success, walking down the corridor to Kirsten.

What had begun as an impulse – phoning, getting out her street directory, finding the house and walking up to it, raising her right hand – an impulse born of rising bills and rent to pay, and a determination not to ask Andrew for more money – was beginning to gain the solidity of an occupation.

She'd had some trouble with Marshall, and with customers over timing. But the delight was fresh, the triumph of having accomplished what nobody, least of all herself, would ever have imagined that she could.

Inside her garden flat, Sophie shoved the night's takings in a drawer. Banknotes fluffed themselves in a papery, feather-light way. They sank down into others of their kind. Imagining a magical, discreet, entirely new form of interest, her soft, thick notes multiplying by proximity, by rubbing against each other, Sophie pressed the marvellous invention that was money down into the drawer with both hands. She studied her treasure before she went to bed.

Its colours, red and yellow, portraits of Edith Cowan and David Unaipon, raced up to meet her, like the carpet roses on the side room floor, but so much clearer, brighter. The confidence in them! Play money. She could buy Mayfair and Park Lane. The sufficiency in that! The strength and keep of it. How fat and jolly, full, the drawer of money was, ready to be played with!

The Model Room – A Drawing

Tamsin ran out the preschool gate, red-cheeked, surprised, checked in her flight. It really is you! And Sophie thought, My daughter!

The sticky melting footpath, hot metal of the preschool gate, shade reduced to scrawny half lines between casuarinas, sharp smell of resin – all of this Sophie took in with freakish clarity, a clarity which made her realise that, in spite of her secret, she was a mother still.

The teacher followed Tamsin to the gate to tell Sophie that she'd refused to take a nap. 'The heat exhausts them.' She nodded briskly to emphasise her point.

Tamsin had not slept during the day since she was eight months old.

She pulled her mother's hand, and asked, 'Where are we going?'

'To Ann's,' Sophie said.

'Are we walking?'

'We've got your bag, remember?'

The teacher listened, as though there must be more to this exchange than met the eye, as though there was something in, or underneath it, that she ought to know about.

Sophie fetched Tamsin's bag from the office. She knew that Tamsin wanted to carry it herself, but it was heavy, and she did not want to stay there, under this woman's eye, for any longer than she had to.

She did not like the way the bag was kept beside the desk, though she knew this dislike of hers was unreasonable. She also did not like the way the woman followed Tamsin with her eyes. Sophie could not believe that Tamsin was the only child at Lyneham preschool whose parents were taking it in turns to look after her, but the teacher behaved as though this was the case.

Sophie's friend Ann was dark – dark skin, dark hair. The slight sideways tilt of her head and her brown eyes were welcoming, full of anticipation, full of questions, as she said hello.

Swarthy, Ann was fond of calling herself, rolling the word around her tongue. The two women were at an age, a stage in life, where complaining to each other about their looks was a source of pleasure and irritation. Sophie considered her looks to be nondescript, forgettable, whereas people remembered Ann's frowns, the thickness of her eyebrows, and, when she smiled in a certain way, the tremendous sense of election, more than a favour bestowed.

Ann smiled and said, 'Come and take a look then.'

The blinds in her workroom were closed against the afternoon heat. It was a room built to trap winter sun and hold it, large windows facing north and east.

A fan whirred. A lamp was trained on her design table, making it a stage.

Tamsin ran forward with a sharp intake of breath.

'Don't touch!' Ann warned her.

Tamsin pulled her fingers back as though they'd been burnt. Sophie rested her hand on her daughter's shoulder for a moment, to soften the command.

'Go outside and play. We won't be long.'

Tamsin's light brown hair, Sophie's hair, stuck to her temples, and her face was hot. She glanced from Ann to Sophie, then grabbed a strand of hair and began to suck on it. She took a last look, over her shoulder, at the drawing underneath the lamp.

There were no toys in Ann's house or yard, nothing to amuse a four-year-old, but Tamsin was good at amusing herself. In the raw time, after Andrew had told Sophie what he wanted, and made clear she had no part in it, Tamsin had spent hours making up games under Ann's big gum tree, while Sophie cried buckets in the house.

Ann had been kind and patient, beyond her natural inclination. She'd offered Sophie money and a place to stay. Sophie was glad, now, that she'd accepted neither, though she felt grateful to Ann for putting up with those long afternoons of tears. Ann knew nothing about living with children, and was not interested in learning. It was Sophie's great good fortune that she'd found the garden flat.

As for the house at Number 10 – Ann had wasted no time, but created drawings that looked, to Sophie's eye of a non-architect, to be complete. Yet she struggled to connect the house with these authoritative black lines, verticals and horizontals laid out in two dimensions. Here was the side room, its contours overwhelming. The new fourth bedroom was behind it, closer to the back of the house. And the reception area Marshall was so keen on – Ann had made it a rounded, feminine-shaped alcove, with indoor plants, expensive couches and soft lighting. Marshall in his element. Sophie had no trouble picturing this part. She imagined herself walking up the corridor, insufficiently glamorous in her blue and brown sarong. She felt the bed rock, in the side room, on its uneven leg.

'Well?' asked Ann.

'It's great. It looks great,' Sophie said.

Ann frowned at the hesitation Sophie fought to overcome.

'They're just sketches. If Marshall likes them, I'll make a model of one of the rooms. You think it's what he wants then?'

'I'm sure it is.'

Ann walked over to the east-facing window, which looked down over the lake. Sophie followed her line of sight. It always surprised her, no matter how many times she stood in Ann's office, to notice how high up they were.

Ann turned to Sophie, one hand steadying behind her, on the ledge, to ask, 'What's it like – working there?'

'The money's good.'

Ann waited. Sophie laughed defensively. She wasn't sure if it was the question, requiring her to step over a line she didn't feel ready to step over, or her surprise at Ann asking it just then. She didn't feel ready to tell Ann what it was like, was suddenly convinced she could not.

She walked over to the drawing and, very gently, did what Ann had forbidden her daughter to do. She ran her fingers over the black lines, tentatively staking out possession.

Ann watched her, without comment, from the window. Sophie bit her lip. She owed Ann a decent explanation. She looked up, hearing a noise outside. It was a mistake to have brought Tamsin, not that Tamsin had done, would do, anything wrong.

She made an awkward face, ashamed of fobbing Ann off with half, or a quarter of an answer. She'd been looking forward to discussing the renovations. Ann hadn't said much on the phone, only, 'My God Soph, the place is falling down!' They'd laughed with delight at the idea of Ann disguising a suburban brothel, though what the word meant in a day-to-day, working way, had been left blank between them.

The need for discretion had been implicit in Sophie's invitation, not needing to be stated in words. 'It's just an ordinary house,' she'd said. And Ann, 'I guess it needs to stay that way then.'

'Until the law's changed, yes.'

Ann had laughed and said, 'I can do disguises.'

They'd giggled at the thought of the Bellamys at Number 13 working up a sweat over their protest letters.

Sophie had also been looking forward to hearing Ann's opinion of Marshall, who'd shown her around one morning.

'I like the other girls,' she said now.

'Tell me about them. I was hoping they would have been there, I'd have liked to meet them.'

'I will,' said Sophie. 'Only not today. I should go and check on Tamsin.'

'And Andrew?'

'What about him?'

'You still haven't told him.'

'Why should I?'

'Because this is a small town when it comes to gossip, and you're a lousy liar.'

'Don't bet on that,' said Sophie, going red. 'As for Andrew, whatever he's got coming to him, he's asked for it. Now I really must go and see what Tamsin's up to.'

'But Soph, be careful,' Ann said.

'Don't worry. I will.'

Sophie fetched Tamsin from the garden, where, surprisingly, she'd fallen asleep under a tree, and Sophie was confronted, as she had not allowed herself to be till then, with the child's fatigue. Quickly, affectionately, she said goodbye to Ann, their hug a continuation of all the hugs they'd shared in their years of friendship.

That night, as soon as Tamsin was asleep, she rang Ann.

'It's me.'

Ann said, 'I've just been watching that Civil War documentary. It's amazing.'

Sophie said, 'I'm sorry about earlier.'

'That's okay.'

'It's just that I don't know how to put it into words.'

'Well, when you do.'

They'd been through the obvious motives and dangers when Sophie first told Ann about the house. Ann had been wary. 'You always make them use a condom? What if it broke?' That afternoon she'd repeated her warning to be careful, but she'd never once said to Sophie, 'Don't.'

Recalling these earlier conversations, it was as though even then, at the beginning, Sophie had foreseen a connection for Ann, that Ann would become involved with the house in her own way.

She began to describe Elise, her yoga mat and soft men's shirt, her athletic appearance, her swinging hair that brought the clients running. Ann laughed and said, 'Jesus, what's *her* secret?' Then there was Marshall, with his tight black thighs. Marshall, Elise's boyfriend. Elise, who could have anyone, but had chosen him.

Sophie told Ann about Kirsten and the armchair, Tracy Chapman, and the view to who knew what. Then there was the side room, to which Ann had not paid close attention, seeing rather what needed to be changed than what spoke humbly of its own existence.

'Soph, I don't know how you can – '

But Sophie *did* know. The knowledge came to her as she was concentrating on the details for her friend. She explained, or tried to, the satisfaction of moving on, in that house, from one hour, one customer, to the next, the feeling of achievement, and how she was, somehow, defying fate. The pleasure of secrecy as well – apart from Ann, nobody from her old life knew. She'd lost touch with other mothers of young children, and was scared to remake contact with them, in case they could tell what she did by looking at her. Ann might tease her about being a bad liar, but the pleasure of secrecy was one, she realised, she had no intention of relinquishing, not yet. Then there was Andrew. She'd meant it when she'd told Ann that it served him right.

The phone freed Sophie's tongue, and they laughed out of a shared sense of adventure.

'That Kirsten sounds as though she knows a thing or two,' said Ann.

Sophie agreed, measuring her own ignorance against Kirsten's skill. She almost said, 'The only way to find out is to try it for yourself.' She could imagine herself saying this, but not Ann's response.

Saying goodnight, hanging up the phone, she pictured the windows of Ann's workshop opening wide. The drawings to which the house at Number 10 had been reduced floated down and rested on the lake.

Andrew and Sophie have Coffee in Civic

Andrew was sitting with the light behind him. His sunglasses gleamed and winked. He'd appeared in front of Sophie without warning, as though from a country far away.

Quick on his feet, he'd asked, 'Have you got time for coffee?'

Hesitating, Sophie knew her chance of saying no convincingly was gone.

'This *is* nice,' Andrew said.

His voice summoned up a general niceness and placed her, his ex-wife, inside it. It suggested that life without her was going very well.

Sophie forced herself to smile as she ordered an iced tea.

Andrew watched people from his seat on the footpath, underneath a wide cream awning. Sophie was glad she had her back to the shoppers, to girls of all shapes and sizes. It made her feel civilised to be drinking iced tea, especially since Andrew had said, 'That's what I'll have too.'

They spoke of Tamsin and the preschool. Their opinion of the teacher was the same, that she was nosy and rule-driven. Andrew had also argued with her about sleeping in the daytime. They were afraid their daughter would be singled out. Once, Tamsin had hit another child, and the teacher had exchanged words with both of them. They'd insisted that Tamsin was polite and obedient at home. They were conscious of the shaky ground of parental separation, aware – they agreed about this, nodding – that it was important not to antagonise the teacher.

Sophie drank her tea and studied her reflection in the café window. It seemed that they'd been talking for a long time, though when she glanced at Andrew's watch, she saw that it was only fifteen minutes. She wondered where he'd been going in his lunch hour, what messages he'd postponed to sit with her. She breathed in deeply, saying to herself, Next time I'm angry with him, I will remember this. It will be my pilot light. Nobody will ever care for Tamsin the way we do together.

Light underneath the awning had a cushion's softness. Sophie allowed herself to sink into it a little further.

'More tea?' Andrew asked, as though tea had been his choice in the first place. He talked about the Beethoven sonata he was learning. 'I'd get somewhere if I didn't have to work.' He made a face, self mocking. 'No no,' he insisted, though Sophie had said nothing. 'I'm lucky I've got time at all.'

She watched her ex-husband over the top of her glass. Was he opening the way to saying Tamsin was too much for him – work, and looking after a four-year-old for half of every week? He'd never complained, or hinted at complaint before. The opposite, in fact. She wanted to ask him if he played for his girls, or, more precisely, *what*.

'I'm going out to dinner,' Andrew said. 'Thought we might try the Taj Mahal.'

'Don't,' said Sophie, hating herself for going red. 'The food's lousy.'

Andrew laughed.

Sophie said, 'The service sucks as well.'

The thought of her garden flat was like a small hard charm attached to a narrow bracelet. Mentally, she curled her fist around it and squeezed tight.

'I best be going. You know how that woman hates it when we're late.'

'Don't I,' Andrew said.

Sophie rang Ann while Mrs B was playing a card game with Tamsin.

'I think he suspects something.' She told Ann about the Taj Mahal.

'That was a mistake,' said Ann.

'I know, but it's too late to do anything about it now.'

'You could tell him the truth.'

'Are you crazy?'

'Have it your own way then, but I think it would be better.' Ann's voice lifted with the pleasure of her own news. 'Marshall liked the drawings. I'm making a model.'

High, excited laughter in the background told Sophie that the game was finished, and her daughter had won.

'That's great. Call me when it's finished.'

Ann said that she would.

Rough Customers

It was an occupational hazard. Sophie's chosen position, the doggy Kirsten mocked while at the same time counselling its benefits, left her vulnerable to being squashed against the pillows. She tried shoving them away. The bed in the side room had two fat ones, meant to make, along with a dark blue coverlet, the room look ordinary, which it did already, in other, superficial ways. Elise hinted at the effect she aimed for – there was no need to spell it out – three simple bedrooms in a suburban house no nosy neighbouring visitor could take exception to. Of course the house was old, but why apologise for that? Shabby, old, but clean, and with a facelift just around the corner. Concentrating on the future, Elise smiled as she spoke of it, her smile like Marshall's, confident and young.

So, the pillows must remain, and the coverlet in place, between clients. But Sophie found them too fat and unwieldy, and they got in her way.

One windy night, before she could manoeuvre and resist, the client had pushed her hard between the shoulderblades, and, instead of rocking on her hands and knees, her legs were flattened and her face smothered by the pillow. She twisted, choking. 'No!' she managed to get out.

He took no notice, pumping, breathing harder. 'No!' she said again, trying to move the pillow with her chin. She grasped the bed's side with her good right hand, and struggled to pull the top half of her body from underneath his grip.

His answer was to increase the pressure, and hiss 'Shut up' in her ear.

Sophie had a shower. She drank water standing at the sink, then curled up in the armchair.

Kirsten raised a sympathetic eyebrow at her red face and indignant expression.

When Marshall called her up the front again, Elise spoke to her kindly. She knew that, if she asked them, Kirsten or Elise would do her next one for her.

She took her turn, though it left her feeling faint and dizzy.

Kirsten's advice came from a long way away. 'Start low down, at the foot of the bed. Never let your head get pushed against the wall. Chuck the pillows early.'

Sophie nodded, willing her head to stop spinning.

It became an occupational hazard for her, a task that she must bear in mind, to avoid those men who would push her flat, face down. She tried to pick them in advance, those who would react with a violent thrust when she invited, on her hands and knees, at the toe end of the bed. She tried to suss them out, her muscles tense and ready.

And if she made them suspicious, if they asked, 'Why are you doing that?' when the pillows hit the floral carpet with a small flat sound, caught between a whisper and a sigh, she turned and smiled at them over her shoulder, smiled and rocked back and forth ever so gently, while her muscles strained, her skin was hard and hot, and the fear of suffocating rose up in her throat.

Rough customers were part of the deal that Kirsten was helping her to measure, and to judge. In the kitchen, after another one had left her breathless, shaking, legs refusing to obey her anymore, she lay in the armchair, then slowly turned around and stared at the black belly of the stove where the pretty notes lay, resting one against the other. She imagined them with feathers. She imagined gathering them up and leaving, never to return. For how could her legs and arms, at the moment helpless liquid, withstand the next time, and the next?

Kirsten finished her turn. She made Sophie strong and bitter tea. Tea was for ladies, Kirsten said, and never drank it, but she made a dark brew for Sophie, curled in the armchair, nursing melted bones.

Kirsten heaped in sugar and carried the thick white mug to Sophie, who cradled it in her hands.

'Nobody's making you,' she said.

'I know that,' Sophie answered, breathing in the steam.

'Why then?'

Sophie said, 'I could ask the same of you.'

Kirsten coughed, taking out her cigarettes.

'You ought to give up smoking,' Sophie told her.

Sophie had tried to get Kirsten to talk about her life before she came to Canberra, but Kirsten didn't want to fill the gaps in the little she'd revealed so far. She'd been 'a bit political', she'd said, leaving Sophie to make of the short phrase what she would, and refusing, when Sophie pressed her, to add to her story of bravado at Manila Airport. Sophie sensed in Kirsten, and in Marshall and Elise as well, that their suspended present, between illegal and legal, had put the past into a kind of holding operation too. Memories from before the house at Number 10 could be spoken of, but not at length, and not in detail. Sophie felt the pressure of this suspended animation in herself as well, as her nights spent at the house increased in number, as she sought her level and her place there, as the past before Andover Street began to slip behind her, not only into another time frame, but another life as well.

She was brought up short to recall that Andrew used to be, apart from Tamsin, the most important person in her life. Even Tamsin, on the days when she was with her father, scarcely rose in Sophie's thoughts now, pitched, as they were, towards coping with her new employment.

Kirsten coughed again. Both women were aware that their questions, their curiosity concerning one another, hung in the air unanswered, mingling with the smoke.

Not having to watch a customer's expression was a distinct advantage of Sophie's chosen position, as was the ability to hide her own. Sophie was grateful for the anonymity it lent her. She could make faces, grimace for all she was worth. The walls and closed curtains of the side room would not give her away. She could poke her tongue out, and she did. She learnt ways to hurry along whoever was behind her. The homely, unfashionable room, with its few simple props, became her silent ally. She coped better with her soreness and fatigue, and spent less time recuperating in the armchair.

In small and large ways, Sophie felt herself adjusting, and wanted only space and quiet, the unremarkable continuance of days. But Kirsten coughed too much, and looked increasingly unwell. Kirsten's cough was a reminder that, although bodies might be trained as well as minds, the unexpected could erupt on a suburban street, out of a clear inland sky.

Kirsten went on smoking. She rattled the cellophane around each new pack as she unwrapped it, deliberately provocative. Sophie realised, watching these two who had a history she could scarcely guess at, that the time had passed, before she came on the scene, when boundaries had been put in place, and set. Kirsten teased, and Elise sometimes placated, sometimes lectured her. 'Put that fag out, Kirst,' she'd said on Sophie's first day. When Kirsten came back from the bottle shop with a good supply, Elise said, 'Don't get the new girl drunk. She'll need her wits about her.'

'She's not a girl,' Kirsten replied.

Sophie listened to them talking about her as though she wasn't there, liking the feeling of invisibility it gave her, and said nothing in her own defence. Their bickering was good-natured. They knew its limits and were comfortable with them.

Warning Sophie about Marshall, Kirsten's voice was sharper, suggesting that she resented his presence in the house in many ways, not just the ringed hand, cupped and ready. She resented his ownership, the money he'd set down, the mortgage that was in his name. But here, too, limits had been set, beyond which she would not go. It seemed to Sophie, getting used to being manhandled, working out her own limits and how she might enforce them, that the balance the three of them had struck might make them blind, or, if not blind then complacent, to Kirsten's deteriorating state of health.

Sophie asked, when she and Kirsten were alone together in the kitchen, how long she'd had her cough. Kirsten shrugged and said she couldn't remember. Sophie bought her Strepsils. Kirsten frowned at the small gift. She sucked one noisily and made a face of exaggerated distaste.

Sophie asked if she'd been to the doctor, aware, as she listened to her voice, that she sounded as though she was speaking to a much younger woman, not one older in years and experience than she was.

Kirsten replied that it was 'just a cough'.

The bell rang. A few moments later, Elise put her head around the door.

One of Kirsten's regulars was asking for her. Kirsten lay back in the armchair.

'I'll do him,' Sophie said.

'You?'

'Why not? Marshall isn't here.'

Kirsten frowned, lowering eyebrows that appeared to be much thicker, darker, frowning at an incapacity that seemed to have descended on her suddenly.

'Why not?' Sophie repeated.

'He's fussy,' Kirsten said.

'I'm sure he'll put up with me for once.'

Sophie poured water at the sink. Grumbling, Kirsten got to her feet.

'She ought to see a doctor,' Sophie told Elise.

'She doesn't like doctors.'

Sophie couldn't tell whether Elise was annoyed with Kirsten, or with Sophie herself for encouraging Kirsten to slack off behind Marshall's back.

The check-ups that Elise insisted on every few months were a source of dissension between Elise and Kirsten. Elise had let Sophie know that she should make an appointment for herself. Sophie saw the sense in this, but shrank from facing the questions the doctor would ask. Elise had given her a number. Sophie had it in her wallet.

'Why?' she asked now. 'What's she got against them?'

'They tell her to quit smoking.' Elise gave a short laugh, annoyed to be stating the obvious.

'Has she tried?'

'Not since I've known her.'

'How long is that?'

'A long time,' Elise replied, then closed her lips into a thin line, her signal that she wished to end the conversation.

Routine and Two Names in a Book

Trees blossomed on late summer nights. All along Andover Street, they sprouted copper leaves. Bracelet flowers were talismans against the cooling winds that, with growing strength, began to blow down off the Brindabellas. Out of season blossoms shone and were arrayed in rows, warding off weakness, warding off the cold.

No-one from 10 Andover Street replied to Number 13's letter, but other residents of Kingston did. Brothels in residential areas would not do at all. The letter writers reminded their readers that whatever future might be on the drawing board, no law had yet been changed. Prostitution in the ACT was still illegal.

Marshall read the letters and laughed. He called it 'Prostitution in the act'.

Sophie stayed out of Marshall's way. She purchased a small travelling clock and sat it on the bedside table next to the tissues. It did not face the bed. That would mock her efforts at control. She placed it carefully so that it faced three-quarters away, but she could tell with a glance, a glimpse at this three-quarter face, what time it was.

And she did what Kirsten had told her she should do, clumsily and inexactly. She got rid of the pillows, was constantly on guard against being flattened, and losing control. The customers who took too long she left gaping, open-mouthed. The hole at the centre of the bed that was herself she removed unceremoniously, expecting the tiny, voiceless clock to strike. Night air would rush in, through closed doors and windows. She did not look behind her, but felt, imprinted on her backside, the many truths of the position known as doggy, along with a blankness at the centre of the bed, and the modern, voiceless timekeeper that was an alternative to giving up, or running away.

'Time's up,' she said sharply, with her head down.

He might offer to pay her to continue. She might, maliciously, refuse.

She took home the same amount of money, now she had learnt to say Enough. The gifts of flowers – roses, carnations, stocks and sweet peas – went straight into the bin. They had the strangest smelling bins in all of Kingston, what with the condoms bundled into nests, in huge black plastic bags, their own form of industrial waste, and then, on top of, all around them, these flowers so lately chosen, presented with a bow, or inclination of the head.

'Coal to Newcastle,' said Sophie in the kitchen, wondering if she should explain about her garden flat.

She shared the chocolates with Elise and Kirsten, who had stashes of their own, gift-wrapped. Kirsten favoured a beer and chocolate combination. Elise frowned at Kirsten drinking on the job, though, as Kirsten pointed out, the beer was light and she could hold it well enough.

One morning, for no apparent, no external reason, Sophie filled shopping bags with money and took them to the bank. She had always paid her rent in cash, but this small ceremony she put behind her now. The passing over of the notes – first having plunged her hands into the drawer and picked some out, the way her hand sometimes touched Mrs B's around them, the questioning look in Mrs B's brown eyes that had quickly given way to acceptance – all this had to go once Sophie became efficient with her money. Cheques were written in her small, upright hand, receipts made out. For Mrs B, rising to a situation that was entirely of her tenant's making – she had not minded cash – banked the cheques and wrote receipts. Her expression said she welcomed the new aspect of solidity that Sophie carried back and forth, the sense of greater permanence in her tenant's affairs, though she did not ask, had never asked, about the restaurant.

How quiet the corridor leading to the rooms could be, and then the step, the low voice, Kirsten's or Elise's. Marshall's voice, at the front, was louder.

Tidying up in the side room, Sophie listened to the rise and fall of voices. This was the curious thing – Kirsten's and Elise's were always held just below the pitch that would make words audible. Sophie guessed that hers was as well. Whether or not the others could hear her with a customer was important to Sophie, finishing her tidying up, getting herself a drink of juice, answering Marshall's summons in her turn.

Avoiding explanations, speaking quietly, Sophie's voice sounded just like those other voices through the wall. She was always relieved when Marshall had taken the money, and she could say as little as possible. She hurried over details she didn't like divulging, and lingered on the one that meant most to her. Even for the extended price, even with the extras, half an hour was the maximum amount of time.

Sophie felt the hairs along her forearms rise. A cloud at the back of a client's eyes told her that he wasn't new. She fancied she could now pick this immediately. The light at the back of a first-timer's, be he in his seventies or eighties, was clear, and the man himself restless, moving from foot to foot, or swivelling from his hips, keen to take in the novelty of his surroundings.

Then the few minutes alone, while he walked down the corridor to the bathroom, had his shower. Some tiptoed, believing that way they would avoid the creaking board. Then the minutes waiting, three or five, the hiatus that made her nervous. She wanted to run back down to the kitchen. She wanted Kirsten in the kitchen hugging her, which Kirsten never did.

While she waited, she practised breathing in and out. At first she thought of nothing, then of the strange and marvellous idea of service that the room itself, in its temporary emptiness, seemed to be offering, both her and the man whose bottom might be turning pink beneath the shower rose, who might complain of rust or leaky taps on returning.

She thought of this service, in the service town that gave her a living, as both strange and marvellous, then tipping over quickly into the familiar, into repetition. And of how the familiar was made up of dozens of small, repeated movements – it almost didn't matter which – except that the client, having decided what he was willing to pay for, would need to stick to it. She would have to make him.

She recalled the routines of the government office she had left before Tamsin was born, the hum of computers, public service clerks answering letters and the phone, the routines and all the small famil-iarities which now seemed so unlikely they were scarcely believable. Much less real, less practical, than this house, the kitchen and the side room where she waited, picturing what she was soon to deal with, the pink balls of old, or ageing men. She thought that, if she could make the transference, anybody could. All it needed – this was a discovery that ought to shock, but didn't – was a setting down, then taking up again, of habit.

Later, in the kitchen, Kirsten's skin would be tight along her cheek-bones. The darkness under her eyes, and in them, would speak of trials overcome. She would reach immediately for her cigarettes, though she might have smoked one, or several, in the front room.

Elise's skin would also be tight along her cheekbones and around her mouth, younger skin than Kirsten's, but Sophie recognised a sameness, knowing the changes that had taken, and would shortly take place again, beneath it. They had no mirror in the kitchen. The house's only mirror was a shaving one, above a basin in the bathroom. Sophie soon learnt that she did not like looking into it, but she recognised that facial tightening, and the care her own flesh took, returning to itself.

Elise would unroll her yoga mat, Kirsten light a cigarette, while money rose like damp bread, yeast-filled, in the stove. Neither spoke, nor wanted to, until some time had passed, and each woman had followed her routine. If they'd both been in the rooms and Sophie hadn't, if the phone rang when they'd just come back – it happened once or twice – Sophie was struck by their determined silence, and the expectation that, without hesitating, she should be the one to answer it.

Kirsten sent herself up, as soon as she'd had a few puffs, getting up to put some music on, bowing her legs and pretending to bend, to buckle, under the weight that issued from her groin. She hobbled over to the CD player like a woman who'd been so long in the saddle she'd forgotten how to walk without it, saying 'Hi Ho Silver' to Elise in the middle of a spine twist on her mat. These were the words that broke the silence between them, not Sophie's on the phone. Elise frowned, ever so slightly, so as not to jar the concentration that was settling behind the tightness of her skin.

Or, if Kirsten went on sitting, smoking, and did not get up, Elise might break the silence herself a few minutes later, by opening the fridge and saying in a low voice, the voice in which she spoke to herself, and to the emptiness she found there, that they were out of juice, and be buggered if she should be the one always going to the shop for more.

Most clients took the substandard bathroom in their stride, though they avoided heavy footfalls and could be put out by meeting one another. Thus the need for careful listening, careful timing, knowing who had gone before. Footsteps in the corridor pit-patted, as though by scarcely making any sound – but the shower was old and cracked and noisy – the client could pretend it wasn't *him* in there. Some, having noticed the condition of the carpet, asked about footwear, thongs, or those woven slipper things you found in the wardrobes of expensive hotels.

Sorry, no, it was bare feet, unless they wanted to replace their own shoes, Sophie told them.

Others made disparaging remarks, disdainful comparisons with *Club Goldfinger*, or *Mimi's*. Sophie pictured them flicking at the shower curtain, and wondered if they would expect more of her body as a consequence.

Preoccupied with sounds and half-sounds, with the adjustments of the house around her mimicking her own – or perhaps it was the other way around – pitching herself forward to being numb, then to the end, driving home with a wad of money in her bag, some nights Sophie hardly noticed the clients any more. They made an impress on her, certainly, but that was all. She knew enough now to be confident that whatever they did would be over in half an hour at the most.

One man kissed her nipples, fingered her, and told her that he'd like to make her come.

'Kirsten?' Sophie demanded in the kitchen when he turned up again, one night when Marshall wasn't there.

Bruce Springsteen's voice of soft seduction lifted from the CD player. He sang his images of women's bodies, gardens, all mixed up.

Kirsten stared out towards the dark boundary of their property. Reluctantly, she turned to Sophie, who, for once, trampled on her need for privacy.

'Help me out.'

Kirsten frowned, then made another face, of resignation, willingness, goodwill, and hitched up her sarong.

Sophie listened to low voices, and, a few minutes later, soft footfalls in the corridor. She made herself a cup of tea and sat in the armchair, watching the undulations of the backyard and the fence, the grey and yellow of the city night.

He came back and asked for her. Elise was in the front room, Marshall absent once again. Kirsten gave her a long, considering look, then said, 'I'll tell him you're busy.'

Sophie nodded, feeling her nipples lift and sting.

He returned a fourth time, when Marshall was back holding the fort, and Kirsten was off sick.

'Just take pleasure,' he told Sophie, who laughed in angry disbelief, then said, 'We must give you a name.'

'Oh, call me anything. Call me John,' he said.

Sophie considered for a moment. 'You can be John the Cyclist.'

She was ashamed of wanting him, impatient both with her desire, and her shame. She wished she could leave them on a chair, folded under her sarong.

She arched her back and felt the bed beneath her tip and roll, though she'd checked the newspaper, meant to make things even.

He said, 'You like it then. You do.'

She laughed to cover her confusion, thinking, If Kirsten was here, behind me in the kitchen, if only Kirsten wasn't sick.

He hoisted himself above her on his cyclist's shoulders. His shadow framed her passionate humiliation.

He liked to make appointments. Sophie wondered if part of her arousal was to do with this. She enjoyed looking at his name in the diary, which Elise called their day book, though all of the appointments were for after six o'clock. It was a very big diary, with a whole page for each day, except Saturday and Sunday, designed for an office, nine to five. Elise overcame this by sticking a page from an ordinary exercise book at the bottom of Saturday.

Elise ruled a line down the middle of the page. She did this first thing. Sophie liked the balance of it. John the Cyclist one side, Sophie on the other. No-one had laughed when she'd given him the name. There was John the Butcher. He'd been Kirsten's. Now Elise had him, but he still asked after Kirsten, hoping she was better. Funny the loyalty, if you could call it that. Butcher. Baker. It was like a children's rhyme, but no-one thought it funny. You had to differentiate. John the Cyclist fitted, recalling a former prowess still very much in evidence – while John the Senior Public Servant, which he'd told Sophie he was – recalled nothing of the kind.

The regularity of it. Public service payday. The big deposit in the bank, or credit union, and then the withdrawal. The whole commerce of the town was geared to this. Woolies put on extra check-out staff. You never went near a bank on payday if you wanted to avoid the queue.

Sophie knew about the deep pleasure of wages just acquired. Her body beginning its slow rise to satisfaction, she hung up the phone and wrote the names in, or, if Elise had taken the call, looked over Elise's shoulder at her large, back-sloping writing, not the kind of handwriting you'd expect Elise to have.

It began then, as wages were transferred from dozens of pay office computers to thousands, tens of thousands of accounts. Her steady, slow anticipation began with picturing full supermarket trolleys, small and bigger treats, takeaway lasagna for dinner from the gourmet deli, full restaurants, food everywhere, and this other treat that was her, and hers. She looked at the two names side by side in the diary, the ruled, dividing line between, and felt the slow, strange, spendthrift and profligate changes that the sight of them began.

Always for late in the evening. Where did he go first? To dinner with his wife? A movie? His age was somewhere around fifty. Were his children grown? He'd noticed her stretch marks, but men carried no such evidence of reproduction. None of these questions she felt like asking, or could ask and expect a straight reply, though he had told her, with some pride, about his work. Maybe before Andover Street, he went to the gym. He had a shower because it was the rule.

Aware of Sophie peering over her shoulder, breathing down her neck, Elise turned round and smiled lightly, raising a pale eyebrow. Sophie smiled back, wishing at the same time to keep her feelings to herself, and to hand them over to Elise. Shame rose again, in her throat, between her legs. Of course Elise knew she fancied him, knew she'd asked Kirsten to take care of this John who made her nipples sting, then changed her mind.

Elise's raised eyebrow was as eloquent as need be. Sophie let her smile fade. The phone rang again. It was payday. Sophie moved away from the kitchen table while Elise answered it, her voice rising in anticipation.

Restless, unable to keep still, Sophie wondered whether her response to John the Cyclist might have something to do with Elise and Marshall. The sex between Marshall and Elise was bound by commerce, public, yet they were a couple. Perhaps it was this that had given her the wrong idea. A couple, public-private, who blurred the boundaries it was dangerous to blur, rubbed out, or threatened to, the carefully ruled line.

Sophie closed the side room door behind them.

'Good evening,' they both said at the same time.

John smiled. His greying hair was damp. Sophie undid her sarong, folded and left it on the chair.

He was heavy-shouldered and the muscles in his calves immense, disproportionate you might say, if you had another idea, ideal of proportion.

His tongue was the right size and shape. She opened her legs to it, to him, and the place between them, that had been climbing all evening towards this, and the writing of their names together, divided, in the book.

The Model Room

It was an idea of a bedroom that Sophie had never associated with a room, or house, before. An idea leapt off the table, taking wings. Its colours were those of the sea at night under a full moon, in a country where it rained a lot, the land beside the water a deep, unthinking green.

Sophie bent over, studying the whole and then each part. Ann had fixed her lamp so that it shone directly on the model, which took pride of place in the centre of her design table. Sophie recalled the drawings in that same spotlight and exalted position. Shadows leached into one another. Drawn curtains and semi-darkness made other objects, including the two women, indistinct.

'Jesus, Ann,' said Sophie.

The bedroom's ceiling was fan-shaped, the edges of the fan decorated with a carved design, repeated in an archway between it and an adjoining bathroom. Yet the archway was more like a tunnel. Its ceiling too, Sophie noticed, looking up from inside, as she was meant to do, was intricately carved. The walls weren't just one colour, but greeny-blue on one side, and a brooding purple, almost black, on the other.

From the ceiling hung, not mobiles – they weren't free-floating – but moving panels, their colours echoing the walls. The room lifted off the table, out of the surrounding dimness, yet its wings were inside, folding, shell-shaped, right up near the ceiling, right height for a person lying on her back.

Sophie was conscious of Ann's shape just behind her, waiting. She stood up and smiled.

'It's beautiful.'

Ann smiled back, relaxed, but there was a shadow at the back of her smile, as though she'd expected something more, or different.

'I kind of went overboard,' she said.

Violet, indigo, colours of a paintbox such as Canberra's dry skies, dry land, seldom saw. But too flat, too matte, these names.

'Do you think they'll like it?'

'They'll love it,' Sophie said.

She touched the overlapping panels, made them move against each other, ever so gently, ever so softly, as wind could, or a shaft of air-conditioning. The panels moved with the tiniest, gentlest of sounds, sounds that could not be made by wood. They had to be made by some sort of material too thin to be wood, and far softer, more flexible than paper. It was the music of expensive lingerie, discreetly, never-endingly removed.

But what about the need for disguise, or at least discretion, the need to make the house look ordinary to passers-by, and to neighbours who would poke their noses anywhere, in order to condemn?

Sophie reminded herself that they'd never come inside, that couple at 13, or their supporters. Unless camouflaged as clients, none had shown their faces inside Number 10, to judge what the rooms were used for, to count beds, or track the feet of strangers from the dripping shower.

Ann's room sang its purpose. No casual visitor would be fooled by it for a second. Sophie looked, and it was like falling in love. She hugged Ann and they grinned with the pleasure of tossing subterfuge aside.

Ann switched the light off. She walked to the east-facing window and opened the blinds. Poplars thrust their spear heads up the hill. It seemed both women had the same thought at the same time, that the trees were marching, that they couldn't wait to get where they were going.

'It's just the light,' Ann said.

Sophie nodded. With a newfound sense of belonging in Ann's house, she made the tea she had not stayed for last time.

Ann was not domestic, but there were tea bags in a canister, a carton of not-yet-sour milk in the fridge. They took their tea outside, to drink in the striped shade of the gum tree.

Sophie leant back against the tree. The smell of resin prickled the insides of her nose.

She told Ann stories of her clients – Doctor Tate and his surprising announcement concerning her uneven legs. Ann rushed inside for a tape, made her stand up, circled her with great solemnity, while she measured with her tongue between her teeth.

'No Soph! It's bullshit! Really!'

Sophie collapsed laughing, and upset her tea.

There was John the Butcher. Sophie described him as a large, fumbling, tentative and modest man, who brought gifts of meat, which she cooked for Tamsin, but found she could not eat herself. There was the big foot man, who had to leave his shoes on because when he got excited his feet swelled up, and he could not get them back on again. He was humble too, after his own fashion, though unapologetic when it came to his curse. And the shadow-men, who faded into one another as Sophie recounted their common histories to Ann – the impotent ones who kept returning, though she could do nothing for them. They made her feel guilty. Kirsten told her not to be silly, and Elise, in a companionable moment in the kitchen one night, while Kirsten was sick, had said, 'It's a business, Soph. They pay, and we do our best.'

All this variety Sophie offered up to Ann as conversation to go with their tea. But she left John the Cyclist out of her account.

They took the empty cups inside, and Ann began to talk about her own work. There was nothing wrong with renovations. They were her bread and butter. But it was her ambition, some day, to design a whole building. When she'd gone into business as an architect, she'd longed to create something beautiful from scratch, from the dirt up, in this city of architectural mistakes, to set her stamp on a clean slate, ground to sky.

Ann said, 'I know I'll never be remembered for working out where to put partitions in an office.'

Trouble was, there were too many architects. She made a wry face, mouth downturned, that reminded Sophie, fleetingly, of Kirsten.

'Maybe one day someone will commission me to build a toilet block,' she said.

'Or a scout hall,' Sophie added.

'Or a bike shed. Yeah.'

They laughed again, and just then could have been any two young women, facing the first hurdles of a promising career.

Ann quoted Louis Kahn. 'The city is a place of availabilities.'

'Well, exactly,' Sophie said. 'What about the new suburbs?' For the town was poking its long fingers right out into the bush.

Ann said, 'Sure, but why pick me?'

'It will happen,' Sophie said, a change to be the one offering reassurance.

A couple of hours later, Sophie picked Tamsin up from preschool.

'Mummy?' Tamsin asked uncertainly, studying her mother with her feet apart, legs sturdy under red overalls crisp as new banknotes.

'Dad's taken you shopping,' Sophie said.

Tamsin was dragging her bag behind her. Sophie felt relieved that there was no sign of the teacher. Her daughter sighed exaggeratedly, and waited for Sophie to tell her how strong she was, which Sophie did.

'I've got a new aunty. Aunty Claire.'

'Did Aunty Claire go shopping with you?'

Tamsin nodded. 'You know her favourite colour? Red!'

Sophie laughed. 'Did you tell her *your* favourite colour?'

Tamsin nodded again, this time with less conviction.

'I'll always be your mummy,' Sophie said, unlocking the car.

'*I know that*,' said Tamsin, with perfect, four-and-a-half-year-old scorn.

Tamsin fell asleep over her dinner. It was all Sophie could do to get the child to wash her face and brush her teeth. She took her tea outside to drink, the evening cooling fast, but still just warm enough.

Elise rang as she was finishing it.

'Can you come in? Kirsten's sick.'

'I've got Tamsin,' Sophie said.

It was a source of irritation that Elise seemed blind to what this meant.

'Soph? I'm here on my own.'

Sophie hesitated, then said, 'I'll see if my landlady will sit for a few hours.'

She felt queasy on the way to Kingston. She hoped she wasn't coming down with something. Too many people were suspicious – Andrew, that woman at the preschool, her landlady Mrs B, who had the kindest heart, whose kindness Sophie must not stretch any further. Sophie knew that Mrs B thought she had a lover, was going to meet a lover – *that* was the sudden need. She recalled the question in Mrs B's eyes that lived below politeness and affection for Tamsin. Why, Sophia, when you could have been with him last night and the night before? Doesn't he know you have a daughter?

Sophie had not wanted to do anything that evening except sit in the garden which, owing to her good fortune and Mrs B's generosity, she and Tamsin were allowed to treat as their own – to sit outside while the temperature dropped, and float back into the model room.

When Elise rang, she was sitting in a garden chair, half in and half out of the porch light, in easy reach of Tamsin and the telephone. There was the dark green garden, watered to the gills, and the sense it always gave her of luxury, repleteness, a deep satisfaction with its own existence. She liked the dark beyond the porch light – her porch, her light, belonging to the flat she rented from Mrs B. It was the light that had reminded her of Ann's model, and made her want to sit there, the way it shone so brightly on the tiny porch and three steps leading up to it. She'd wanted to drift back to that tiny, voluminous room, to surround and pamper herself with it.

For that was the meaning of the folding, fan-shaped panels, Sophie decided on her drive to Kingston – their meaning and their gift – to make *her* the seductress, the active one, the one who chose. And enchanted, like someone in a fairytale, as young men were, in fairytales, even if they managed to escape. Ann's model room was perfect, she decided, for her purpose, for theirs.

Sophie parked at the back of Number 10. The suburb she had come from, the rest of Canberra, faded. The hypnotic rhythm returned. Sophie's knees made way for it. The bed rocked, her knees balanced and made way. The fan whirred. Her arms were the right distance apart, coiled spring in each of her elbow joints, should a spring be needed.

Potential

If potential could be measured in the precise lift of an eyebrow, the timing of it, so that whoever was watching smiled, and Marshall smiled back, showing corrected teeth, then such potential Marshall harvested now that autumn was just around the corner. He set about making something of it.

Whether or not Elise was in love with him, whatever was between them, they complemented one another in a business sense. Elise went to the front of the house to meet the customers her partner had welcomed. She wore silver lycra tights. Performing for him, she became effervescent, blonde ponytail and swinging thighs. She rubbed herself against him, legs spread, laughing.

Marshall might kiss her, grab her by the crotch. Sophie might be standing at the kitchen end of the corridor, thinking of the phrase 'eyes only for each other'. If Kirsten was watching, she might say something. Sophie never did. Kirsten might say, 'Fuck her in this house and you'll have to pay for it.'

Kirsten had come back to work saying she was better, but she didn't look it.

'Potential' was Marshall's favourite word. He used it of girls, who did not always recognise the compliment. 'You've got so much potential,' he told Sophie, his casual tone belying the hooks underneath. These hooks intrigued Sophie. She could not have described quite what their shape was, or their power.

Marshall preferred the carrot to the stick approach. He wore courtesy like a glove that hid a malformed hand. He took pleasure in introducing Sophie to new customers, calling her from the kitchen in a voice he kept especially for her.

Sophie, in her blue and brown sarong – she had two now, and never felt cold in them – made her way to Marshall's foyer, to the plain chairs and coffee table, on which might be, if the evening's business had progressed a certain way, some glasses and a bottle of wine.

Marshall introduced her as 'our new girl', though the adjective was wearing thin. Whoever was waiting there might lean back, to study her at ease, perhaps with disappointment. She was growing a second skin to this reaction. He might half stand, out of politeness.

Marshall waved away the gesture. No need for formalities, his expression said.

Sophie fingered the knot of her sarong, and kept a prudent distance from both men. She breathed a sigh of relief once a service was agreed on, and she could shut the side room door.

It was the flash of Marshall's bloodstone ring that struck Sophie most forcefully, one evening, as she walked up the corridor with an armful of fresh towels. The smell of soap powder filled her nostrils, and she recalled the latest in a series of discussions about whether it was worth sending the sheets and towels to a laundry, or whether they should invest in a good washing machine.

Marshall appeared from nowhere. His ring hand flashed, cupping her right buttock. He smiled at her over the top of the towels. The door to the side room stood open in front of them. Marshall's hand directed, not to be put off this time.

Kirsten's voice rang loudly.

'Phone, Marshall Matt. For you.'

Marshall hesitated in the act of shepherding Sophie into the side room. Kirsten advanced. 'It sounds official.'

Marshall grunted with annoyance, and his fingers went limp.

Quickly, Sophie dumped her pile of towels and followed him to the kitchen.

Marshall picked up the phone, then glared at Kirsten.

'Funny,' Kirsten said. 'Maybe he got sick of holding, or maybe something happened to the line.'

It was Elise's smell that Marshall carried when he sat at the front of the house, in the dingy foyer, chatting up a client, boasting about the proper reception area that would soon replace it, projecting himself towards this in his style and manner. It would be an asset, then, to have the right kind of man about the house, a man to take the money who smelt, faintly, not of having just released his own semen, nothing so obvious as that – of a finer promise altogether.

Marshall's open hands, his knees not quite together, promised sex with beautiful young women, how much of it there was available, and he, the man who managed them, what proof he was of this, in the cut of his clothes, the bulge of his never-to-be-exhausted manhood. His skin was perfumed with the bodies of young women, various and thrilling, the pads of his fingers, when he took the clients' money.

Sophie overheard him saying to Elise one evening, 'If it keeps going like this, we can both retire at forty.'

Yet the three women breathed a sigh of relief when Marshall left the house. Kirsten took charge of the armchair, turning up the sound on Tracy Chapman. Elise seemed to grow in height, in stature, filling out her role as acting manager. There was a chill between her and Sophie, where there had never been affection, and Sophie wondered if Kirsten had told her what had happened, what her quick thinking had only just averted.

Kirsten smoked, mistress of the CD player. She swallowed two Panadols with a glass of water. The plastic they were wrapped in gave a small click as she released them. Taking her turn in the chair, Sophie wriggled her buttocks into a more comfortable position. Elise finished talking on the phone. The doorbell rang.

They relaxed in Marshall's absence, but Kirsten left early, after a dispute with Elise. 'I need the money,' she insisted, and Elise, 'For Christ's sake, I'll fiddle with the book! Now go home and tomorrow find a decent doctor.'

Undressing in the side room, Sophie entirely forgot where she was for a moment. She was sitting in a concert next to Andrew. There was music in her ears. Her heart lifted towards it.

'What's that you're humming?' John the Cyclist asked.

'Oh,' said Sophie, wrenched from the pleasure and comfort of the melody. 'I can't sing in tune,' she murmured. 'Do you know what it's meant to sound like?'

Instead of answering, he looked at her curiously. His shirt was half undone. He'd pulled it out from the waistband of his trousers. Neat they were, his actions and the waistband, resting now against his singlet and his skin.

Sophie walked across and undid the next button.

He smiled down at her and dropped his hands, palms outwards.

She lifted his right hand and studied it between her two. The summer had left bracelets of freckles round his wrists. Age and many summers had coarsened his skin, and it was hairy too, with thick, fair hairs running up beneath the shirt. She ran her fingers over them and felt them lift, like hackles.

She finished undoing the buttons, and slid the shirt away from his wide, sloping shoulders. She pulled his singlet out, and he helped her remove it by raising his arms over his head.

She had a quick, uncomfortable flash of Marshall's bloodstone ring, yet there was a deliberateness to her movements now, a steady pedestrian advance. She reached up and kissed the bend of his smile, just where it turned a corner.

Taking his left hand this time, she led him to the bed.

He was not a passive man. His way of smiling down at her, while she undressed him, wasn't passive. She put his hand between her legs and closed her eyes, shut them to the anchor of the watermarks. She did not think of the position known as doggy, or what her upturned face, eyes closed, might reveal. She gave herself up to sensation, to the familiarity of hands which she had just now studied, and also to what could not be studied or anticipated in the abstract, the surprise at the ends of his fingers, just where her skin began.

There was a small wait while he took care of the condom. She knew that it would fit, that he would be careful. She'd watched him before, and she didn't have to bother with this now. He entered her sideways, her back against his stomach. Knees braced, he made it all seem effortless. He crossed his hands around her chest. She rejoiced in not having to consider her own knees, braced or otherwise. Having offered pleasure, he now took his own.

Sophie lay leaning on one elbow. With her free hand, she smoothed the ruffled sheet between them. He was lying on his side, facing her, having taken off the condom and dropped it in the bin.

'Are you married?' she asked, staring at her ringless fingers with their short nails, the line of freckles at her wrist.

'I was,' he said.

'I was too,' she offered. 'Children?'

'Two. Grown up,' he said, changing his position, rolling over on his back, and leaning against the pillows with his arms behind his head. He stared up at the ceiling, which was all in shadow. A bordello pose, she thought, smiling to herself.

'Grown up, but sometimes they still act like three-year-olds.'

'Oh,' said Sophie, wondering if he was giving her an opening to tell him about Andrew and Tamsin.

The hair under his arms was brownish, rough. His sweat smelt strong and sour. She was glad that he did not seem embarrassed by it. There was a sweetness to him, to the smell of him, that ran counter to the sweat, and to the sweet-sour smell of semen retreating to the edges of her senses, emanating from the bin, mingling with others of its kind, common to the room.

Sophie looked over at their two piles of clothes sitting neatly side by side on chairs – well, her sarong hardly made a pile. That's a statement in itself, she thought, and will be more of a statement when he stands up and starts replacing layers.

She glanced again, this time under her eyelashes, at the man lying naked and relaxed beside her, hands behind his head. She thought how, in another room, another situation, she might roll over, roll against him, he might open his arms to her and they might lie there, forgetting about the time, telling each other stories of their childhood. She wondered if his parents were both dead, like hers.

She did not want him to see her thinking this, to guess that she might be imagining anything along these lines.

She wondered about his particular brand of indifference, how it might show itself more clearly as she got to know him better, in small gestures, in the steps he took, the way he gave her pleasure. He only needed to look at her undoing her sarong to know that it was already working in her, what he was about to offer.

Kirsten would say it was simple. Kirsten would say she liked him too much. But Kirsten wasn't there.

'Look!' Sophie admonished, sitting up, aware of John's surprise, grabbing the lamp from the table by the bed, and tipping the shade at arm's length so its dull beam grazed the ceiling.

'Look,' she repeated, making sure he did. 'Soon, this room will be transformed. See those marks, the ceiling's practically covered with them – well, the light's a bit too dim, but you know they're there. They'll be marvellous colours, dark but glowing, colours you can lose yourself in.'

John smiled. 'That will be nice.'

Sophie smiled back, responding to the catch in his voice.

'Go ahead and tease me. You might see them too,' she told him, putting the lamp back down, giving his shoulder a quick nudge. 'You never know your luck.'

'There'll be ceiling panels,' she continued, 'right where those marks are, the darkest ones that look like thunderclouds.' She laid her hand against the side of John's face, against his cheek, and turned it slowly, so that he was forced to look straight at her. 'Sh, sh, they'll say, those panels to each other.'

'And when will all this happen?' John asked, still smiling underneath her hand.

'One day,' Sophie said.

Compromise

Late afternoon sun shone through kitchen windows that Elise had cleaned. She went over every centimetre of the windows with a fist of paper towels and the liquid cleaner.

Sophie opened them as soon as she arrived at Number 10. She rushed around, letting the stale heat of the day out in a rush. It was her self-appointed task, quickly, before the doorbell rang, to cool the rooms down, freshen them with outside air. It could still be warm outside at six, but not so much now. Daylight saving had just ended.

Clients did not like open windows. An open window was a threat or insult, noise of traffic in Andover Street, a child's voice, tired, returning from the bus or hockey practice, lilt in a child's voice to be going home.

'When we have airconditioning in the rooms – '

Marshall liked to begin this way, planning aloud to Elise, Sophie if Elise was busy. *When we have this, when we have that.*

They were making money to pay for the renovations, accomplish all these things that Marshall planned. Sophie thought she would miss rushing round and opening the windows, those few minutes when the house breathed in and out, and she with it, banishing neglect, as Elise did with the paper towels and Windex.

There was a tacky brown blind on the outside of the kitchen window, which faced west, looking out onto a backyard of thistles and dead Salvation Jane, long grass with the thin pointy seeds that burrowed into dog fur, caught between your toes and pricked when you walked out to hang something on the line. Sophie walked barefoot to hang tea-towels, fancy knickers, on the rotary clothes line, or the corset they kept in the cupboard in the front room, for clients who liked dressing up. Marshall said that when they went up-market, there'd be a great deal more variety, but for now there was just the one piece, a white corset with cups of scratchy lace, bought at a Target sale. Sophie disliked the corset, but she didn't mind watching it going round and round on the line.

Elise was on the phone, assuring Kirsten decorously, in a low voice, that she didn't need to come in. The few days before payday were usually quiet.

She'd been swimming that afternoon, in the Murrumbidgee, out at Kambah Pool.

'I saw a black snake,' she said, raising her voice. Sophie couldn't tell if she'd been frightened, curious, exhilarated.

'Swimming alongside me. I just kept going. I could have turned round, but I was nearly at the other side.'

Elise and Marshall were meeting Ann next morning, Kirsten too, if she felt up to it. Ann would present them with her plans, which were now complete. They would see the model room.

Elise laughed. Her voice changed. She said, '*Then* we'll be in clover.'

There were a few minutes remaining before the sun disappeared behind the lake, behind Black Mountain, neither of which could be seen from the kitchen window. Sophie sat in the armchair, facing the setting sun, happy at the way everything felt normal, this last span of daylight unremarkable, holding nothing special. There was no fore-taste, in or underneath it, of the night ahead, only Elise talking on the phone. A moment of *not yet.* Yet still Sophie was preparing, in her bones, her skin.

Next day was sullen, thundery. Sophie had planned to take Tamsin to the pool, but held off because of the thunder. Tamsin had her swimming bag packed, but was reduced to watching 'Playschool'.

A knock on the front door announced Ann, bringing the hot, sweet, thundery stickiness of the afternoon inside Sophie's flat.

Tamsin stood in the doorway, twisting a lock of hair round her right forefinger. She balanced on the balls of her feet, knowing trouble when she saw it.

Ann twirled and stamped, flinging her arms about. Elise had hated her plans, and the model.

'But why on earth?' asked Sophie.

The problem was the kitchen. In Ann's plan, the kitchen was shrunken, merely functional, reduced to a kind of nook, or galley, with a microwave, a bench, power point for an electric jug – all to allow for a fourth bedroom and the ensuites.

'You see!' cried Ann.

Sophie said, 'Oh no.'

Too late she noticed her daughter's open eyes and ears. 'Tamsin,' she said. 'Ann and I will just be in the garden.'

Was it the first time this had happened? Surely not. Tamsin with her quick wits, her taste for new words. She could have heard, could have repeated anything.

Like an usher with a late arrival, Sophie shepherded Ann out the door, one hand at her back. Behind the crab-apple tree, grey-black clouds were boiling, immense.

Ann had shown her the plans and drawings. How had she missed something so obvious?

'What are you going to do?' she asked.

'You know her, Soph. You work with her. *You* tell me.'

But the other problem was uppermost in Sophie's mind. Danger hit her with the first roll of thunder off Black Mountain.

The word 'brothel' had been out and about, aired between them in Tamsin's presence, with Sophie not stopping to think of the folly of this, of a four-year-old's talent for mimicry and the long hours spent with Andrew. Sophie had only thought with pleasure of Ann as a friend she could confide in. Up to a point. But the point of discretion – what you should and should not say in front of your daughter – this had long been passed.

The mood was gone, Ann's flung hoop of adrenalin. She lifted her chin towards the flat, half hidden behind rhododendrons.

'I've got kind of an idea. Don't know if it'll work. I have to think it through.'

'Ring me,' Sophie said. 'I can come up to your place without Tamsin.' She reached up to kiss Ann goodbye.

Ann made a face, not rejecting the kiss, not accepting it.

'I'm sorry,' Sophie said.

Ann's lips were pursed, holding in emotion, though it was changed now, the need and the direction. 'I think you ought to tell them. Not Tamsin of course, but Andrew.'

'But – ' Sophie began.

'I suppose it depends on how serious you are.'

'And you?'

'Oh, *I'm* serious. No-one speaks to me like that muscly little sheila did today and gets away with it.'

Muscly? Sophie thought. Was Elise muscly? She said, 'I'll talk to her. And Kirsten.'

'That's the dark one? She didn't say much. She laughed at my model.'

Sophie turned to go inside as the first great drops of rain, heavy as dollar coins, hit the apple tree.

No trip to the pool then, this hard rain instead. 'Captain Planet' had replaced 'Playschool' on the television. Tamsin sat in front of it. Lightning made the flat's small living room a stage. Normally bored by 'Captain Planet', Tamsin appeared to be giving the cartoon characters her full attention.

Sophie hugged her daughter quickly, apologetically. 'We'd better hurry up and close the windows. It's going to *pelt* down.'

Tamsin turned around and smiled at Sophie gratefully, and it was this, suddenly, that Sophie couldn't bear, her daughter's gratitude for a weak and cowardly offering.

Tamsin jumped up and ran into her bedroom. She wound the window closed. Sophie heard her talking to herself, but could not make out the words.

Later, after the worst of the storm had passed, she let Tamsin put up the folding umbrella in preparation for walking up to Mrs B's. She made herself be patient, silent, while Tamsin worked at the umbrella, figuring it out. She might jam her fingers, but the lesson would be worth it, her expression said. Sophie, for her part, was conscious of a dry, dead patch inside her, that the rain would not be reaching.

She rang Ann as soon as Tamsin was asleep, and they talked over and around the blunder. Ann's confidence was shaken. Sophie heard the catch in her friend's voice, and felt ashamed of her oversight, her failure to pay attention. She should have realised that Marshall, who, she was sure, *had* taken note of the diminished kitchen, would use it to stir up trouble. They talked until Ann said she was sure she could work out a compromise, but Sophie saw purple panels folding in on themselves, collapsing, as though the force that acted against gravity had been removed.

Elise said, 'Whatever were you thinking?'

'I didn't think,' said Sophie. 'I wasn't thinking. Sorry.'

'You could have warned us.' Elise's voice was hard. Her manner said, you brought that woman into it. The *architect*.

'Actually.' Kirsten smiled through her smoke, primping, hand behind her head. 'I quite liked it. Tarty, but nice.'

Kirsten had come to work with unhealthy skin, and thick black-purple rings under her eyes.

Elise frowned, but Kirsten was in a mood to provoke.

'It could grow on us. Seriously. I can see us in the *Good Weekend*.'

'Shut up, Kirst,' Elise said.

'Ann's got an idea,' Sophie told them. 'She'll work something out. It was my fault anyway, for not explaining to her about the kitchen.'

She didn't add that Marshall ought to have explained, that it was as much Marshall's fault as hers, for choosing to show Ann around the house one morning on his own.

Elise and Kirsten studied her with expressions which met, then mingled resolutely. Kirsten hunched her shoulders. Elise got out her yoga mat. They did not say yes, or no.

Sophie felt disoriented. Sometimes it seemed to her that the last words she'd spoken coherently had been to Andrew. 'Go ahead then. Leave.' Which of course he'd done, would have done, whatever she'd said, or not said, at the time.

'What does Marshall say?' she asked, aware that to bring up his name, as things stood now, was to take a further risk.

'He thinks it's great. What did you expect?'

Elise and Kirsten exchanged another glance, Elise still angry, Kirsten letting Sophie know that, if it came to taking sides, she was on Elise's.

Sophie pictured Marshall being swayed by Elise's arguments, the force of her personality, but then recalled the bloodstone ring, the cupped hand, Marshall standing just outside the kitchen with his arms crossed, the jealousy in that, the stealth and at the same time cruel challenge of it. She remembered Marshall sitting at the table with them, establishing his right to, knowing how it made them squirm. He staked out, then expanded his territory. But when did the stake become binding, and who decided that?

When the doorbell rang, and Marshall called Elise to the front of the house, Kirsten said, 'He saw where your friend had pinched the space from. That's why he never showed us the drawings till the other day.'

Sophie nodded. She wondered how long he'd expected to get away with it. Had he expected the renovating work to start before Elise got wind of what was happening?

'He's a bastard, Soph.'

'Why does she put up with him?'

'Who bloody knows,' said Kirsten.

Kirsten let Sophie do all but her last remaining regular that night, and left early again. Sophie worried about her driving home. She worried about Kirsten alone in her flat, which she'd described as spacious, airy and expensive.

It was a strange night's work. The sky filled with a bronze light after midnight, a light that, in the summer just behind them, might have blown down from bushfires on Mt Ainslie, Mt Majura. After it was over, Sophie ran the gauntlet between trees covered with metallic blooms. They threaded her way home, these posturing, decorative trees, from Andover Street, across the lake.

She opened the door of her flat quietly, though no-one was inside. She put her money in a drawer, just this night's takings now. She imagined the drawer's arms around the notes, keeping them safe till morning.

She lay in the dark and looked back on an older version of herself, a woman who'd mourned a broken marriage. This mourning period was coming to an end. She'd done certain things to speed it up. She'd telescoped consideration. She was aware – was Andrew? – that a raft might sink.

Walter Burley
Griffin

Walter Burley Griffin had brought his vision of democracy to Canberra, his gift that was not recognised as such, that was refused, then ruined by bureaucrats, successive changes of minister, a world war – Ann said.

Sophie listened. She loved it when Ann talked about architecture, history, planning – and then contingency, pragmatism, loss of vision – all this Sophie loved to hear Ann talk about. The Griffins had come to Canberra at the wrong time. Why should a raw upstart town mean anything when there was Gallipoli? An idea out of kilter with its time was still an idea. Ideals and visions remained, though turned into a dog's leg broken in three places.

Ann wasn't quite ready to forgive, not yet. She said, 'You might have warned me.'

Sophie heard the echo of Elise's voice, and repeated, 'I'm sorry.'

Ann waited for Sophie to apologise properly, while all Sophie felt like doing was making excuses, calling herself the meat in the sandwich, though she didn't like the phrase, knew it was inept, inaccurate.

She felt the buttered bread sliding over her, however, across her sides, her front and back. What kind of meat would she be? None appealed.

She said, 'I somehow never noticed the kitchen being so tiny.'

'The dimensions were all there.'

Sophie felt the pull of dishonesty, a sharp pull, and strong. If she liked to think of Ann and Marshall as two slices of bread, then, meat or no meat, it was she who had brought them together.

Ann took up her favourite position, hands balanced for leverage on the window ledge, back to the lake.

She smiled at Sophie then, dispelling irritation. They talked about the compromise. 'Easy once I worked it out,' she said.

'And the kitchen,' Sophie said, to make quite sure, 'is – '

'There was all that space in front, you see, just going to waste. There'll be enough for each bedroom to have an ensuite and still keep the kitchen.'

'Have you shown it to Elise?'

'I'm seeing her on Wednesday.'

In the end, thought Sophie, I wasn't needed as a go-between. Well good.

'Up the front,' she said, 'I take your point about the wasted space, but Marshall uses it as kind of a reception area.'

'That's cool. I won't get my fingers burnt twice in the same place. You don't need a whacking great barn of a reception area. Couple of chairs. Coffee table for magazines. Complimentary bubbly if he's into that.'

'He might be,' Sophie said, thinking of Marshall's ambitions, what form the next one might take. 'He was talking the other day about a video room.'

'Well he never said anything to me about *that*. He'll have to use one of the actual rooms for that. I don't see how I can squeeze out a fifth one.'

'Better not to mention it.'

Ann nodded.

Sophie glanced over at the model, which Ann had moved to a side table. Now it stood in shadow, but she recalled the way the lamp had shone, how the moving panels had seemed to herald a magical performance.

Ann followed Sophie's line of sight. She nodded again briefly, as though settling something in her mind.

'I can work around Marshall. It's that Elise who's the wild card.'

'He deliberately went behind her back. He showed you the house when he knew she wouldn't be there.'

'I did wonder about that,' Ann said.

'I think he likes to set women up against one another. He's got some notion that it keeps them on their toes.'

'He may have met his match in that Elise. How old is he?'

'Early to mid twenties.'

'Young to be buying a house. Where did he get the money?'

'I don't know.'

'We're marginally older,' Ann said, with an air of comfortable finality.

Sophie and Ann considered one another, through their marginally older years and looks. They laughed, and Sophie began to relax.

They talked about Ann's latest commission, a bedroom for another single woman. Ann said, 'We single women are growing on the trees.'

Sophie had never heard Ann complain, not seriously, about a shortage of men. She plucked one every now and then, tasted and then dropped him. Whether or not she was casual with all of them, she was casual in her recounting of their episodes to Sophie, making light of what perhaps already was, what she did not allow to weigh more than a single ripe fruit in season.

This single woman had contracted Ann to create a bedroom with windows placed so that the moon path could be followed every night of the year.

'Is she a hippy?' Sophie asked.

'An old rich one, maybe.'

'Can you do it?'

'Of course,' Ann said, 'but I'm letting her think it's a bit harder than it is.'

'Do you think she wants a room like that for entertaining lovers?'

'Maybe. She's not *that* old, actually.'

They went through the single women they knew, criticising some, speaking respectfully of others. Only Sophie, it seemed, wished to run from the arms of one husband straight into another's, and was going about it entirely the wrong way. But she did not envy Ann. This lack of envy occurred to her just then, completely, without before or after, as though envy might have auditioned for a part and been turned down.

She wondered what Ann would make of John the Cyclist, but still did not feel ready to confess. She watched Ann closely, as though Ann was about to do something unexpected.

Ann tossed her hair back, narrowing her eyes. She'd hennaed her hair, which Sophie thought was a mistake. She pictured Ann in Elise's lycra tights on the yoga mat, copying Elise's stretching exercises, Ann lumpy, frowning, saying 'shit'.

She said, 'Did you see that movie about phone sex? Well, there was phone sex in it. This bunch of women, paid to talk, sitting there with their hair in curlers, in their pyjama pants and slippers.'

'No, I didn't.'

'Well that's the point, I guess, that it doesn't matter. That it's all in the guy's mind, on the other end.'

Ann turned away from the window ledge, pushed herself away from it energetically, using both hands as a lever.

Sophie said, 'I wonder if they realise.'

'If they did, it wouldn't stop them.'

'You wanted to know what it's like,' said Sophie suddenly. 'The whole thing – it's to pitch against drift and aimlessness.' She hurried on in her wish to explain this much at least, knowing pitch was the wrong word, inappropriate, it made you think of baseball. 'You're confronted with that, your body is,' she said. 'You begin to learn its limits, or get an inkling of what its limits might be. It's a matter of endurance. And that's interesting, you see.'

Ann was silent for a moment, then she said, 'Jesus, Sophie.'

Sophie recalled a conversation she'd had with Ann, a long time ago, when Ann, a recent graduate, along with many other young architects, was working on the new Parliament House – a magnet of course, and not only for local talent. She remembered Ann telling her about the architect in charge, Romaldo Giurgola, his insight and generosity. What had charmed and excited Ann had been the unexpected curves hidden deep inside the building, its green internal courtyards that only MPs and their staff would be allowed to use.

When they'd talked about Giurgola and the secret feminine curves, Sophie had listened with pride in her friend, pride in what she was doing. She glanced once again at the model. In just those few minutes while they'd been talking, and the sun had slid behind Black Mountain, its colours had noticeably darkened.

Soon, she would be crossing the lake to go to work. She would stand at the kitchen window, or sit in the armchair if it was free. The setting sun would light her face. The bell would ring. The door would open on a stranger.

She forced her attention back to Ann, and Ann's career. Moon windows could be a person's bread and butter, should not be scorned for that. Neither should they take the place of what Sophie believed to be her friend's greater scope and reach. Could renovations ever be more than icing on a less than perfect cake?

Ann asked, as though their conversation had been running along different lines, had arrived somewhere quite different, 'How are things with Andrew?'

'Okay,' Sophie said. 'I guess.'

Perhaps it was something about visions, she thought on her drive across the lake, that you became aware of them most personally, most precisely, in the ways that they were turned aside, and turned aside *from*. She recalled the Griffins once again. The unmarked, unsullied vision – that was general, for a whole city, or a continent. It could be blinding, or a person might slide out from underneath it.

Here we are in the 1990s, she reminded herself, with self-government upon us, big government and little, the little carving out its own agenda, concerned not to waste police resources, concerned with the spread of AIDS. Soon, despite objections, prostitution would be legal in the ACT.

She thought of Mrs B, who'd buried a son and husband in baked, unyielding, suburban Canberra dirt, which she had set about transforming, watered, fed. Ann and Mrs B had liked one another, the one time they'd met by chance in Sophie's flat. Sophie had listened, smiling, while they talked about European architecture, in that raw early time, after Andrew had said he didn't want to be married to her anymore.

A Weekend at the Coast

Andrew rang. 'It's me.'

'Hi,' said Sophie, pleased to hear his voice.

'We're going away for the weekend,' Andrew told her, 'and I want to take Tamsin with me.'

'Where?'

'The coast. We haven't booked yet.'

'Who is *we*?'

'Jenny,' Andrew said.

Questions rose up and filled Sophie's mouth, burrs and thistles, grass seeds with pointed ends.

'Where's Tamsin now?' she asked.

'In her room.'

'What will Jenny think?'

'She likes kids.'

I bet she does, thought Sophie, wondering what Tamsin was doing in her room, if the doors were open, whether she was listening.

She put the phone down, thinking that Andrew's voice had been eloquent with lack of interest in her, and whatever she happened to be doing.

Yet it was a treat to be sitting in Ann's kitchen drinking freshly ground coffee on a Sunday morning. Ann's face glowed in the early light. Sophie thought of Tamsin at the coast with Andrew and 'Jenny' – which one was that again? She sighed and let Sunday morning seep into and wash over her. They were going to the Kingston markets, and after that, if they still felt like it, for a walk around the lake.

Sophie felt nervous at being in the same suburb, close to Andover Street, with Ann. She would not go there though, would not sneak a look. She had not told them about her free weekend, telling herself, instead, that she had earnt a holiday.

She put down her mug. It was one she'd never seen before. She had often noted how Ann accumulated possessions without apparent effort, certainly without pointing out their acquisition. It seemed to Sophie, sitting in the direct and calming sun, a new-minted mug between her hands, that a reversal might be possible. It might well be *her* kitchen they were sitting in. They might be drinking out of mugs that she had paid for, out of her legal and legitimate income. This seemed to be at her fingertips, as though the heat of the liquid, contained and trans-mitted by the clay, had itself produced an astounding leap of fortune.

Ann asked, 'What's she like?'

It took Sophie a second to grasp her meaning. 'The new one? Beautiful. Clever. Rich. Likes children.'

'Rich?'

Sophie improvised. 'Father owns a chain of chemist shops in Queensland.'

'What's she doing here?'

'Snaring my ex-husband.'

Ann's laughter was sharp-edged. Sophie almost believed in her inventions. She hoped their morning wasn't going to be spoilt.

She stood in Ann's workroom while Ann fetched her coat.

Ann had moved the model once again. It was still on a side table, but adjacent to a window. The morning light seemed especially drawn to it. Sophie smiled. The miniature room was fragile, yet enduring.

There were the colours of the sea at night, never to be observed directly from her land-locked city, the panels that folded in on themselves discreetly, yet opened out as well, as wings did, of generally unnoticed creatures, when aroused.

Ann came up behind her, red coat over one arm, a pure wool coat Sophie regarded covetously. Perhaps, this winter, she would buy one.

'Come on,' Ann said, 'or the morning will be gone before we know it.'

'How's Jenny?' Sophie asked, the next time Andrew phoned.

'Who?'

'Jenny. The coast. Remember?'

'Oh fine,' Andrew said lightly. 'Fine.'

Waves of bitterness flowed, and it was all Sophie could do to keep her nose above them.

Her pleasure in her daughter was a recompense, but more than that, it altered time. Having Tamsin in the flat with her altered their existence in minutes, hours and days. With the coming of the cooler weather, Sophie's life fitted snugly in around her daughter's. She picked Tamsin up from preschool and they walked, bought treats for dinner, revelling in Canberra's golden autumn. After dark, they lazed about the flat. Mrs B would have cooked for them every night, but Sophie didn't want this. For a few hours in the evening, she wanted her daughter entirely to herself. Tamsin had not said anything about the weekend at the coast, and Sophie was too proud, too careful in the wake of past mistakes, to press her for descriptions that were not volunteered.

But at work, the waves of bitterness came back. In the side room, Sophie became taciturn, then silent. She sat in the armchair, resting between clients. She did not want to talk to Marshall, or Elise. When the phone rang, she lifted the receiver and spoke automatically. When a client equal to her bitter energy turned up, she would be ready for him.

Kirsten's Eyrie

Sophie learnt that Marshall was a man quite willing to bide his time. If one opportunity failed to produce the desired result, then he would try another.

It was so quiet in the kitchen that the humming of the fridge might have been thunder. Sophie wished for Tracy Chapman or Bruce Springsteen, Kirsten smoking in the armchair, Elise in the middle of a bow posture on her mat.

Marshall closed the door behind him, then cupped her buttock with his hand. No hesitation on the threshold this time. Elise's customer, regular and elderly, would keep her busy for a good half-hour. Even if the phone rang, it wouldn't save her.

She sidestepped away from Marshall's hand, and turned to face him, saying, 'You don't want to do this.'

With a smile of victory already assured, Marshall said, 'Nobody will know but you and me.'

Didn't he realise how delicate the balance was, between her and Elise? Of course he did.

'Elise will know. I'll tell her,' Sophie said.

'You'll get the blame. She'll kick you out.'

'Then I'll go. Is that what you want?'

Her firm voice threw Marshall momentarily off balance. She moved quickly towards the back door. In less than a heartbeat she was there, and had it open. Cold air blew a magazine lying on the table.

'You can tell Elise I'm sick, and I'll be back tomorrow. But touch me once more, and I'm telling her the truth.'

The wind bit through Sophie's simple cotton garment. Hurrying around the corner to her car, she looked down at her sarong and thought, How foolish. A single knot, and then. She did not normally consider herself brave, but hugged the secret pleasure of standing up to Marshall.

She went home and sat in silence in her garden flat, and told herself, If I have to stop, I will.

The phone rang a couple of hours later. 'How are you, Soph?' Elise asked politely.

'I started throwing up,' said Sophie. 'Must be something I ate.'

'Will you be okay tomorrow?'

'I hope so.'

'I hope so too,' Elise said. 'It's tough here on my own.'

Kirsten's flat was modern, clean, on the fourth floor of a new brick apartment block. It would have fitted Kirsten like a glove had Kirsten possessed the strength to wave herself around and fill it out. Kirsten barely had the strength to move her fingers some days. Others, she was better.

She sat up in a white bed that filled her bedroom, the rest of the flat seeming to contract around it. 'My eyrie,' she called it, something in her of a hawk's sharpness still.

Considering, dark-eyed Kirsten leant against white pillows in her high, sweet flat, and invited Sophie to sit down on the end of the bed. Which Sophie did, while Kirsten said, 'I've got some sort of virus. That's what the doctor told me.'

She made a face, reaching for her smokes, on a bedside table the same height as the bed, preferring temptation, Sophie guessed, to be right there, underneath her eye. Abruptly, she shoved both hands under her bum and sat on them.

'It can't help,' Sophie said.

'No. Right.' Kirsten bent her head forward, taking in Sophie's edgy seat, her need for reassurance.

That great drop under the words 'virus', 'doctors'. The decision to have, or not to have, a cigarette.

'What exactly did the doctor say?'

'A low level virus. Not the big one, naturally.'

'Do you trust his judgment?'

'Hers. I suppose so. She told me to give up smoking.'

'Is there anything I can do?' asked Sophie.

Kirsten couldn't think of anything precisely, not right now. 'It's nice of you to drop by though.'

'Shopping?' Sophie wondered. 'I could drive you to the doctor.'

'Thanks.' Kirsten coughed. 'Maybe next time.'

'Do you like living here?' Sophie asked.

'I do,' said Kirsten, with a smile that, for her, was unusually compliant, willing to meet Sophie halfway with regard to whatever errand Sophie had embarked on.

She gave her shoulders an impatient shake, and reached again for the table by the bed. Her eyes slid towards the blank eye of a television at its foot.

'You can manage by yourself?'

'Manage,' Kirsten repeated, as though the word, and all it suggested, was beneath her.

Kirsten looked thinner, but the shadows under her eyes were less heavily incised, as though the tension of keeping up appearances in the Kingston house, now lifted from her, had brought relief. Perhaps, thought Sophie, she has enough money in the bank to cover her rent, and to ride out this illness, whatever it is.

'Can I get you a glass of water?'

'Sure.'

Sophie watched Kirsten drink her water slowly. She would have liked to lay down a plan for the future, and discuss it. Her plan would be in long straight lines. She multiplied them in her head, watching Kirsten's throat move up and down.

All those men intent and focused on their pleasure. Each one would pay well. Sophie pictured, beyond the regular, bright lines, herself young, strong, in command. She would be well off if she devised a plan and saved, independent even of her landlady, who had been kind, and cared for Tamsin. She would work longer hours, build up a reputation. She'd be able to afford the deposit on her own flat, perhaps a small house. She imagined Tamsin in a house which her mother owned, a house with white curtains moving in the breeze.

'Marshall came on to me again,' she said, without knowing she was going to.

'I told you to watch him.'

'He bailed me up in the kitchen. I ran away. Do you think Elise knows?'

'She knows, but she doesn't want to.'

'What does she see in him?'

'He's got money, he's ambitious.'

It was the first time Kirsten had said anything implying criticism of Elise.

'What about you?' asked Sophie.

'What about me?'

'Are you an exception?'

Kirsten laughed, then coughed again. 'I piss him off,' she said, as though she'd forgotten she'd already used this answer.

Sophie felt as though she was sitting on a cloud, so high up, so white, so easy to fall through to the street below. She was glad, feeling suddenly light-headed, that she and Tamsin lived on the ground floor.

After she'd said goodbye, Sophie folded two fifty dollar notes and left them under the sugar bowl on the kitchen bench. She didn't say anything to Kirsten about them, nor did Kirsten mention them, the next time they spoke on the phone.

Rabbit Glare

In the photograph, they were all running away. They *were* all running away. This was factual, correct. Only in the photograph it looked so much more so, caught in the flash bulbs, even Marshall, last one out and turning to make sure the door was locked. Marshall had been snapped in profile, responsible and solemn, his lip ring standing out.

Sophie was glad that Kirsten hadn't been at work. Kirsten might have faced the camera, tried to grab it, hit the photographer over the head. Sophie could not imagine Kirsten desperate to escape the flash, or the push of bodies in the driveway. As for herself and Elise, they were legs flying, they were pale limbs in motion. Elise's long hair swept forward over her face as, with a cry, she recognised an ambush. Athletic Elise sprinted down the footpath, Sophie and Marshall bringing up the rear.

Sophie rang Ann.
  'Have you seen it?'
  Ann said, 'Nobody would recognise you.'
  'I recognise me.'
  It came out a wail, a cry, long keening on the 'I'. 'I – eeee.'
  Ann said, 'I'll come over.'

They sat outside, though it was no longer warm enough to do so comfortably. Ann had brought wine.

Sophie said, 'I have to think.'

'What is there to think about? You've had men lining up to pay for sex. You've got a kick out of deceiving Andrew. You've made your point, haven't you? Just quit.'

Sophie lifted both hands to her temples, raked her fingers through her hair, aware that the gesture was inadequate, yet overdone.

'There's this man,' she said.

'One of them?'

'I haven't fallen for him.'

'What then?'

'It's business. Unfinished business.'

Ann said. '*What* about this man?'

'John. His name's John.'

'John then.'

'I told you, it's business.'

'But harmful,' Ann said irritably, 'in the long run.'

Sophie said. 'I'm not ready to give up yet.'

'Vengeance is mine,' said Ann, but instead of sounding defiant, or cynical, a note crept into her voice that had not been there before, of querulous uncertainty.

Sophie said, 'If I left now, I'd never see the new rooms.' She meant work in them. She expected Ann to grasp the difference.

Ann frowned. Sophie studied her expression. 'There's a problem?'

'Nothing I can't handle.'

There was something odd in the slant of Ann's reply. But Sophie was too concerned with her own problems to pay attention to it.

Ann did not understand the practice of the house, daily, hour by hour. But then, in fairness, Sophie thought, when Ann *had* asked questions, her answers had not led to understanding. So the fault lay with her as much as with Ann. Or else it lay between them.

After Ann had left, Sophie sat feeling empty, limp, and thought about what she might no longer get away with. How short the time of getting away with seemed, now that it might soon come to an end. She thought of Andrew, Mrs B, and what she owed them, individually, and also, peculiarly, together, as though they were bound for a second, like twins joined at the hip. Until she got over her confession, they would be like this, the two people, two adults, to whom she owed an explanation. Perhaps they would join further then, in judgment, condemnation, solid as a deformed tree trunk, as two humans linked by fresh and flowing blood. At any rate, she must say something to Andrew.

Photographers and reporters pranced up and down Andover Street. In daylight, the rundown house put on a show of sameness for them, for its neighbours, and those who'd taken it upon themselves to protect that corner of the suburb. The square house, angled in the sun of morning or of afternoon, gave up nothing special, and was not yet famous, or infamous enough, to be interesting in its own right. Yet the cameras kept on turning up, as though a big story was there, if only they could find it.

They'd been conned by the vigilante team. This was Marshall's expression. He wasn't at all put out, either by the renewed campaign, or the media's reaction.

The Bellamys from 13 and their supporters were angry that their letter writing had not produced the desired result. The 'dump', as they now referred to it, was still operating right under their noses. The police hadn't done their job. Community action would get the place shut down, and persuade the police that the time for turning a blind eye to a brothel on a residential street was past.

They lobbied politicians, marched with placards, fifteen, twenty at a time. They wrote press releases, handed out flyers at the Kingston shops, gave long interviews.

Sophie stayed away for a week. On the nights when she did not have Tamsin, she sat with her hands folded in her lap, lacking the energy to read, or watch TV. She sat in the darkness in her tiny living room, listening to the night sounds of the garden, straining towards the traffic in Andover Street.

As though to spite the protesters, Number 10's custom increased and looked set to keep on climbing. Elise phoned Sophie, sounding desperate, and Sophie said, 'Okay. I guess it can't be *that* bad.'

Men who, until now, had not done a rash thing in their lives – or so they told themselves – drove late at night to the lane at the back. They lined up. This was worth a picture, though in the dark, in the flash, a line of cars was all it was, with shadow shapes emerging, the suit of one and casual attire of another.

The white rabbit glare. Men, who never in their lives had been so daring, persuaded themselves that now it was their turn. For a hundred bucks, it was cheap at the price. Nervous clients scuttled in, red-faced, or pretending unconcern. Marshall still liked to open around six, to pick up punters on their way home from work. Some stopped to look. They might return on payday.

They came and went around the back, through the kitchen door, some with faces down, embarrassed, some with defiance urging a stretching of the shoulders, a taller walk that Marshall, not particularly tall, had to hurry to keep up with.

Marshall the escort. When Elise complained, he called it an emergency. He said they were lucky with the house's position, next to a vacant block. He secured the back gate, met customers and escorted them himself. The brown blind was lowered over the kitchen window.

'For a day or two,' he assured Elise, 'till we work out something better.'

Clients stood in the kitchen's spotlight, blinking and disoriented, while Marshall said, 'This way.'

They stood, driven and arrested, some aware of having made a mistake, now it was too late to back out without abandoning what, a moment ago, had seemed so important. Some walked along the corridor smiling, as though the very suburbanness of Andover Street had been the lure, the promise that would not disappoint. They marched forward with undimmed excitement, needing no escort, certainly not Marshall, to one of the rooms.

Marshall called a meeting in the kitchen. They could hold a press conference, he suggested, give the interviews the media were clamouring for.

He paused, to study both his girls. Sophie wished that Kirsten was there, to give her views on clamouring.

Marshall warmed to his subject, arguing that they should tackle the whole question of legality head-on, prove what a farce it was to prosecute, and how behind the times their Kingston neighbours were.

He smiled slyly as he said this, hinting that he and the police had arrived at an arrangement agreeable to both.

Look at Fyshwick, Mitchell. *Club Goldfinger* had been operating out of Grimwade Street for a decade. The Yellow Pages were full of advertisements, while all *they* dared, so far at Number 10, was a name and phone number.

'Our paparazzi,' Marshall said, 'won't hang around forever.'

Elise had her own views. 'The publicity's dying down again. Soon we'll get our kitchen back.'

Marshall pursed his lips, then ran his tongue experimentally over the upper one. His lip ring was gone. It had left a tiny hole.

He fixed Sophie with his black eyes. 'And there's the plans our architect has submitted to the building office. We have to show them we mean business, and we're here to stay.'

He grinned, then mimed the action of taking a bull by its horns. Testing the hole in his top lip with his tongue, he raised the question of needing to hire a replacement for Kirsten. Their future should be planned and plotted out. If Kirsten wasn't up to it, they needed someone else, had put off finding someone else for far too long.

His expression said he understood and accepted Sophie's circumstances. 'With the kid. And you give good value Soph, the nights you're here.'

Sophie said, 'I'll work as often as I can. But I agree with Elise, about the publicity.'

She looked from one to the other, Marshall making a face of wry acceptance, and Elise tight-lipped. Their disagreement over the kitchen was there, in summary, in the drain of colour from Elise's temples, her lips a thin unpainted line.

'Okay,' Marshall said, 'but get a new girl. Tomorrow, or I'll find someone else myself.'

John rang and asked to speak to Sophie. She smiled, lifting the receiver. 'All quiet on the western front,' she said.

'Are you sure?' His voice was petulant, a child's.

'It should be fine,' she told him. 'I think they're giving up.'

'The demonstrators or the press?'

'Both. There's nothing doing tonight, anyway.'

Elise smiled her own form of encouragement, from the middle of a triangle posture on her mat.

'After all,' said Sophie, to keep him on the line, to stretch out anticipation from her toe-tips to her short, housewifely nails, 'how much more mileage can they get?'

'Don't bet on it.'

Sophie laughed into the phone. She hadn't been about to bet on anything, but was aware that she was taking a huge gamble with the man on the other end, inviting him to play the same game of chance that roused, and threatened her.

John the Cyclist shook off Marshall's guiding arm.

'Jesus,' he said, safe in the side room at last.

'A bit of publicity. We're managing the best we can.'

John's blue eyes were tense. They sat down side by side on the bed.

Sophie took his hand in hers and turned it over twice. The thick fair hairs were there, offering protection. She wriggled closer so their knees were touching.

She noticed something she never had before, that John had pixie ears, pixie ears on a broad-based, solid man. 'You made it anyway,' she told him.

He inclined his head, and raised one eyebrow slightly. Anxiety transferred itself, from skin to skin, but she did not want to let his hand go.

'I must not be recognised,' he said.

Sophie stared. He was a bureaucrat, not a politician. A senior one then, very high up, whose embarrassment would embarrass, perhaps mortally, the government he served? Maybe it was more personal – the wife, in spite of having been referred to in the past tense, still very much around.

Sophie was glad the room was dim, the ceiling in shadow beyond a small circle of lamplight. She would have turned the lamp lower, to hide behind, to emphasise the need for anonymity. At the same time, she felt her own fear of discovery lessening, in response to his. If she was afraid of Andrew finding out, then here with her right now was a man who had as much, or more to fear. She shivered. A little of the excitement she'd felt talking on the phone came back.

She turned his hand over once more, then pushed him back so that he lay full length on the bed, arms by his sides, head against the pillows. Not a passive man, in his encouragement, in better times.

More difficult undoing the buttons this way, but she managed it.

The belt and waistband, everything in order. She wondered if he realised how important it had become for her to accomplish things one after the other.

He looked at her, then down at his recalcitrant erection.

'Relax,' said Sophie.

The condoms were ready on the table. The old-fashioned travelling clock faced the wall. Outside ceased to matter to Sophie, and she willed it not to matter to John either. She unknotted her sarong and slid away from the small blue-and-brown comfort of the cotton.

She reached forward and kissed him behind the ear, then went to work, feeling confident, as any professional might, of the hundred workings of a similar nature she had put behind her.

She smiled, fearful of too many words.

He sighed and closed his eyes.

She got the condom ready, and then climbed on top. Her knees were strong, her thigh muscles reliable. She balanced, hands firm on the sheet and mattress, on either side of his shoulders, where the freckles, fading now that it was autumn, danced.

His eyes were still closed, his expression troubled.

'Sh, sh,' she whispered, dreaming words of encouragement and reassurance.

Was it just loss of anonymity that he was afraid of, this man with his worried face? Moving up and down, she imagined him cycling up a long, steep hill, then resting at the top, arm raised in a salute of triumph, guarding his Achilles heel.

She buried her face in the side of his neck. She bit the top of his pointed earlobe, and he drew his breath in sharply. He held her buttocks in his hands, firmly, pressing her against him. When he came, she felt him throbbing high inside her.

'That's my girl,' he said.

She dropped the condom in the bin. He lay still, as though he was asleep. She traced the outline of his body on the crumpled sheet. At the bottom of the bed, her sarong lay where she'd pushed it. She cupped her hands gently over his calf muscles, fascinated by their spherical and perfect hardness. It seemed that she might hold them in a belonging way. She leant over and traced their outlines with her tongue.

At the sound of Marshall's raised voice, followed by Elise shouting, 'Get lost drop kick!', John stiffened in the act of tying up his shoelaces.

'I knew it.'

'Stay right here,' Sophie said.

The front room's door was open. There was a loud noise by the window, followed by a man's cry of alarm.

Sophie peered between the slats in the blinds. It was dark, the nearest streetlight blocked by trees. Their porch light had been switched off since Marshall began bringing clients through the kitchen. She heard another thump, and running footsteps, then saw three flashes in quick succession.

A sound behind her made her swing around. John was standing in the doorway of the side room, dressed for battle, with the jacket of his suit covering his head like a hood, but looking as though he would much prefer to leave by the secret trapdoor Sophie wished she could produce in the middle of the floor, underneath the carpet roses, just for him.

She took his hand and led him back into the room, shutting the door softly, leaning against it and letting out a long-held breath.

'I'll give it five minutes,' he whispered.

'Is there somewhere else you have to be right now?' she whispered back, registering, with a small surprise, that it was much earlier than his usual appointment.

'Not urgently,' he said, his tongue making a small click around the 't' sounds.

'I'll check the back way,' Sophie said.

She returned to say there was no-one out there, wondering where Elise and Marshall had gone.

John rearranged his jacket, which he'd let slip off his head, pulling it forward so his face was hidden. His eyes accused Sophie from its depths, as though the whole embarrassing scenario was her fault, as though she'd conjured up a rogue photographer, after promising him they'd lost interest and moved on.

She followed him to the kitchen, phrasing words of farewell, then discarding them.

The kitchen was silent and empty, the blinds fully drawn.

She opened the door, conscious that, in less time than it would take to draw her next breath, the invisible swaying grass heads would swallow John the Cyclist.

She willed him not to look back, and he didn't.

'What was all that fuss about?' Sophie asked Elise.

'Just some smart-arse amateur.'

'Amateur?'

'Yeah. Some creep who thought he could sneak in through the window.'

'What happened?'

'I hit him with the diary.' Elise giggled. 'I heard a noise and rushed up the front. It was the first thing I grabbed.'

'Where was Marshall?'

'Oh, he was there,' Elise said vaguely.

'You're lucky you weren't with a customer.' Sophie wondered why Elise had heard the sound of the front window being forced, while she, concentrating on her John, had not.

'So,' Elise said. 'I'd still have chased him off. But I tell you what, I'm sick of this. Next one to try some monkey business, I'll brain him good and proper.'

All the rest of that night, Sophie waited for the knock on the door, the bell that announced, not another customer, but the police. What if the amateur photographer had gone to them with a complaint, or the pressure of publicity had become too great?

Once the police were inside, what more could be said? Would Marshall, summoned from his to-and-fro-ing, his please-and-thank-you in and out the gate, gracious Marshall, hand extended and 'Good evening gentlemen', persuade them to hold off a little longer? Grease the palm a little more, offer another bribe, as Sophie suspected he'd been doing? The police would laugh. They'd say, come on girls, you've had your little joke.

The house without John. She smelt him in the corridor, and at the kitchen door. She smelt him on the doorjamb, as though he'd brushed it with his hood in passing – shoulder height, neck height for a solid man.

She stood on tiptoe and breathed in deeply the cold air of the yard, picking up anxiety as it passed over neglected earth. Apprehension filled her nostrils and her throat, and she almost cried out, almost ran across the thistles, the grass heads with their pointy seeds pricking soles and instep, making clear, once and for all, where her flesh ended, where another's might begin.

Shame

Sophie caught and held her breath. She decided she would not run away, transform herself into one of those rabbits, boggle-eyed and beating her feet against a cage. She breathed out again.

They did not take the bull by the horns and go after publicity themselves. In this much at least, Sophie and Elise had their way. But neither did they buckle under pressure. Unless forced to by the law, they were not about to close.

The traffic in the rooms spoke of itself, pit-pat of feet and murmuring of voices just below the level that would make words audible, the voices and the feet and everything that was familiar, in the dying down of this second, inconclusive, flash of the public eye.

It had been good for business, Marshall reminded his girls, referring to the flurry of publicity as 'our second wave'.

There was a coolness, crispness, between Marshall and Elise over how it had been handled, over luck and whether, when, it might be expected to run out. But they did not discuss their differences in front of Sophie. And Sophie, listening for hints of what was said in her absence, of what these two, her employers, decided when she wasn't there, was attracted to the wave idea and thought it as accurate as any. The publicity had scared off some old custom, and had washed up new.

It had carried John the Cyclist away.

Though she schooled herself against it, Sophie kept expecting to hear John's voice on the phone, the precise ring of the doorbell made by him and no-one else.

She stood in the kitchen with her back to Elise and the new girl, who was called Marika.

Elise said, 'Go *on* Soph.' Or, 'It's your turn. Don't just stand there.'

Marika said nothing, but her eyes mocked Sophie. Brown eyes they were, like Kirsten's.

Sophie got herself through one half-hour, then the next. She avoided looking at the day book, with its carefully ruled lines. She sat in the armchair whenever it was free. She kept on wearing her sarong. It was her work dress. She could not think of a better one. She placed it on a chair, and, at the end of each session, lifted it carefully so as not to dislodge the small packet of shame folded underneath.

She fancied she saw John in Civic. She would not have said till then, or not with such conviction, how many men there were who shared his features and physique. Her eyes swivelled after long legs, an athletic walk, calf muscles that bulged under fine merino wool.

Jack

A man came to the door. He rang the bell and waited, rocking backwards and forwards on the balls of his feet.

'My name's Jack,' he told Sophie, in the side room.

Sophie smiled. She liked a client who introduced himself. It was better than just standing and staring, so that even the small offering of a name was left up to her.

'Hi Jack,' she said. 'I'm Sophie.'

Jack rearranged his feet in dust-covered work boots. He lifted his chest and tucked in his belly. His denim shirt was open one button too many. Ginger hair curled out away from it. He had three sleepers in a thin-as-thin-can-be right earlobe, and an excuse for a moustache. He took a deep breath, lifting the top half of his body out of his hips.

There was Elise's yoga teacher, who encouraged, 'Lift yourself out of your hips!' There was Elise, who liked repeating such advice in the kitchen.

Jack said, 'I like a good strong massage. None of your butterfly fingers. I like my pubic hair pulled. Leather across the buttocks.'

'I don't do bondage,' Sophie said. 'Did you tell Marshall what you wanted?'

Jack puffed his chest out. 'Maybe you can learn.'

Sophie stared. He was tallish. The hair on his head was wavy, the colour of plane leaves in autumn.

His pale eyes flicked towards the bed and back again. 'I'll teach you,' he said.

'What – ' Sophie began, but did not need to ask. He meant, to hurt me.

She felt uncomfortable and said, 'You've taught a girl before.' A phrase came to her and she repeated it. 'Put her through the paces.'

Jack laughed. 'I'm not a horse trainer.'

'If I go along with it – what then?'

But this was not a question Jack would answer.

'It's up to you,' he said.

Not the Taj Mahal

The crab-apple leaves were falling. Sophie and Andrew sat under the tree. Andrew brushed at the table and dodged a falling leaf. There was something on his mind.

'I went to that restaurant,' he said. 'No-one's heard of you. You don't work there. You never have.'

'Which restaurant?' asked Sophie.

'The Taj Mahal. Why did you lie to me?'

Sophie thought how short a marriage could be, a single season, less, and the rotting season, how short! Blink, and it too would be gone. She thought of what she'd said to Ann about not being ready to give up, and Jack, whose appearance she had spoken of to no-one outside Number 10.

Tamsin was a small, hard fruit that she and Andrew, singly or together, had the power to spoil. But spoiling had not been Andrew's way. His way had been to cut her, Sophie, loose, sail off into a future that held no place for her. Oh, she'd used the phrase herself – Andrew's way – allowing it to act as both summary and conclusion. He would be free, yet was proceeding according to a plan.

The small fruit between them, ripe for spoiling. Tamsin had followed her own path into the flat that was her home for half the week. She insisted on carrying her bag for as much of the distance as she could manage. The most important part was dragging it across the threshold. She shouted at her parents if either of them tried to help her.

Andrew stopped fidgeting and sat calmly, waiting for an answer. Sophie was conscious of a hardness that had not matured, against it a dull, ineffectual crackling. It would have been different if he still wanted her, even in the way of nostalgic recollection. It was his interference in her business, in the absence of desire, that she couldn't bear.

She would not ask if Tamsin had alerted him, what their daughter had said. If Andrew knew about Andover Street, let him be the one to bring it up.

'I don't want you checking up on me, following me around,' she said, calm in her own way, yet wanting him gone, off the property, with an intensity which made her hands shake. 'You don't *have* to know where I work. It isn't any of your business.'

'You're Tamsin's mother. I have a right to know.'

'No, you don't,' said Sophie.

Behind them, Tamsin sang as she put away her things. Was it always to be like this, Sophie asked herself, wishing, as Tamsin's voice caught, stopped and started again in a lower key, that she had kept her own voice down. She hated the prospect of two parents arguing under an apple tree, now one season, now another, Andrew pushing from one direction, she pulling, or simply wishing that he wasn't there. That day they'd met by chance in Civic seemed impossibly remote.

Andrew smiled the lopsided smile she hadn't seen in a long time.

'Come on, Soph,' he said. 'If it's any comfort to you, the guys in the restaurant took your side. I said I was looking for my ex-wife. You could try me, you know.' He waved a hand with generous expansiveness around the garden. 'Why did you expect me to believe that a part-time waitressing job pays for all this?'

'I have an understanding landlady.'

'So I've seen.'

'What are you looking for?'

'A good time.'

Andrew smiled again, but this time it was the smile Sophie associated with rejection.

'We got married too young,' he said.

'I didn't,' she replied.

There seemed no way to bridge the gap, and then have Andrew walk on, and not blow up the bridge.

Sophie rang Ann.

'Andrew knows.'

'What?'

'That I'm not working at the Taj Mahal.'

'Is that all?'

'Isn't it enough?'

Ann did not say, I told you so, but these words somersaulted down the line.

'You couldn't recognise me in the photos.'

'It's borrowed time though, Soph.'

'Borrowed?' Sophie echoed. 'I prefer to think of it as stolen.'

'Have it your way, then.'

'He's such a prick.'

'I've got to go,' Ann told her. 'I'm meeting someone. I'm late already.'

Afterwards, it occurred to Sophie that Ann might have been referring to the model rooms, for which time needed to be borrowed, so that they might see the light of day.

The phone rang a few days later, when she was getting ready to go to work.

'I never lied to you,' said Andrew.

Sophie wanted to point out how many different ways there were of lying. She strained for the sound of Tamsin's voice behind his, in the background.

'I won't keep on asking,' he said.

'Don't then.'

Jack in the Side Room

How seductive the side room was, holding Jack and Sophie captive, holding them in tension. How it pulled, and how Sophie felt this pull, savouring it, in her calf muscles, her knees, beginning early on the morning when Jack might be expected, though he didn't make appointments. How this pull and her pleasure in it strengthened through the day, so that when the doorbell rang, and Marshall called her to the front, and Jack stood in the foyer with his shirt open to just above the navel, she was ready for him.

The side room welcomed them with its simple props, its air of anticipation, what she and Jack together began teaching one another.

Jack undressed and knelt on all fours against the far wall, opposite the door, his opening gambit and his starting point. Her whip arm not yet tingling, not yet warm, Sophie ordered him to the centre of the floor, where she'd already laid a towel. Jack measured Sophie's distance from it, his as well, seeming to prance there, on his hands and knees, eager for the race ahead, the starting gate still locked, but tinder merely, sticks brittle and soon to be broken.

A flick of Sophie's whip, a little crack like the sound of a twig breaking, signalled that the race was on. She ordered Jack to move to the middle of the room.

Jack took no notice. His destination was the door. He crawled towards it vigorously and with clear intent. Sophie's fingertips began to beat. She took up her position. He tacked to out-manoeuvre her. The walls were his friends. He moved with confidence and speed along them. Sophie raised her whip and brought it down. The seeking tongue just caught his heels. He let his breath out sharply.

Sophie learnt fast. 'Come here,' she said. 'Go there', with cold intensity.

Jack had his own ideas. He had his orders too. If he was swift, then his pursuer was as fleet of foot, and swifter. He pranced. She circled, coming round behind him. She raised her whip and brought it down, tasting heels and buttocks – oh, the pleasure in that! Coming back for more.

It was a lot to do with footwork, Sophie decided as she became more skilled, her judgment of distance more acute, and her pleasure clarified, in a performance with a shape to it, a job well done. She had to circle swiftly and *make* Jack kneel over the towel. He begged, and she replied with the words he'd taught her. She concentrated on her feet and where to place them, on the warmth shooting up her arm, the whip whose tongue must light within a centimetre of Jack's back and buttocks. She must feign indifference so successfully that it became a habit, to his whimpering and sharp intake of breath.

Sophie faced Jack, standing over him. His body ran with sweat, thighs trembled, knees chafed against the carpet. His expression changed, taking in what before might have been held to be distinct and separate, the twin desires of surrender and escape. He did not look at her. She would have been disconcerted had he looked up, caught her eye. She would have lost her place. *She* looked down at *him* – the dance allowed for this. It had moments of stillness, longer ones towards the end. She looked down and noted the high, red flush along his cheekbones, the sweat along his hairline that beaded, dropping on the floor.

Here was one with whom she could clear a bright, accurate path between herself and Andrew, cut a swath behind the husband who'd rejected her.

This Jack, who faced her with his raised, haughty diaphragm and his heron's eyes, would have no truck with whispering panels, or colours of the sea at night. Jack cleared his own space. He made her see afresh, and with meanings she had scarce divined, old, worthless items in the room, and how she might make them part of her dream of revenge.

Sophie walked with an elastic step back to the kitchen. Elise was in the front room. Marika's smoke circled the back of the armchair. Bruce Springsteen's 'Secret Garden' rose from the CD player. The old, close-fitting kitchen door had effectively shut the song off from outside.

The Whip

Next time Marshall called her to the front for Jack, Sophie's right arm tingled in anticipation, and her fingers opened to take hold of the whip.

In the side room, they spun the wire of tension out between them. Sophie's thigh muscles urged her forward from the moment the race began. Jack sprang from his corner, and she moved to block him. She watched his upper arms, feeling the blood flow through them as though it was her own, a thrusting, wonderful warmth.

Their bodies were joined by the whip. This was the wire, the spring. Gladly, Sophie lifted it and brought it down again, cutting the air too close to skin for the eye to make distinction. But she knew how close, and satisfyingly, from Jack's sharp intake of breath. He never looked up, never looked at her, but her hands and feet knew the next steps to take. She seldom made mistakes now, trusting that space of air the whip created, the split second of not being quite sure before it landed on the carpet, dead against his toenails, or flayed the air just above his back.

How worried she had been, when she first raised her whip, about where it would land, the darkness that its tongue sought, with her right arm behind it, as though her arm and the instrument it raised were made of the same mixture of flesh and leather. She knew the pleasure of the hunt, of moving with assurance towards victory. Her breath heaved, and relief flowed over her, as Jack's hand pumped, as he brought himself to climax on the towel.

They sat next to one another on the bed, using up the half-hour.

In the underwater light, Sophie traced Jack's fish tattoo with her right forefinger. 'I suppose it hurt, getting it done,' she said. 'I suppose you liked that.'

'A bit.'

Jack had his small habits, quirks, Sophie called them, wanting to provoke. He was annoyed if, when he arrived, someone else was using his room.

'Why don't you ring beforehand?' Sophie asked.

But this he wouldn't do. He liked the early evening, payday or the day after. Sophie pointed out that these were their busiest times. As she traced the small fish with her finger, Jack's pale skin contracted. It was freckled like her own. He shivered underneath her touch.

'Why?' she asked. 'Why did you like it?'

Jack pulled away and laughed.

Sophie laughed with him, but she thought, Fancy getting to that point, and after you'd got to it, what then? A shabby house in Kingston, waiting to be legal, a girl to teach, to break in.

Jack took no notice of photographers or letters to the editor. They meant nothing to him. He shrugged and the fish moved on his shoulder.

He said, 'If the police were going to shut you guys down they'd have done it months ago.'

'You don't care, one way or the other?'

Jack shook his head to show his boredom with the question.

He's passing through, thought Sophie, and wondered how, or if at all, a photographer would catch him. It was his nerve that interested her, along with his purchase of sharp, calculated pleasure that had a beginning, a middle and an end.

When other clients asked her questions, Sophie affected indifference to publicity of any kind. She said, 'We'll have to wait and see.' She no longer wished to be reminded of John the Cyclist's disappearance, or to think about the future in a general way.

She asked Jack, 'But when you've finished, when you come back down, then what?'

Jack said, 'What is this, the third degree?'

And Sophie, 'When did it start?'

'For Christ's sake!' said Jack.

How odd it was, thought Sophie, that pleasure in the half-hour, with the evening closing in, should offer itself up here, now, with this man, his wavy red hair, his fish tattoo. He would stay until his time was up, getting his money's worth, resting in the echo of their dance around the floor.

Sophie thought of Andrew, in his ignorance, his innocence, how she added to this wilfully, unfairly. Relaxing with Jack, she pictured Andrew on his raft of girls, in an Hawaiian shirt perhaps, a straw hat. She ran her fingers ever so lightly, ever so gently, across Jack's tattoo, and imagined her ex-husband in a shirt covered with hibiscus flowers. She saw Andrew floating with his mermaids, in his swimming pool of ignorance, and smiled, and told Jack that his time was up.

The power that being with Jack gave her, that her new skills lent, followed Sophie down the corridor with its creaking board. She stepped confidently past the bathroom door, whether it was closed, or open to let the steam out after a customer had had his shower.

She stood in the kitchen doorway with her whip in her right hand, her arm glowing, raised as though to seek another target.

The new girl, Marika, watched her with an expression of contempt.

Marshall flexed his shoulder muscles under a black T-shirt. He looked up from counting the night's takings and said, 'You're raking it in, Soph.'

Sophie waited, guessing how they talked about her when she wasn't there.

'This SM guy,' said Marshall. 'It's every second week.'

Still Sophie waited. Her point of view was simple. Why should she pay Marshall more for Jack because Jack paid *her* more? She worked hard for the extra. For a silly moment, she imagined Marshall chasing Jack on all fours, Jack's look of horror should she suggest it as a joke. This money that Jack paid belonged to her. It seemed the notes he handed her had a special glaze.

A feeling of greed took hold of Sophie then. She argued with Marshall, watching him stretch and then contract his fingers, recalling the pressure of his hand that day in the corridor, how Kirsten had rescued her, and how she'd found the courage to stand up to Marshall the next time herself.

Greed met her anxiety and steadied it, holding it in place. In her mind, she followed the passage of the notes from Jack's hand to hers, to the stove and then her handbag at the end of the night, accompanying her home, then to the bank next morning. Greed warmed her deepest organs. It lent a metallic light to trees. Marshall's ring flashed. He let the subject go for the time being.

Sophie recalled how, before she'd got around to opening a bank account, her notes had fluttered and spun like tame birds settling in a wind. She remembered the light in Mrs B's brown eyes when she'd handed her a stack, and wondered whether Mrs B had ever coveted, schemed, lusted for *her* independence, the way that she was doing now.

The lust of customers – it did not rank, or, if it did, was only a tiny measure of what Sophie was beginning to suspect lust could be – this burning towards the freedom money bought. Scarcely were her customers aware of their lust, it seemed to Sophie, than they took steps to satisfy it. Of course, she never saw the ones who didn't, who were too poor, or frightened.

Mrs B was lonely. Her loneliness struck Sophie as she stood her ground with Marshall, and returned Marika's disdainful stare with one of her own.

Paying for a Violin

Andrew could play any musical instrument you put in front of him. Once, in Ireland, he'd picked up a lute at a Dublin market, a spur-of-the-moment purchase. Their flight to Heathrow was leaving in two hours. Andrew taught himself to play the lute while Sophie was checking out of the hotel, then in the taxi and departure lounge. By the time their boarding call was announced, he was playing it as though he'd been doing so for years.

Tamsin was learning the piano. Andrew thought the violin might be a good idea as well. There was no such thing as starting too young. Andrew had an old Randal upright that he'd learnt on himself, that he loved and kept well-tuned. He owned an up-to-the-minute Yamaha keyboard as well. Tamsin was musical. She'd inherited the gene, Andrew said, and it was a sore point that she was unable to practise during the half of the week she spent with Sophie. They were negotiating transferral of the Yamaha, but Andrew wasn't keen to give it up.

Sophie might say – she got as far as planning it – 'I could buy a violin for her'. Andrew would be speechless, or else he would scoff. 'Do you know how much a decent violin, even a small one, costs?' Sophie would explain that she wasn't short of money. She would be forced, then, to continue with her explanation. Her offer to shoulder responsibility, to pull her weight in the matter of a violin, would be her burning bridge. She would tell Andrew about Andover Street. She would have to. The violin that she would buy, her ability to, would become the threshold which, once passed, could not be crossed again.

Sophie circled her new purchase in her tiny living room. She corralled it, as though it might sprout legs and walk.

At last she heard them. Tamsin hummed along the path, dragging her bag. She kissed Sophie hello.

There was the car door closing, there was Andrew bringing up the rear. Now was the moment for courage, not to lose it.

Andrew caught up with his daughter and kissed the top of her head. His eyes met Sophie's over it. Tamsin's hair smelt of the shampoo he kept in his bathroom. Sophie wondered if his girls used it when they visited. Maybe, afterwards, one of his girls skipped down a path, and tossed her hair.

'Come inside for a moment,' she said.

The morning shone like new coins from the Yarralumla mint. And the violin in its case as well, a golden, lacquered gift.

Tamsin dropped her bag and ran. She hugged the case, and then its precious contents. It wasn't even Christmas, or her birthday, which was months away.

She picked up the bow and drew it lightly, lightly, first across the strings one way, then another, her small round face intent and focused. Andrew's daughter.

'Dad will tune it for you,' Sophie said.

'Where did you get this from?' Andrew's voice was pleasant.

'It's my violin,' said Tamsin, letting both parents know, in three words, that she'd absorbed every nuance of friction concerning her musical education.

'What?'

Sophie lifted her chin in Andrew's direction. Tamsin held the bow more tightly.

Andrew took it from her, repeating, 'Where did you get this?'

'I bought it.'

'What with?'

'Money.'

'Don't give me that,' said Andrew.

'I'm not obliged to give you anything.'

Tamsin was staring at them, wide-eyed, stricken.

'Tamsin, go to your room.'

'That was unnecessary,' Sophie told him, after Tamsin, with a last glance at the violin, had obeyed her father.

It had taken only seconds, from the first, joyful surprise to Andrew's reaction. But Sophie had anticipated it. She made fists of her hands. The moment for courage was upon her. If only she could grab it, as it skipped humming by.

Andrew waited, mouth half open, teeth ready to clamp down on whatever words she chose.

Sophie glanced towards the closed door of Tamsin's bedroom.

'I borrowed it,' she said.

'*Borrowed* it. Who from?'

'The bank.'

'So you took out a loan?'

'That's right.'

'Why?'

'Because I wanted to *do* something, don't you understand? You left me. You left *both* of us. Oh, you may think you haven't, you may think it doesn't matter to Tamsin that every time she goes back to what used to be her home, there's another aunty. You wrecked our family, then insulted me by insinuating that I couldn't provide for my daughter, and then quibbled over that piano – '

'Leave my music out of it.'

'Why should I? And it's not your music that's at issue here, it's Tamsin's.'

'Why should I believe you? You're devious and sly. Why should I believe anything you tell me?'

'Get out,' Sophie said.

Andrew threw the bow down. It caught the light and, instead of falling straight, seemed to fly, but a flight that was over before Sophie had time to blink. Air caught it, from a fugitive, unnoticed wind, as though it struggled to return to its owner's hand.

Sophie turned her back. Andrew slammed the door. Sophie's legs were shaking and would not hold her up. She took three steps and leant against the closed lid of the Yamaha, struggling to get air into her throat and chest.

No sound came from Tamsin's room. Slowly, Sophie straightened up and opened her daughter's door.

Tamsin was sitting perfectly erect on the edge of her bed. There seemed to be no blood in her face at all.

Sophie bent and hugged her.

'I'm sorry, sweetheart,' she said.

Sophie cried as quietly as she could. It was a skill to cry quietly when you lived with a four-year-old, and she had learnt it.

Someone was knocking at the door. Didn't they know it was important to be quiet?

'Sophia?'

Sophie opened the door and stared at Mrs B. She wiped her nose on her sleeve.

'Sophia, what is it?'

'It's Tamsin's violin,' Sophie said with a sob. 'I bought Tamsin a violin.'

Mrs B came right inside and closed the door behind her. She opened her arms and folded Sophie into them.

Sophie bent over. How small, she thought. What a small, wiry person.

Mrs B was out early in the morning, in her long, mud-coloured skirt and boots, mulching the azaleas. She didn't turn her head as Sophie approached, though Sophie knew her footsteps had been heard.

'I'm sorry,' Sophie said.

From behind, Mrs B looked to be a much younger woman, straight legs and supple back. Underneath the skirts Sophie had never seen her without, her legs would be strong, but with clotted veins that sometimes gave her trouble. Wild hair stood out around her head.

She turned and looked at Sophie, shading her eyes with her hand and asking, 'Who, child, who are you sorry for?'

'Myself, I suppose.'

'Good,' said Mrs B. 'That you have got so far is good. You're young. You have your life ahead. Don't waste it feeling sorry.'

Mrs B looked down at the freshly turned compost, which was full of worms.

'You will do what you will do. Just don't pretend that someone force you into it.'

When Sophie began to walk away, Mrs B called after her, 'Sophia? Bring Tamsin after school. I have her favourite. Ice-cream with home-made syrup.'

Sophie smiled over her shoulder, feeling sad, disappointed with herself, and grateful.

She had not been able to tell Andrew about Andover Street. When the moment came, she had not. She gave herself excuses. It was a mistake to try when Tamsin was there. Lunch on a weekday, when Tamsin was at preschool. She would ring Andrew and apologise, invite him to lunch. He would come prepared. It would be another way to burn her bridge, to start on the no-going-back road of explanation.

But yet and still. Underneath her disappointment, she was aware of the seductive pleasure of *not* telling Andrew, risking him finding out some other way, being grossly and deliberately unfair. This was the sticky bottom of her lack of telling, lack of coming clean, this pleasure in continuing to deceive a man whom she'd once believed she loved.

The violin was not mentioned the next time they spoke on the phone. Tamsin did not touch it during the three days she spent with her mother, and Sophie did not try to make her. When the time came for Tamsin to pack her bag, she asked if she could take the violin with her.

'Of course,' Sophie said.

Andrew's voice on the telephone was cold, and Sophie's unapologetic. She passed on a message from Tamsin's teacher and left it at that, telling herself she'd taken the first step back towards a civility they needed to re-establish for their daughter's sake.

When the time came for the next switch-over, the violin was missing. Tamsin did not explain why she hadn't brought it with her, but mentioned, in answer to Sophie's questions, that Dad was teaching her to play, and that he was going to arrange for another teacher, 'a proper teacher', too.

Sophie accepted this. She saw herself as having tried, and failed, on one level, and as having escaped detection on another.

No more was said about bank loans, but it was understood – gaining ground with dignity, Andrew made this clear – that the violin would stay at his house. He would arrange the lessons. He would pay for them. No point in Sophie incurring further debt. It was lucky that she'd chosen a good instrument, when she knew nothing about them, and had no ear. It was very childish of her not to tell him how much it had cost her.

The violin and its shiny case left an emptiness in Sophie's flat after it had gone. It had been there such a short time, but its absence was curiously felt. The fact that Tamsin never once volunteered information about it added to Sophie's sense of loss. Tamsin hadn't asked for a violin. Its eruption into her life had brought argument and tension. Still, there'd been those seconds when she'd run forward, when her face had shone.

Sophie came back after dropping Tamsin off at preschool, and sat with her hands folded in her lap, wanting no distraction or activity, quite still. She looked around bare walls she had not thought to decorate, sniffed, and smelt expensive lacquer, well-seasoned by time. Four yellow cups and saucers that she'd bought one morning, giving in to an impulse of delight, looked forlorn, too solitary and fragile to make any kind of independent statement, seeming instead to mark the swift removal of her later, lavish, and most foolhardy purchase.

She sniffed again, aware of scents that were fugitive and foreign – she was now used to her habit, since her marriage ended, of fixing on some sideways thing that others would dismiss. It had got her into trouble. She recalled Ann's drawings, and how she'd ignored, or hadn't even seen, what ought to have been obvious. She wasn't very good at paying attention to the obvious, and look at the mess it had landed her in. But that morning it did not feel to Sophie as though she was surrounded by a mess. It felt rather like a breathing space, a clear space ahead, into which she could continue to venture.

Tamsin was at preschool, and the violin, unless she made a fuss about it, gone for good. Why had she lied to Andrew? Why, after cranking up her courage, had she been unable to follow through? She was well aware that she'd made Andrew more suspicious, that he did not believe her story, concocted on the spot, offered instead of what she'd intended to say – I work in a brothel. She'd even relished these five words, with their cumulative power to shock, rolling them around her tongue. But, when it came to the moment, she had not brought them out.

Andrew had ordered Tamsin to her room. He'd been so swiftly and completely angry that it had put her off balance. But this was no excuse.

She made tea, no longer sorry that she'd confessed to Mrs B instead, but thinking over all she had relinquished, blowing through the steam.

She'd surrendered the pleasure of watching Tamsin play the violin, of observing the fingers of her left hand, already strong and sensitive to the piano, pressing on the strings, her right hand managing the bow, her look of concentration which was all her father's. Sophie could not recall when – except, possibly, with Jack, and when Tamsin was new-born – she had ever focused on a task as thoroughly as she imagined Tamsin doing. She felt herself becoming invisible while Tamsin played, as though the sound had form and substance, along with the person who produced it, while all else turned to air.

Sophie blew on her tea again. It was still too hot to drink. She had given up the satisfaction of telling the truth. She had halted halfway. Why? Where had the lie about the bank loan come from?

Then she understood. It came to her all of a sudden. It was because of the house itself, what she must go on to say, once she breathed the first decisive words. A proper explanation would require as long a telling as the time she'd spent there, a rightful description, not only of the rooms and their temporary inhabitants, but Elise and Kirsten, Marika and Marshall too. And not only individuals, but their feelings, and how all of these combined. And Jack – Jack most of all.

Since she could scarcely hope to lead Andrew to an acceptance of even a small part of this, she had not offered any of it to him, preferring to pluck a lie out of the air instead.

She tried to picture exactly the instrument she'd paid for, and found that she could not. There was the case, the lingering abrasive smell, Andrew flinging the bow down, and the way the bow had whooped and bucked, in protest, but with a kind of joyful energy.

The Garden Centre

Autumn ought to hold damp mornings, mist, if only as potential, ought at least to be able to provide this much. It was a golden autumn that year, but too dry. Trees quickly dropped their leaves. People with orchards watered them daily, and, in suburban gardens, turned up the sprinklers to swell apples, figs, the chestnuts coming on.

Collecting Tamsin from Sophie's flat, Andrew looked about him, at the fruitful trees and bushes. He smiled with tolerant forbearance, inviting Sophie to put past disputes behind them.

Sophie caught Mrs B's eye across the path, where she stood waving and blowing Tamsin a goodbye kiss.

Andrew saw the look that passed between the two women, and turned his smile off with a quick, efficient twist.

Mrs B pulled up at 10 Andover Street in her white Datsun, and opened her boot to bags of manure, long green hoses, spades with whopping handles. She showed her khaki skirts, her wiry rump, to Number 13. Her Datsun sat there all afternoon, a small car with a dented boot, looking as though it might belong to a client who had special privileges, or had overstayed his welcome.

Mrs B worked in Number 10's backyard, while all stayed quiet across the way at 13. There were no more photographers. The story had dried up again. Even the letter writers seemed to have run out of things to say. The vote in the Assembly had been postponed, no explanation given.

Mrs B hacked at Salvation Jane and thistles, ripping them apart. When it was her turn in the armchair, Sophie sat looking out the window, admiring her landlady's rhythm with a mattock.

On her working days, when Tamsin was at Andrew's, Sophie and Mrs B took to arriving around lunchtime. Sophie helped carry tools and hoses round the back, smiling at the strength in her landlady's arms. She had burnt one bridge and discovered, under it, another. She had to pinch herself sometimes, in order to believe that Mrs B had taken such revelations in her stride.

Sitting in the armchair, staring out the window, it seemed to Sophie that the overgrown backyard had been waiting for just such skills as Mrs B was offering. She let her eyes go out of focus, waiting, not waiting, for the doorbell to ring. Since they'd started opening in the afternoon, a surprising number of clients found it suited them.

Marshall said 'Wow' when he added up their takings.

Elise had suggested making over the garden while they were waiting for the building plans to be approved. The rest happened easily, Sophie mentioning Mrs B's long experience, picturing her hands flung up in horror, but then suddenly certain that they wouldn't be.

Elise had asked, 'How old?'

'Seventy something.'

'She's the one you live with? Who babysits your kid?'

'Not *with*,' said Sophie. 'A flat at the back.'

'A granny flat.' Elise smiled. 'Except that she's the granny.'

'I think she'd like to be,' said Sophie.

'She won't go running to the cops?'

'What would be the point of that?'

Elise made a wry face. 'Just checking,' she said, and then, 'Why not? Let's give it a try.'

Sophie held her breath the first time Mrs B and Marshall passed each other on the back steps. It could have been a confrontation, Marshall sarcastic, Mrs B immediately on her dignity, her high horse.

But Marshall grinned, squinting a little in the soft, clear light of noon. 'G'day there,' he said.

Mrs B grinned back, responding to the catch in Marshall's voice, the new season of his olive skin.

Marshall laughed before Mrs B had even spoken, prancing and impressing, sensing in his own way how this was a woman who liked to be impressed.

Mrs B laughed back and suddenly they were a pair, unlikely coupled, delighted and surprised. It was an added pleasure when Mrs B held out her calloused, work-stained hands and told him she was helping with the garden.

Elise bobbed and ducked. She squatted in a long smooth movement. Her navy cotton pants stretched, so that anybody watching could make out her kneecaps. She turned over her shoulder, blonde plait swinging, drawing stares as she called out, 'Come and look at this!'

Mrs B and Sophie were in another section of the garden centre. Mrs B had made a list of what she thought might do. There were many practicalities to think of. She might not always be around to lend a hand with watering, or weeding.

'Low maintenance,' Sophie was explaining, holding a pot balanced in her hands. The plant inside had dark green leaves like question marks, small blue pointed flowers.

They'd bent their heads together over leaves of a surprising thickness and opacity, over labels which displayed white or pink blossoms in amongst the green. But Sophie fancied this blue flower, pointed as a pixie's chin, belonging to a native bush which promised good ground cover. Writing at the bottom proved too small for Mrs B, even with her glasses on, so Sophie had been reading instructions – how to plant and when.

They looked up at the sound of Elise's voice, and went to find her.

Elise was examining a piece of garden sculpture, a cupid holding a bow and arrow, other arrows waiting, ready to be fired, in a bag on his back. The stone looked weathered – it was a technique, Elise said – already with a tinge of green in places, giving potential buyers an idea of how it would appear, in time, with lichen, moss, with water flowing.

'Look,' Elise said, 'a fountain.'

Mrs B rubbed the pads of her fingers across the cupid's head.

Elise sprang to her feet, throwing her arms around them. 'A pretty fountain Soph!' she cried. 'Not like that great gush in the middle of the lake!'

Present at the kitchen conference were Elise, flushed from her visit to the nursery, the excitement of discovery fresh along her cheekbones; Sophie, watching her and thinking, but she's beautiful; Mrs B as expert gardener; Marshall to oversee proceedings.

A bond sprang up, immediate and strong, between Elise and Mrs B over the fountain. Mrs B understood what Elise meant, at the nursery, in the car, while Sophie remained quiet, muted in her enthusiasm, listening to them. Sophie had thought of Elise as like Marshall in many ways – a business person, ambitious, user of others if need be. She hadn't seen before the impulsive fancy that filled Elise when she talked about the garden, had not imagined that Elise might have this in her.

The fountain would be for them, for the girls, in the middle of a walled, private garden full of lovely things.

Marshall couldn't see a problem. 'Why not, if we can afford it?' he said.

He speculated about a mini fountain in the new reception area, proposing a pair, one big, one little. Gurgling water and glossy indoor greenery. It would have a calming influence, and might just be fitted in. Clients would appreciate that, arriving so often, as they did, in a state of nervous tension.

Marshall grinned. 'Let's do it.'

His hair had grown and he no longer gelled it. He took in Elise and Mrs B, two scheming women, seeing where their scheme might lead, having this in him – not to deaden the bright ideas of others, not to squash them, though there was still the business of the kitchen between him and Elise, and Sophie was careful not to catch his eye.

Feeling her way towards assurance of a place at this kitchen cabinet, Mrs B was solemn, nodding agreement, her willingness to help.

Ann's plans and drawings were still waiting for approval, but once approval had been given, carpenters and plumbers could be contracted. Marshall would take *their* – he smiled at Sophie – architect's advice on who to hire. He also had some contacts himself. He was getting to know people in the building industry.

Sophie kept her eyes lowered. Marshall slipped in information, patting Elise's hand across the table. He was about to begin visits to each member of the Legislative Assembly, which surely must be voting soon. They'd had enough delays.

'Girding my loins for it,' he told them.

'The act,' he said, repeating the old joke with a cursory lift of his eyebrow, giving Elise's hand a gentle rub.

The house would be unusable for weeks, its insides pulled apart. They were looking at renting a place in Fyshwick.

'We can still work in the garden,' Elise said.

Elise would love the fountain, Sophie thought, the play of water over stone – but not to gaze at. Rather, Sophie saw Elise ministering to the fountain in a thousand active ways, loving in equal measures the smallness, the activity, and the privacy of her ministrations.

Marshall smiled, wanting to please, and to be pleased. The phone rang and he said, 'One of you girls answer it.'

Sophie picked up the receiver. The caller sounded young and nervous, swallowing his words. Reassuring him, Sophie thought, It's over, my probation. If I want to, I can count it as being over now.

'I rang Kirsten last night,' she told Elise when they were alone together in the kitchen. 'She still doesn't know what's wrong.'

'Fags and a shit lifestyle,' Elise replied, moving restlessly from fridge to yoga mat and back again.

Buoyed up by having received a clean bill of health, but, even more, by finally finding the courage to undergo a full medical examination, Sophie had taken the chance to talk to her own doctor about Kirsten.

'I found a specialist,' she told Elise. 'All Kirsten needs is to get a referral.'

The doorbell chose that moment to ring.

Pulling up in her car at 3am, Sophie noticed a light on in Mrs B's house and thought, Something's happened.

Mrs B was sitting in her kitchen, fully dressed. The kitchen clock was ticking loudly, but there was no other sound. Her head was bent over a photograph album. Her calloused hands held it open at what might have been a favourite page, and there was a stack of albums beside her on the table. They were old, their covers red and yellow.

She looked up at Sophie's knock and said, 'Come in.'

She studied Sophie with a distant look, a look that put Sophie in her place. And Sophie held her breath because that place was suddenly unknown, unexpected. She feared to step forward, or speak into it, in case it evaporated, or took her wholly in.

Then Mrs B blinked brown eyes that were very dark under the kitchen bulb and said, 'See here, Sophia.'

She moved across, indicating that Sophie should join her in front of the album.

'This is when we first come to Canberra.'

There were the flatlands, yellow and immense, the plains that did not yet carry buildings, and the scrubby bush.

Mrs B pointed with a forefinger. With so much time spent in the garden, some of the earth that had winkled its way into seventy-year-old fingers could not be removed.

'And this,' she said. 'The flooding of the lake.'

Slow brown water edged its way forward. There were dozens, Sophie realised, possibly as many as a hundred, photographs of the same scene. Put them together in a pile, flick them, and muddy water would move forward over the tops of shoes.

'Why so many?' Sophie asked.

Mrs B had had one child, a son, she said, by way of explanation. Her boy, just turned thirteen, had been riding his bike along a suburban street, had, as young riders do, with the wind behind him, dashed out at a crossroads, met a car head on.

There were pictures of the roadside shrine, garden flowers, the fresh face of a smiling boy.

'It was the first in Canberra,' Mrs B said of the shrine. She had newspaper cuttings, folded, in case proof was necessary.

'I put flowers for years, together with my husband.'

She turned pages, to show where both were buried. Yellow grass heads framed the picture. The cemetery looked raw, surprised to find itself there.

Mrs B's hands moved restlessly, yet with the rhythm of long habit.

After she had talked for a while about herself, and her own childhood, Sophie said, 'It's late. We should both be in bed.'

Sometimes, Sophie went to bed and masturbated, wanting, or needing her own touch, that particular release which had been teased and courted through a night's work, a practical way of relaxing, bringing herself down, her fingers ready and finding that place, those places, so lately and vigorously occupied, still open for business.

She used the time as well, these movements, to say goodbye to John the Cyclist, the goodbye he had not offered her. It was kind of a salute, two fingers or three, bittersweet, as familiar, shocking on the tongue, as the names she had given her men.

John had had a name and character. But courage? The kind it took to keep turning up under the photographers' flashes, the cameras' glare? This her John had not thought it worth his while to cultivate. He had not been thick-skinned, was one way to look at it. There were simpler, safer, more discreet ways to get what he was willing to pay for.

'Bye John,' she'd say, before she arched her back. 'Goodbye and good luck.'

Tonight she thought about, but did not do any of these things.

She thought about the failure of imagination which could overcome a person creepingly, and how, if she wished to, from this moment on, she could picture Mrs B with her albums, sitting in a clock-loud kitchen, where previously she, Sophie, had not imagined much going on at all. Imagination had been lacking, and Sophie had thought, if she'd thought at all, of Mrs B sleeping soundly in her bed.

Mrs B had been the youngest of her family, she'd told Sophie that night. She'd had no particular claim to it, but survival had, for whatever reason, claimed her. Of the DP camp, of the Polish town, she had no photographs at all.

A Whole House

Ann had been asked to design a house. No longer would it be necessary to pour her energy into ceilings shaped like fans or shells, a clutch of private lunar windows, partitions breaking up an office floor. Still private and domestic, her new commission, but a whole house. Her name on a yellow board at the front of an empty block, her ideas taking shape above it.

A lawyer had commissioned her. They'd met at university. He'd made a lot of money. Ann did not say break, didn't use the word, but it was there, in the light behind her, as she pushed herself away from the window ledge. A breaking light modelled itself on their side of the lake. Trees, shaped like antique weapons, a few yellow leaves left clinging to them, pointed up the hill.

Sophie felt the expansive view the new home owners, the lawyer and his pregnant wife, would share, for the house Ann would be designing for them would also be built on a hillside, not far from where they were standing now, the same suburb and a choice location. Expansiveness. Not that needle point of pressure on which all of Ann's energy had been focused, her time and talent paid for, to step into a house already built and say, This I will alter and not that. *This* I am being paid to alter, and not *that*. Instead, a yellow board on a hillside, underneath it virgin Canberra dirt. Rooms would take shape on a drawing board, their relation to each other needing to be worked out, the relationship of outside to inside on a suburban block. Scarcely to be remarked on surely, by passers-by, except, it might be hoped, one on the lookout for an architect. But a logical progression, for one in Ann's position. One customer would lead to others, in time and with a small but growing reputation.

Ann's voice was clipped and businesslike, having been given the opportunity to move on, suggesting that renovations, now behind her, were cosmetic surgery, like breast implants.

Sophie smiled at the flush along Ann's cheekbones, the way she shook her hair, back to brown and longer, the way she stood with her strong legs apart, hips forward to meet a challenge.

'To your brilliant career,' Sophie said. They drank a toast, the champagne in Ann's best glasses, pale liquid reminding Sophie of the lemonade Mrs B had made on a hot Saturday morning. Was that the morning Andrew had begun to suspect she was lying about the restaurant, or when suspicion had solidified? He'd been pleased, so far as Sophie could recall, with the small ceremony Mrs B had made – cool liquid on a wooden tray, Tamsin running across the grass to meet her new friend, through the deep green of the garden, with the crab-apple in full, delicious leaf above their heads.

Champagne bubbles got up Sophie's nose. She sneezed. The light was fading quickly. She wanted to leave Ann's workroom, though she'd only just arrived. She wanted to walk home down the hill before Ann switched on electric lights. If she stayed, even another twenty minutes, it seemed she would be obliged to witness Ann's preparations for the evening – ringing friends, perhaps arranging dinner. Of course, Ann knew Sophie had to go to work.

Ann leant forward to fill Sophie's glass. The champagne was in a bucket with legs, a peculiar contraption, the kind you saw in posh restaurants, the kind Sophie might have served customers from had she been working at the Taj Mahal.

'Just a wee drop,' she said, with a poor attempt at a Scottish accent.

They sipped their drinks and spoke of Ann's good luck. The lawyer was influential. 'A great networker,' Ann said. 'He's made his own drawings. He knows what he wants. People like that do.'

Sophie asked about the Andover Street plans. 'How long will it be?'

Ann shrugged. 'You know what they're like.'

'But about how long then?'

Ann shrugged again. 'Few weeks.'

The phone rang, and she went into the next room to answer it. Sophie had the feeling she'd been expecting the call, and that it was from a man.

She walked over to the model, sitting once again in shadow on the side table, ran her fingers lightly over the thin walls, then looked at her forefinger and licked it to make sure. No dust. Ann's approach to housework was hit and miss, and Sophie knew that dusting was not part of her routine.

When Ann came back, she said that it was getting late, and she had better go.

As she made her way downhill, she thought of Ann moving up into a different, bigger league. She looked back at O'Connor Ridge, outlined against the sun. Could different leagues be pictured as contours on a hill, an upward climb? And then what? Movement, at any rate, away from her, thought Sophie, testing her feeling about this, not sure whether she wanted to bury or face up to it.

It startled her to realise that five years had passed since Ann had gone into business on her own, and that now, with this next move, she seemed about to put the last five years behind her. With another backward glance, she saw that Ann had been marking time, designing the Andover Street renovations, a coda to this period of her life and work.

It seemed to Sophie, grabbing something to eat, getting in her car for the drive across the lake, that it had never been Ann's intention to stay in one place for long, as far as her career was concerned. The butterfly dance of the cosmetic architect had never been her destiny, or plan.

Sophie wanted to feel happy for her. Any congratulatory toast, even the most casual, between old friends, was a kind of pact with the future, fingers clasped around a glass, liquid raised, not in mockery or bitterness, celebrating the courage that floated in small, optimistic gestures.

The New Girl

Jack pulled on his jeans and balanced on the edge of the bed. Sophie knotted her sarong under her left armpit and sat down beside him. It was her good fortune, she was coming round to thinking, that Jack never questioned her about her life outside the rooms. He never asked her why.

She asked him, 'What do you get out of it?'

He scoffed and would not answer. They laughed at 'why' and repeated it, in the voices of insistent crows. *Whywhywhywhywhy.*

He'd noted her stretch marks and said, 'You've had a baby.'

'A daughter,' Sophie had answered cautiously. She did not know whether Jack's question came from curiosity, or alarm at what the presence of stretch marks might suggest.

She wanted to know how it had begun, this business of him kneeling on the floor while she stood over him with a whip in her hand. She needed to know the story of how Jack had arrived at Number 10.

His semen was soaking into the towel, already bundled up and out of sight, when she said, 'But you *could* stop, if you had to.'

'Oh, *had to*,' Jack repeated, bending over and reaching for his boots.

'You could smarten yourself up a bit,' she said.

Jack laughed. 'I used to be smart once. Quite the ladies' man.'

He pushed against the side of the bed. Sophie felt it move on its uneven leg.

She wondered if Jack was an only child. She was interested in the problems only children might confront. She thought of child abuse, so much in the news these days, imagining a sadistic school teacher, or a bully, some older child who'd inspired both fear and admiration. She stared up at the ceiling, observing a line between herself and Jack, made not by the whip but circumstances that might descend on any person, hurry them along, so that they woke up one morning to remark, So *this* is where I am.

The way back might be bright and clear one minute, covered in cloud the next. The way forward might beckon with a golden finger. Bank notes might whisper, then settle like contented hens.

Sophie began telling Jack about the garden centre, and their plans. Not only flowers and shrubs would fill the decrepit and neglected yard, but a fountain would spread its tinkling, silvery largesse.

Jack listened, looking interested. His features took on a simple dignity and his light, thin form a kind of grace.

Sophie sat beside him. She felt their garments matched, easily slipped off then on again. She smiled and took Jack's hand, turned it over once, then again. Autumn shone becomingly on a backyard cleared of weeds.

The new girl, Marika, was a poacher. She poached Sophie's regulars while her back was turned. Pay weeks, the three girls were on together, but off-pay weeks Sophie and Marika shared between them. This arrangement made it difficult for Sophie, who took to doing what she'd never done before, which was to try and arrange her next appointment with her regulars while she had them there. Except for Jack. Marika didn't want Jack, though he paid so well.

Sophie sat at the kitchen table looking through the diary, reading the names that used to sit opposite hers, the lettering like crosses. Of the names and bodies that had grown familiar through the long last days of summer, the yellow drop of autumn, many had transferred to Marika.

Sophie thumbed back through uprights and horizontal bars, black letters in her writing, or Kirsten's or Elise's. She thought about what Marshall still referred to as their second wave. She didn't like to think of herself limping past the finish line, last year's horse, a superannuated nag.

But Marika was striking-looking, she had to admit. Very dark. Hair with a natural wave and large, dark eyes that looked straight through a person to what was out the other side. Marika had another job, in Fyshwick, on the nights when she was not at Number 10. She made comparisons that showed up their house in all of its bad lights, its hopes as well as present making-do. She expressed no enthusiasm for Ann's renovations, but instead told stories of *Parliament House* in Fyshwick, of a luxury and glamour which Number 10 could never acquire. She added tales of Roman spas, jacuzzis if they wanted water, complimentary champagne for the girls as well, beds designed for foursomes – had they thought of that?

Marshall said he didn't see why they couldn't give foursomes a try.

When Sophie returned to the kitchen from her half-hour with Jack, Marika studied her with a superior expression.

'You're not strong enough,' she said. 'You need to put on muscle.'

'Oh, muscle,' Sophie said airily, as if she could call some up at will.

Kirsten's shadow and her smoker's cough followed Marika, who was a smoker too. 'What's that old woman doing here?' she asked.

'Helping in the garden.'

'What is she, some kind of pervert?'

When Sophie replied with, 'No, a friend of mine,' Marika smiled as though this was just the answer she'd been waiting for.

Sophie got ready for her next client in a special way. She lit the lamp on the small table in the side room. A lamp denoted cosy evenings, though it was Tuesday afternoon. With the curtains closed, the room dim past the lamp's modest gaze, it was possible to shut out the amenities it lacked. The carpet's stains were masked. It did not look so frayed.

Lamplight made an inviting circle of the bed, but Sophie's client regarded it with apprehension.

'I've got the extra towels,' she said, beginning to undress.

She set them out along the bottom of the bed. He had to have plenty, could not abide a mess.

He removed all his clothes, then quickly replaced his shoes. These he inspected critically, though he'd wiped them on the doormat. He had to have his shoes on, he'd explained the first time he saw Sophie, because when he got excited, as he was about to do, his feet swelled to almost twice their size. It was an affliction, in a case like his, having to return to the office for the afternoon.

'Oh leave them on,' Sophie had assured him.

Now there were fortnightly memories of the big-foot man's surprising agility, the need to keep shifting the towels around, the hump and groan, afterwards spent and pale and slack in the lamplight's circle, the pretence at evening and what it might allow. Spent and pale, two feet enormous at the bottom of the bed, while Sophie lay beside him, watching them quiver and relax.

This day, this Tuesday, the man with his shoes on regained his steady breathing and enquired, 'The dark lady? The one with – '

Great tits, Sophie added silently. 'Marika,' she said.

'I might try Marika next time. Do you think she'll mind?'

'I'm sure she won't,' said Sophie.

Will I miss you, Sophie wondered, when I read and remember your name in the book?

What was the point of a fountain in the back garden? Marika asked. Or, indeed, a back garden at all? Who will see it out there, be impressed?

'We will,' Sophie said.

Although Elise shot wary, calculating glances at Marika from her yoga mat, she found a way to get on with the new girl. Sophie heard them laughing together through the kitchen door. Elise had bought a gas heater. Small fan heaters did for each of the rooms for the time being, ducted heating being part of the plan.

When Sophie opened the door, Elise and Marika were standing shoulder to shoulder, in front of the heater. They looked up and did not share their joke.

It may have been Mrs B's presence, her involvement. She made them two and two, not counting Marshall. Elise liked Mrs B. Marika didn't. The antipathy was mutual. Marshall was amused. He liked it when his women showed their claws.

Antipathy made shards of female malice in the kitchen. Marika knew how Sophie minded each time one of her regulars switched over. Sophie tried overcoming the division, finding out what Marika was interested in, starting conversations. Marika made short work of her attempts. Sophie wondered how, and when, Marshall would approach her, with his cupped hand, his bloodstone ring. She wondered if he had already done so, one night when she wasn't there, and Elise busy in the front room.

Whatever her feelings and suspicions, Elise was not allowing jealousy to get in the way of business. Photograph her with Marika, as an advertisement for Number 10, and words would be redundant.

Marshall leant in the kitchen doorway with his arms crossed. It was payday. Marika and Elise had customers lined up.

He asked Sophie how things were going, and she told him they were fine.

'With Jack,' he probed. 'How are things with Jack?'

'Everything is fine,' she said.

'You must have a flair for it.' Marshall smiled. 'We could advertise. Discreetly.'

He looked her up and down, openly provocative, as he had not been since the last time he'd caught her alone in the kitchen. 'Whoever would have thought it. A skinny little thing like you.'

'I can hold my own,' said Sophie.

Marshall took a step inside. 'Show me. Come on, I'd like to see.'

Sophie refused, praying that he'd disappear. 'Is that someone at the door? I thought I heard a knock.'

Marshall smiled again. 'The bell's in perfect working order, Soph. A blind cretin could find it.'

Sophie sidestepped, deft and fast.

The bell rang loudly. That's my nine lives, she thought, and I can hardly hope for more.

Marshall went to answer it, throwing over his shoulder, 'I'll get that demo sometime, you'll see.'

Sophie stood in front of the window. The reflection looking back at her contained the skinny little thing Marshall had described, grown into an unexpected and surprisingly lucrative potential. Her face and form were fluid, wavery, yet hardened as she watched them. Sophie could not, as she stood there, believe that the person looking back at her was Tamsin's mother. How could she be both the woman Marshall had described, and Jack paid for, and a good mother to her daughter?

Marshall was taking a long time to call her. She knew the customer must still be there, or else he would have come back. She hoped he'd asked for Marika, and that Marshall would stay and entertain him until she was free.

She blinked and rinsed her eyes under the tap, then returned to the window and opened it as wide as it would go. Her breath caught in the cold air. Her whip stood by the door. It seemed that the yard had already been planted out in rows, as straight and clean-edged as though a delicate machine had fashioned them. She saw through the earth to seeds that were already swelling, feeling herself stripped and hardened against other people's expectations.

She moved through what remained of the night as though nothing could touch the fine, hard place inside her.

Doctor Dare

Sophie looked forward to the days closing in, the longer nights with Tamsin, the excuse for staying home. Most of the daylight hours, before and after preschool, she and Tamsin spent out of doors, the crystalline daylight at the end of autumn too precious to waste.

They walked, mother and daughter, or rode their pushbikes, Tamsin with her first, Christmas two-wheeler that Andrew had taught her to ride. She still sometimes used the training wheels, though she didn't need them. Andrew might teach, but Sophie was keeping up the practice.

'How are your lessons going?' asked Sophie. 'On the violin.'

She had been thinking of this question for some time. It was the way the light fell on the path ahead that made her ask it now, the feeling that the two of them, Tamsin and herself, might overtake and then be bathed in it, and afterwards never need to move; the feeling that they would be held suspended, having set off on with quite another destination in their minds.

'Okay,' said Tamsin, wheeling her bike towards the gate with the same purposeful consideration she applied to everything nowadays.

'What's your teacher like?'

'He's got brown hair and a – a ring through his nose!'

Tamsin screwed up hers and laughed, turning to face her mother squarely with direct, bright eyes. She held the handlebars easily, and her feet were planted on the path in a way that suggested it would take more than a quarrel between her parents to dislodge them.

'I want to go that way,' she announced, pointing with her left hand up the hill.

'Are you sure you can manage it?'

'Of *course.*'

Reassured, Sophie fell in behind her daughter, not so close as to run into her if she wobbled, or stopped suddenly, but close enough to be on hand if she was needed.

The Yamaha was installed in Sophie's living room, in front of the window.

Sophie and Tamsin looked at it, then at one another. 'For rainy days,' they said.

If the weather was bad, Tamsin sat down at the instrument of her own accord. The sound of scales, now hesitant, now forthright, filled the air of the small flat, which seemed grateful for them, as for the fulfilment of a promise that had been long withheld.

Tamsin never sought her mother's approval when she practised, never looked at her or asked for acknowledgment of any kind. She existed wholly for the task while she performed it and, when it was over, her face and small body looked washed clean.

Nights when they'd had tea early and were already in their pyjamas – Tamsin's were decorated with pink and aqua bears, Sophie's with stars and moons – Sophie might say, 'There's nothing on TV. Absolutely nothing!' And Tamsin, who had asked for her own calendar so she could cross off the days till her fifth birthday, obedient and careful Tamsin, with her own reasons for doing things, would take her seat at the keyboard. Tempered melodies and scales would fill the flat to bursting and meet the dark outside.

There was Mrs B, tapping on the door, calling out hello.

Turning on the high piano seat, legs swinging in their flannel bears,

Tamsin jumped down and took Mrs B's offered plate carefully, with both hands.

'Anzac biscuits. Yum,' said Sophie. 'I'll put the kettle on.'

They ate the sticky, treacly, still-warm biscuits. Tamsin got crumbs all over her pyjamas, and didn't mind. She licked each of her fingers right to its base. She cleaned her teeth and sat up in bed while Mrs B read her a story.

Sophie turned the television on, then off again. Tomorrow she would have her daughter to herself, all day apart from preschool. This would be the good time.

'So,' said Mrs B, when Tamsin was asleep and they were sitting over a second cup of tea. 'How are you, Sophia?'

'I'm okay,' said Sophie, 'thanks.'

'And Tamsin?'

'I know. I *know*,' said Sophie.

'Have you spoken to your husband?'

'Ex-husband. I'd tell you if I had.'

'Well then?'

'He'll be furious. Enraged.'

'If he finds out from someone else – ' said Mrs B.

But Sophie was insistent. 'He'll never forgive me.'

She thought, after Mrs B had rinsed her plate and left, that her friend's questions were well-meant. But the advice annoyed her, all the same. Nobody who gave the matter a single minute's thought could expect anything other than disaster to result from telling Andrew. Yet Sophie was courting disaster by keeping quiet, and she knew this too.

She woke sweating in the night, straining for the sound of Tamsin's breath in the next room, struggling from the nightmare that was Andrew finding out, but felt that she was, at the same time, struggling up and out of a precious luminescence. It enfolded and stuck to her, to her skin and eyelids. It held her, fascinated, even as she shivered, even as the breath caught in her throat.

In the passenger seat of Sophie's car, Kirsten sat blockish, upright, with a curious fixedness, as though she was made from wood. She'd been sitting on the edge of her bed, fully dressed, when Sophie came to take her to the specialist.

'That Marika,' Sophie said, pulling out of the driveway of the flats with a sideways glance at Kirsten, 'what a bitch.'

Kirsten laughed and asked Sophie what she'd done.

'She pinches all my regulars apart from Jack.'

'Tell her not to.'

'All very well for *you*.'

The midday light on the lake was clear and clean, intense. Kirsten's eyes flicked from the view out the passenger side window to Sophie's face, and back again. She leant forward stiffly, with a shrewd cast to her features. 'What is it with Jack then?'

'I like getting my own back,' Sophie said.

Kirsten laughed again.

Sophie remembered Kirsten helping her out with Marshall, and said she suspected he'd had sex with Marika.

Kirsten nodded, unsurprised.

'What does Elise think?' asked Sophie.

'He lies to her and she believes him.'

'Should I tell her?'

'If you dare,' said Kirsten.

Sophie looked down at her arms under the fine wool of a new, expensive jacket. The muscles there were strong. She looked at her hands on the steering wheel. Her nails were short and businesslike. Her hands were strong as well. She concentrated on turning into Marcus Clark Street. There was the car park ahead of them, and the Westpac Building, doctors top to toe.

In the waiting room, Kirsten turned pages of the *Women's Weekly*, and ignored Sophie's attempts to restart their conversation. But she came back from the consultation smiling, a line of colour at her hairline, the shadows underneath her eyes less black.

'Took heaps of blood,' she told Sophie as they walked out to the car. 'He's after doing more blood tests than you can poke a stick at.'

'But what did he *say*?'

Kirsten made a face. 'Told me I should give up smoking.'

'Well, he's right.'

'Yeah, yeah,' Kirsten said.

Andrew in a Good Mood

Andrew in a good mood seemed to fill the whole of Sophie's tiny living room. It occurred to her that she had never entertained him inside it before.

Tamsin played the Yamaha. She did not miss a beat. Notes hung in air already saturated with her father's presence. When the last one sounded, she sat facing the keyboard with her hands on her knees. She sat that way for a long moment, then swung round and looked straight at Andrew, who leant back in his chair with an attitude which asked, What next?

Sophie pictured a reversal – Andrew's house, the violin, Tamsin standing to perform, holding the bow correctly, as she had been taught. Try as she would, she couldn't make the picture fit.

Tamsin jumped down from the piano stool.

'Where are you off to?' Andrew asked.

'To my room.'

There was an awkward moment, then he said to Sophie, 'You're looking well. That's a nice jacket.'

Sophie thanked him, resisting the impulse to apologise for Tamsin, or ask about the violin. Andrew's magnanimity, the effort he was making, flowed out around her, and she found herself wishing to gather up whatever was left between them that might one day turn into affection. Maybe he's between girls, she thought.

She offered to make tea, which she'd taken to drinking black with a small dish of jam. Andrew smiled. It was a new sensation, that he might think her stylish in her jacket, with her borrowed Polish custom. She flexed her fingers and felt the muscles in her arm respond.

Andrew twirled his cup by its narrow handle and asked, 'Where did you find them?'

It was the colour of the glaze that had caught Sophie's eye. Four yellow cups and saucers had brought the sun out on a cloudy morning.

'They're my landlady's,' she lied, pouring quickly to cover her confusion, wanting to ask Andrew if he'd play something for her, but, in the second before he spoke again, understanding that it was too late for this.

'Have you got a bloke?'

'No,' she answered carefully.

'You'll feel better when you do.'

Sophie bit her tongue. 'All in good time,' she said.

She recalled how it had blazed up at her that she could walk into a shop and buy a violin, how she'd acted on that impulse, and where it had led her. Items shone in windows and on shelves. Their price tags made them luminous. She blinked at the common magic of what was daily bought and sold.

Tamsin came when she was called, and accepted her father's goodbye kiss with a blank face, a calm control.

Banking

The subject came up of how to bank the share of money that was Marshall's and Elise's, money that paid the mortgage and kept the business going. It wouldn't do, had never really done, to leave it in the stove for Marshall to collect. And Marshall was increasingly busy now, about the town.

When the question arose, nobody wanted to do the banking. Nobody liked doing it. That was why the notes sat in the oven waiting for Marshall. The account was with the St George in Kingston. The tellers would know, they would soon work it out.

Sophie thought the problem over and suggested Mrs B.

Elise frowned, her eyes hard, then said that it might work. They had to find a better system. The present one was a robbery waiting to happen. And what would they do then? Go to the police?

'Officer, we've been robbed.'

'And what is your address?'

Sophie was nervous, once she'd dobbed in her landlady, but Mrs B took the suggestion in her stride. Nobody at the St George Building Society, in the heart of Kingston shopping centre, up-and-coming Kingston, would dare raise so much as an eyebrow. Just let them, said Mrs B. Of course, jokes might surface after she had left the building.

An old lady who turned up every day with a bag of money. A pickpocket? Highway robber? A regularly successful, very successful punter.

Marshall agreed to the arrangement 'until we can work out something better', meaning that once the house was legal, any one of his girls could, and should, turn up at the St George in Kingston's main street, give sniggering tellers the finger.

Mrs B ministered to the waiting fountain in the afternoons, and Elise did too. Nothing Elise liked so much when she had a spare few minutes, than to relive the morning at the garden centre. She calculated water pressure, where the pipes and pump would go, made phone calls, arranged for quotes, and wrote down figures in the back of the diary. She ordered a small shed to house the fountain temporarily, and the gardening tools.

On the days when he was there, Marshall followed Sophie with his eyes as she made her way in and out of the kitchen, up and down the corridor, watched her with a question that did not demand an immediate response, but was ready to take advantage of the next opportunity.

No-one with Jack's tastes turned up, as he had, on the doorstep.

Enjoying her break at the kitchen window, Sophie glimpsed Mrs B through the doorway of the shed. It was amazing how her arrival and the garden project had opened up the whole back of the house. At any time, Sophie, Elise or Marika might walk into the kitchen, might look up, and there would be Mrs B heaping weeds into a wheelbarrow.

Marshall teased his gardeners, saying, 'What next, ladies?' His expression said, Surprise me, if you can.

One late afternoon, after Mrs B had left, Sophie heard her name called. Marshall was right by the fence. He waved her over.

With the sun going down behind him, with his face and form in shadow, Marshall looked solid and immovable. His feet in good shoes on the chocolate soil said – there could have been a drum roll – here I will also make my mark.

Sophie shaded her eyes against the setting sun. There was a runnel of freshly-turned earth between them. Soon the sun would be gone.

The night's work would begin. The garden taking shape both gave the lie to this night's work, and welcomed it.

Marshall put his arm around Sophie's shoulders. He smiled and told her, 'Things are ticking over.'

Sophie pictured the earth as a clock. Her stomach cramped. 'That's good,' she said. She heard the echo. Digging. Dig.

But then she felt herself beginning to relax. What could Marshall do to her, out here? Hadn't he taken Mrs B in his stride, appreciating what she'd done? Women did not have to be all of the one type, for Marshall. It was one of his talents, that he did not try to guess, in order to circumvent, what a woman might accomplish.

Sophie recalled Marshall and Mrs B kidding one another, Mrs B tiny and supple, prodding him with her gardening fork, Marshall's smooth, unhurried laughter. Boundaries were suspended, along with the rules they rested on. Regulations past and present were tossed in the air to see which ones floated, which might sink.

Carefully, she removed his hand from around her shoulders.

'Why did you buy this house?' she asked.

'It was a bargain.'

'Why Canberra?'

Marshall smiled, undaunted. 'You know the three of us drove down here with only one case each?'

'What about Kirsten?'

'She was as keen to get out of Sydney as Elise and me.'

Elise came to the back door as if her name had summoned her, though Marshall had been speaking quietly. She beckoned him with her pointed chin.

Sophie watched Marshall's back and buttocks swing purposefully away from her, thinking how used she was to being interrupted, and how so often it had been a blessing. Marshall disappeared inside, a flash of shapely buttocks, well-shod heels. The set of his head suggested that no woman would corral him, not for long.

She walked over to the garden shed.

The cupid's knees were dimpled. His legs were very plump. Sharply-angled light picked out every line and curve. Sophie wondered why Elise had not given him a name. She ran her fingers round his face, and allowed them to rest in indentations that might one day fill with moss. Between his legs was a small oblong pouch, a match for the larger one holding the store of arrows on his back. And below the pouch another arrow, precise and downward pointing, almost hidden by the way his thighs were crafted, one against the other. Sophie ran her fingers over it, and the grooves on either side. She tugged and nothing happened. She smiled to herself at the thought that the sculptor had not considered such a baby prick important. Far better to have the water bubbling from the sturdy bag of arrows on his back.

Jack in the Front Room

There was Jack's ginger snap bobbing up and down along the fence. He'd come round the back.

'Guys!' he called out, taking in the three of them and grinning, taking in Elise, with gumboots up to here, and Mrs B, but hers were hidden under a mustard-coloured skirt. Sophie had borrowed Elise's second pair. They were too big. She'd stuffed the toes with tissues.

Jack said, 'I like your wellies!'

Sophie leant on her spade and asked, 'What are you doing here?'

'A welcoming remark!'

Jack ducked his head and nodded, one half of an impromptu Punch and Judy show.

He held a punnet of seedlings out towards her with another nod, shyer, less confident this time, as if the inspiration of his gift, now that he was in the act of offering it, seemed suddenly in doubt.

Sophie took the seedlings, thanking him. She felt flustered, aware of Elise's and Mrs B's attention.

'Did you try to ring?'

'Bugger that,' Jack said, dismissing, at once and completely, any need for telephones. 'Go round the front, Jack. Please. I'll be with you in a minute.'

Jack bounced off. Sophie put the seedlings in the shed.

This was what came of leaving the house empty, not having anyone sitting by the phone, listening for the door. There'd been a fierce shower of rain at midday. Then the sky had cleared, offering a respite, what might be a last opportunity, before the temperature dropped heartlessly, before nightly frosts turned mud into resistant blocks, and the vigour of their spadework became a petty, useless chiselling.

They'd rushed out, all three of them, Marshall occupied elsewhere, Marshall the lobbyist in a sober suit.

On her way into the house, a noise behind her, a sharp crack at the ground, made Sophie swing around.

Mrs B was attacking the last big stand of weeds, over by the side fence, hurling abuse at them. Take that and that! Her face was redder than the sprinkler heads, her shirt sleeves rolled up way past the elbow. Her hair had all but left its bun, flaring out around her head, a grey, upstanding proclamation.

In the front room, Sophie thanked Jack again, then asked, 'Why so early?'

'I had a cancellation.'

Warmed by two hours in the garden, Sophie's right arm shone. She wielded her whip with flair and vigour. Sun caught the spring of energy between them. Jack covered the floral carpet on his hands and knees. Oh, he had it covered! He moaned with the remorselessness of four walls closing in. The carpet rose to meet him, and she forced him to the white towel at its centre.

She'd left the curtains open. Winter sun sought out the corners where Jack scrabbled, begging to escape. He cried, seduced by echoes, no strangers' voices through the walls, and Sophie gave herself up to his crying.

Sitting on the bed, measuring his breathing, Jack picked up Sophie's right hand and studied the half-moons of wet earth underneath her nails. She moved closer to him, half in and half out of the sun.

'Don't know if you guys have got plans for a vegie garden. A bit of broccoli and parsley. They'll survive the frosts.'

Sophie pictured the frozen ground, white-crossed, dark green leaves dormant, but alive.

She smiled. 'Do you have one yourself?'

'Yes,' said Jack. 'And chooks.'

He squeezed her hand. Dust moved in generous bands of light.

'Whereabouts?' asked Sophie, hoping she might prod or trick him into revealing something of his life outside Andover Street.

But Jack would not be drawn. 'A suburb, just like this one,' he replied.

He had gentle manners, beneath the panting and the begging. They sat in companionable silence for a moment, then Sophie began to tell him about Ann's model room. He listened while she created for him, with her hands of a novice gardener, the shell and fan shapes, colours you could drown in, the purple susurration.

She sighed and projected herself towards that moment when, having made an introduction, having accepted some new man's request, having agreed a service and its price, having finished with all necessary conversation, she would turn her eyes to the ceiling.

Another architect, with a different imagination, might have chosen to install ceiling mirrors, wall mirrors, confronting Sophie with herself from every angle. She'd learnt, from talking to Elise, that this had been one of Marshall's early suggestions.

Jack bent over to pull his socks out of his boots, saying with his head down, 'You know what you are, Soph? You're an optimist.'

'An optimist?'

'Of course!'

Jack waved his arm, flourishing a sock, uncharacteristically expansive.

'An opthimisth!' He stuck his tongue between his teeth to exaggerate the lisp. 'You've got opthimisth written all over you.'

Sophie pretended to search for the word, on her collar bone, her thigh. She reached across and grabbed Jack's arm, up near his tattoo.

'What's it look like? Does it look like this little bugger?'

Jack laughed and tussled with her, wrestling briefly. 'You may be going through a rough patch, but every cloud's got a silver lining!'

She punched him and he pretended to fall over. They spoke again, with pleasure and enthusiasm, about the garden that would take shape with the warmer weather, the men who would lay pipes for the fountain under great, drenched lumps of clay, in the position Elise and Mrs B had decided on between them.

'The old lady? What's she doing here?'

So Jack had noted Mrs B's trowelled look, her anger. But that was all he asked. And all Sophie said was, 'She's helping with the garden.' Not 'my landlady' or 'friend', not wishing then, or ever, to offer one up to the other.

Jack said, 'I'll be keeping your next gentleman waiting.'

'Can't have that,' said Sophie. 'He might turn out to be my silver lining.'

'Right,' said Jack, still holding his sock. He waved it in front of her, pretended to examine it from inside out. He shook it and said, 'Unfortunately empty.'

'Vamoose,' said Sophie, 'Hurry up, or I'll have to put you out in the street like that.'

It arrived that night, the first of the great flooding rains – herald, promise and arrival of winter in the space of a few hours. The friable brown hole that was Number 10's backyard empty of its weeds, its reigning thistles, became a pond, a mini lake echoing the big one, which swelled, lapping at its borders, out of sight. Jack's gift of seedlings waited in the garden shed for the rain to ease. The idea of growing vegetables as well as flowers pleased Elise, who looked forward to healthy meals augmented by fresh herbs, carrots with the smell of earth still on them, greens that had not been sprayed with pesticides. Marshall had been tickled. 'Good on the bloke,' he'd said, and added that seedlings were a welcome change from chocolates, which only made his girls fat, or cut flowers, which were dead by the end of the week.

Next morning, Mrs B tapped on Sophie's door, under the dripping eaves.

'Sophia! Listen!'

They smiled at one another. Sophie, who'd slept late, was still in her dressing gown, her blue pyjamas with their stars and moons.

'No outside work today,' they said.

Sophie brewed coffee for herself and tea for Mrs B. She took a steaming mug, a bowl of cereal, to a window seat.

Mrs B drank her tea very strong and black. She sipped and complimented. But she did not like Jack, what Sophie did for him, and he for her.

'You only saw his head,' Sophie argued, 'over the back fence.'

'I saw enough,' said Mrs B.

'What can you tell about a person from just seeing him once?'

Mrs B scoffed. She could tell everything. She could tell a person by his walk.

'He walks like this – bounce, bounce! And he sticks his chest out, so!'

Sophie laughed, but Mrs B was not to be laughed at, or dissuaded. It was all there, and she had seen it, what Jack might do to Sophie, how he might twist and corrupt. Sophie called her prejudiced – they'd come this far, that they could toss the word prejudice at one another. There was the matter of clients in general too, Sophie's claims to sum *them* up.

'But what is it Sophia – '

Mrs B was proud and stalwart in her own way, which was a lot to do with stance, the straight way she stood, legs not buckling, not bowed, weight of her upper body precisely managed, but not ramrod either, for that would draw attention of another kind. There was her scorn, by implication, for those whose posture gave them away.

'What is it, that a man pays for you to hit him?'

Sophie said, 'You wouldn't understand.'

Mrs B went red. Her eyes flashed and she looked away.

'I'm sorry,' Sophie said. 'I didn't mean that. Jack and I get along okay.'

'He's crazy.'

Sophie recalled the big-foot man, and the doctor who'd almost convinced her that her legs were different lengths.

'He's not the only one.'

'Hmph,' said Mrs B.

'He's got his own vegie garden. And chooks.'

'So this crazy man will be bringing us eggs next?'

Sophie laughed again, but Mrs B refused to be placated.

After she'd gone, Sophie rinsed her breakfast things. It occurred to her that, however much it might satisfy a certain logic to run together Jack and her ex-husband, they didn't fit. They never would.

Revenge on Andrew's body – oh, it was grand to imagine this! The trouble was, revenge against Andrew left out Jack's ways. It left out Jack's way of lifting himself out of his hips as he walked into the side room. It left out his fish tattoo, and the way he made it swim in the underwater light, the pleasure it gave her to run her fingers through the air above his back. It left out Jack's strange, pale eyes, his decisions and compulsions buried deep, their shared words, and the taste and luxury of adding to them.

In spite of her landlady's warning, Sophie went on seeing Jack, and providing for his needs. This worried Mrs B, who had taken a large general principle in her stride – that men paid for sex, and her tenant took their money, part of which ended up in her own pocket as rent. Mrs B, whom Sophie had expected to shock, at the very least to disappoint, had not been shocked, had been practical instead, and was now offering practical advice, was saying to Sophie, 'Enough.'

Mrs B's acceptance at Andover Street had been so smooth, apart from Marika's disapproval, that it seemed to Sophie a place had been there waiting for her. She'd slipped so easily into the role of gardener that it was as though she'd been preparing for just such an opportunity. The task, the person, the neglected ground were matched.

In 'optimist', Jack and Sophie found another of their repeated words, not the harsh, mistrustful edge of 'why', or the vague trajectory of 'potential', though both of these continued to do well enough in conversation. Optimist provided its own shorthand, and became, though neither would have gone so far as to state *this* in words, a measure of their understanding.

Optimist was a lovely word, thought Sophie, as she raised her whip, as Jack cried, his right hand pumped, as he spurted on the towel.

You could wrap the word around your tongue, or deliver it straight-faced. It looked forward, but not only that, was friendly – Pollyanna-ish of course, that's where the teasing came in – allowing for a person's courage in overcoming setbacks right now, in the present.

Outside at Tilleys
as the Sun Goes Down

Ann leant back in her chair. She wasn't in a hurry. Sophie didn't have
to go to work. They were drinking Cooper's Lite. Ann drank half her
beer in one go, then rubbed her forehead with the back of her left hand.

The sun was going down behind Black Mountain, and the air around
them was a crisp, thin blue. Sitting outside Tilleys with the smokers,
they relaxed in the lee of the mountain and its shadow. O'Connor Ridge
rose above Sophie's left shoulder. You might not notice it – a visitor
might not – seeing only that the street wound up a little. Straggly trees
were outlined against the sky. Black Mountain's siblings, Ainslie and
Majura, turned pink and yellow faces to the city.

Sophie felt privileged that Ann was giving her this time. Privilege
hovered just above the rough, black painted table. They sat with their
heads together and their mouths made rings. Though neither smoked,
there was a semblance of shared breath, of two women enjoying in
public a vice otherwise privately indulged in. Though their table was
in shadow, Ann seemed, by some trick or compensation, to have kept
the sun's warmth in her cheeks.

Tamsin had two straws for her coke and was giving them equal turns.

Her face was carefully composed, so as not to be seen to be listening to her mother's conversation.

It was the best time to be sitting outside at Tilleys. Sophie loved the old black tables with their peeling paint. It didn't matter what, or how much, was spilt on them. A visitor, especially one from the coast, might contract her fingers at the sudden chill, feel how the night was folding itself in against the mountain.

Sophie shivered, partly with cold, and partly with the pleasure of the evening ahead. She and Tamsin had already shopped for, and partly prepared their dinner. She would read, watch television, enjoy the quiet of her garden flat.

Ann had been too busy to meet earlier, and now Sophie was constrained by Tamsin, yet conscious that this restriction gave her a certain freedom, too. For there was much concerning Number 10 that she no longer wanted to discuss with Ann. Particularly, she felt unable to tell Ann about Jack. Yet he loomed large behind her, between her shoulders and the Ridge. She shrugged and blinked to make his image go away, while Ann's brown eyes held a thoughtful frown, and Tamsin sucked her coke, measured through her straws.

'There's a problem with the building office,' Ann said. 'Of course, the house is in the middle of a residential area.'

Startled, and with a quick, worried glance at Tamsin, Sophie asked, 'Where can we go?'

'Fyshwick, Mitchell, Hume. Where everybody else is.'

Tamsin stared solemnly at her mother, then bent her head and took two sips.

Sophie looked through the café's front window to the booth immediately inside, the couple outlined there. Two women. One leant forward urgently to speak to the other. Her hair was spiked like Marshall's used to be.

Ann said, 'If I'm knocked back, I can appeal.'

'You'll do that?'

'Of course.'

'Do you think it will make a difference?'

'I don't know,' Ann said. 'There has to be some reason why the legislation still hasn't been passed.'

Ann smiled crookedly. Her smile, perhaps meant as a belated reassurance, instead reminded Sophie that, in Ann's opinion, flexibility was needed. If one location proved too difficult, best abandon it and try another. But there was no alternative to the house at Number 10.

Sophie remembered a story Ann had told her once, about a set of double doors behind the tapestry in the Great Hall of the new Parliament House. She had been given a bit of the Great Hall to work on. Giurgola had taken an interest in everything, no detail was too small. He wanted the doors behind the tapestry, in exactly that position. It was Ann's job to work out the details. She was told by the bureaucrats that such doors would be a security risk, because of who might need to be entertained in front of them – the Queen, the President of the United States. Doors presented security problems, and there was no need for those there. None at all.

But Giurgola, the master architect, winner of the competition, had weighed in with his argument about democracy and open lines, how certain ones must run through the building. It was important that the doors should be there, and that they *could* be opened, even if they never were.

Ann had told the story out of respect for her old employer. Sophie thought she would see things differently now. It could be a burden, she realised, being placed so squarely on a land or water axis, or that other one, going deep into the earth. You couldn't blame a person for twitching off an axis, or sliding with a backward glance.

The bond between herself and Ann was as thin and fragile, suddenly, as the air around them.

Ann asked, 'How are things with Andrew?'

Sophie said, 'Okay, I guess.'

Ann glanced across at Tamsin, busy with her coke.

'It's getting cold,' said Sophie. 'We should go.'

'I'll drive you,' Ann suggested.

'We've got the car.'

'Well, then I'll follow in mine.'

Sophie sat Tamsin in front of the TV with a bowl of soup.

Ann said, 'It's like this. He came on to me.'

'*Andrew* did?'

Ann blushed, wiped the back of her hand across her forehead, then looked at it, as though it might contain something more than skin with blood flowing underneath. A flush spread along her cheekbones, in and out of the roots of her hair.

It was so unlike Ann to be discomforted, embarrassed, that Sophie found herself almost as surprised by this as by what she was saying.

'You forget what it used to be like. We got on well. I was friends with both of you.'

'Was?' said Sophie, then, 'Please keep your voice down.'

'I had to choose. I *did* choose. Don't get huffy with me, Soph. We talked about all this, remember?'

'You've been seeing Andrew.'

'I haven't been *seeing* him. We bump into each other. We drink in the same places sometimes.'

'You met Andrew at Tilleys?'

'Not there. Christ.'

'Tell me what happened.'

'Last week I was having a drink with Irene. You know Irene from Foreign Affairs?'

Sophie nodded.

'She heard about the house I'm doing. She knows this diplomat who's looking for an architect.'

Sophie waited.

'Well, when Irene said she had to go, I looked up and there was Andrew. He was on his own and we got chatting. He bought me a drink.'

'What did he say about me?'

'Nothing. Not a thing. He never mentioned you.'

'And?'

'He came on to me.'

'And?'

'How would you feel about it? Would you mind?'

Sophie thought of all the things she might tell Ann, that Ann already knew. She might say that Andrew had a new girl every other week. He picked them up, tasted, and then dropped them with the speed of a rosella in an apple orchard. She might say that she did not want Ann in Andrew's house, with Tamsin there, Tamsin coming home to her and telling her about Aunty Ann.

She might say that Ann had had plenty of practice in picking up and dropping, and therefore would not, should not, be surprised when it happened to her. Or ask if Ann had considered what life would be like as part of Andrew's raft, swishing along, it might be, or hitting a snag.

She was pleased at Ann's embarrassment, counting it a small, yet precious, triumph. 'Go right ahead,' she said, 'only can you use your place?'

As Ann was leaving, Sophie asked, 'You know that word cuckold – does it apply to both sexes, women as well as men?'

'I don't think so,' said Ann.

The Andover Street house felt reliable to Sophie, the next time she approached it on her way to work – denser and more solid than Ann's warning in the blue air outside Tilleys, and her other warning, her laying down of the cards, in the garden flat.

A maze of narrow-fronted rooms in Bunda Street housed 'the Lost Boys', Ann's name for the building office clerks who were withholding their approval. Building regulations were strict, as everybody knew. They ought to have been taken more carefully into account by Marshall and Elise, and Sophie, and by Ann herself. It occurred to Sophie that the Andover Street renovations might have been no more than a game to Ann. Yet she'd found a way to keep the kitchen.

She pictured Ann playing with thin slivers of wood, paring them, the peelings thinner than fruit skin and every bit as supple, painting them purple and blue-black. Delivering her announcement outside Tilleys, she'd been businesslike, her mind on other things, working out whether or not to tell Sophie about meeting Andrew, and her drink with him.

Sophie answered the doorbell at Number 10, offering, over and again, her introductory speech. She was used to Marshall's absence now. The pressure of a client's hand was sudden, pointed, like someone stacking dollar coins. Here was Doctor Tate's hand, old, insistent, on the small of her back. She'd never told the doctor he was lying, or mistaken, about her uneven legs. She was pleased that he had not switched to Marika, pleased at the loyalty, if you could call it that.

Different pressures – some surprising, some familiar – demanded allegiance and belief, when set against the paper plans whose future was in doubt, or the likelihood that Ann and Andrew would sleep together, if they had not already. The old walls with their watermarks were real, and the sly, fading carpet roses, the bed that rocked, Sophie's braced knees and elbows with a spring, and strong arms warmed by gardening.

Men in Leather

Word spread eventually, and men in leather came knocking on the door. They arrived in belts with studs as big as the bullseyes on a Target bag.

Opening the door in her sarong, Sophie confused, or disappointed them. They stared at her narrow throat and pale, bare arms, seeing weakness instead of her growing strength. Their expressions said they expected an outfit as polished and provocative as theirs, at the very least one that displayed muscles acquired in a gym.

Sophie swung her whip with the skill that Jack had taught her, but somehow her sessions with these new men failed to please. She puzzled over this, not knowing whether the fault was in her, or whether it lay between them. Was the solution to do as they did, and dress for the part?

Marika's eyes followed her around the kitchen. 'A skinny little thing like you,' she said, echoing Marshall's words.

Sophie still wondered if Marshall had had his way with Marika, behind Elise's back, or if Marika had had her way with him.

In the side room, she conjured up Marika's scorn to give her movements and her words an edge. Somehow, these fell flat as well. Still, a modest procession of newcomers kept turning up, in response to

Marshall's word-of-mouth advertising. They stared at Sophie, and she read the disappointment in their eyes. Few returned a second time, but occasionally one did. A short tetchy man, with a hard, thick body and no hair at all, asked for her three times. A thin young man, younger than Sophie and far less experienced, apologised for coming back. His anxiety was infectious, and he made her forget her lines.

'Where's the fancy man?' Jack asked her late one afternoon, while he was getting dressed.

'Who?'

'Mr Fancy-himself-at-the-front-door.'

'Oh,' said Sophie. 'Marshall? He's around.'

'You girls getting on okay?'

'Just fine,' Sophie said.

She was tempted to tell him about her failures with the men in leather.

'Are *you* all right?' she asked instead.

'Why shouldn't I be?'

'Maybe you need a holiday.'

'What from?'

'Me. Us,' Sophie told him. 'Yourself.'

Jack abandoned the study of his boots, taking up her hand and turning it over, as though searching for something that might be written underneath her skin.

He chided her gently. 'You're an optimist, remember?'

Sophie smiled, and they spoke in low voices of the garden, what would be planted where, how long it would take to make a showing. They floated themselves out towards this vision separately, and yet together. Sophie knew, by the way Jack spoke, that he was trying his best.

After he'd left, she reflected that the precise intimacy her work demanded might well cancel others out. If Kirsten had been well, she would have asked her about this. Kirsten would have known what to say.

She blinked in the bright light of the kitchen as she replaced her whip, skirting Elise in a cobra posture on her mat. Her feet touched base and scuffed against uneven boards, carrying their own knowledge of items in the house, as did her hands and arms. She felt Marika's eyes measuring her wrists and ankles, the backs of her knees through her thin sarong. She felt able to avoid Marshall, though she still feared what he might insist on, if they did find themselves alone. She could be patient with new customers, and not mind how many switched over.

What happened in the side room between her and Jack took sustenance from everything around it, yet their time together came more and more to speak for itself. This time, this speech, these sensations, began increasingly to define Sophie's moods and thoughts at Number 10 – the baseline she returned to. She was no longer tempted to tell Andrew about Andover Street, or pretended to consider it.

The Blazing House

Ann had that swish to her bum which announced that she was getting her own way in bed. A flush at her temples belied the colder, creeping days. She lit the combustion stove in her workroom and showed Sophie her completed drawings for the lawyer's hillside house.

Sophie admired. Eyes narrowed, Ann considered her work critically. She grabbed an exercise pad and made sharp, quick notes.

She said, 'Some of the calculations are turning out to be more complicated than I thought.'

Sophie wasn't sure how many ways she was supposed to take this. She asked about Ann's appeal to the building office.

Ann, her back turned, said, 'It's not the first time those bureaucratic halfwits have got in my way.'

Sophie tried to recall other times when Ann's plans had been held up for this long. She couldn't think of any.

She stared at the design table, which held the skeleton, the raw shape of a family home. She looked around for the model, then asked Ann where it was.

'In there.' Ann waved her hand dismissively towards a cupboard.

Waves of warm air travelled across the room. Ann's cheekbones bent them, the mass of her dark hair. Next door, the television was on low for Tamsin. The sun was going down behind Black Mountain. At this time of day, at this season, the mountain cast its shadow halfway across the lake.

Sophie took a deep breath, then said, 'So – you and Andrew?'

'It didn't work out.'

'What happened?'

Ann rolled up her drawings. She glanced pointedly at Sophie. 'Have you ever – this may sound weird – but have you ever thought of your ex as a very attractive man *at arms-length*?'

'You mean you fucked him and it wasn't any good?'

'It wasn't terrible,' Ann said. 'I mean, it wasn't a *complete* disaster.'

Sophie laughed to cover her anger.

'He likes me,' Ann said, as though this was the surprising part. 'He wants to try again.'

Sophie and Tamsin walked hand in hand in the thick dusk, down the hill from Ann's house to their garden flat. They walked downhill in step, something they'd perfected, and Sophie listened to Tamsin's account of her argument with John Trickett, a dispute involving a truck, and sand thrown in the eyes. She hoped that it would not mean words between herself and the preschool teacher. She thought they'd have an omelette for dinner, something light, easy and nutritious, and that Tamsin would practise the piano.

Sophie pictured herself washing up, as notes fell in the space behind her, how tonight it might be as it had been before, when the flat seemed too small to contain them. She would rush to open windows front and back, in defiance of the cold. She wished she'd asked to see the model that Ann had banished to a cupboard. Perhaps Ann would let her borrow it. She could ask next time.

She thought of Andrew and his girls, among whom she must now number Ann. A reluctant Ann – or half reluctant, where Andrew was concerned – with one foot on the shore. A foot could stabilise – or push off, if pushing were required. She waited for jealousy to rush in and fill the cracks in the little Ann had told her, jealousy to colour, *quickly,* *quickly*, the space between the lines. She pictured Ann doing a version of the splits, thought, Better you than me, and wondered at her ex-husband's show of preference.

She wondered more, though, at herself, for not noticing an attraction that had probably been around for years. Andrew was serious about his raft, conscientious in applying himself to what he said he wanted. Sophie puzzled over whether he could be serious about Ann as well, if he would apply himself to pleasing her, with more success, next time.

Mrs B's house had all its lights on, front and back. It looked like a huge ship, heading for the lake. That's strange, thought Sophie. Does she realise? Maybe she's losing her memory. Maybe she turns them on and then forgets about it.

Tamsin shouted with pleasure at the blazing house, and ran ahead, up to the door, banging on it with both fists. The door opened. Mrs B's head appeared. She bent to give Tamsin a kiss.

Sophie waved good evening, wondering where her landlady had been, in the midst of all that light, asking herself, Will she come back now, for my daughter?

'Don't be too long,' she called to Tamsin. 'I'll get dinner started.'

A Difficult Customer

'What's up?' Jack asked, when he arrived for his session.

Normally, Sophie would never have left a client alone in the side room while she answered the doorbell, but today she'd been glad to.

'What's up?' he repeated.

Quickly, she told him about the man standing beside the bed as though already in possession of it, a big man, 6 foot 3 or 4, used to getting his own way. Marshall was somewhere in Civic, Elise in the front room. The man was arguing with her. A hundred dollars was too much. Weren't there any other girls?

Jack said, 'It's okay. I'll see to it.'

Sophie stood, hesitating, in the doorway.

The man looked down his nose at Jack, who bounced straight up to him and asked, 'What seems to be the trouble?'

'Are you in charge here?'

'Near enough,' said Jack.

'I'm not paying a hundred for her.'

'Not obliged to, mate.'

'I'll give you sixty-five.'

'That'll buy a hand relief.'

'Look at this room. It's filthy.'

'Just old,' Jack said with an air of comfortable propriety. 'Make up your mind, or move along.'

'Eighty for the full service.'

'No deal,' Jack said, standing aside from the doorway and extending his right hand towards it.

The man hesitated for a second, then marched out.

Sophie shut the front door behind him with a sigh.

'We can manage, usually.'

'Stupid prick.'

'Thank you,' Sophie said.

She sat on the edge of the bed, watching Jack undress. She balanced uncomfortably, not wanting comfort.

Winter sun, low on the horizon, soon to disappear behind Black Mountain, shone a brief, angry red. Jack's long legs might have been a crane's, a heron's. He winced, taking off his shirt.

Sophie ran her fingers over his bare back, through the air just above his skin, teasing herself with her nearness to him, and what they were about to do, with Jack's inescapable proximity, the tiny, measurable, buoyant space of air between them.

His hands were work-calloused, weathered past their years. They reminded Sophie, in certain lights, of Mrs B's. Sophie turned them over in her own hands, examined them critically, compared them with her own. Underneath her nails, right against the quick where the nailbrush hadn't reached, was a thin crescent of earth. She thought of this as one of her trademarks.

Jack's refusal to talk about himself past a certain point could not alter the fact that he worked with his hands. She'd discovered a callous at the base of his right thumb, proof that something had been held or rubbed there repeatedly. She guessed his age to be somewhere around forty. That gave him a working age of twenty-two, twenty-three years, assuming that he'd gone to work straight after school. A builder of some sort, Sophie thought most likely.

Next summer, his neck and shoulders would be burnt. He would have a singlet line. Under it, his skin would be the white she knew. A builder who had once been an athlete – that was a possibility. His calf muscles were strong, though they did not stand out the way John the Cyclist's had. She knew that Jack was swift. She pictured him lifting heavy weights, walking gangplanks, deft and solitary.

His work boots were always covered with a fine coating of dust. These boots came to stand over against the whip, the towel, the choreographed movements of their time together. Sophie had asked Ann about the building sites she visited, the companies she dealt with, but Ann wasn't able to recall anyone answering to Jack's description.

He looked far away sometimes, with the distance in his eyes of travelling, and surprise at where he'd landed. When Sophie had asked him once what he thought of Canberra, he'd said it was okay, but in such a tone that Sophie had pictured him alighting in the city on one leg, having been blown off course like Bogong moths were, in November, having never meant to fly anywhere near her city.

'Are you ready?' she asked.

She curled her fingers in his hair and tugged. She kissed his fish tattoo, then lifted his hair where it curled, surprising as a baby's, and kissed the pale skin underneath.

'Jack, Jack,' she said.

His hair drew into itself what little light was left.

Sophie placed a white towel over the roses in the middle of the floor. Her whip stood ready. For the old, plain, serviceable whip, they had substituted one that was feathered into a dozen thin strips of leather. Sophie at first regarded this new whip with suspicion, and then took to it. She'd learnt how to bring it down to within a centimetre of Jack's bare back, his buttocks that would disappear through a mouse hole in the wall.

She switched the lamp on since, without it, there was insufficient light. It cast its glow indifferently around the room. Jack rocked, toe to heel and back. He eyed them all off one by one, the accoutrements of the room he paid for, lamp and bed twin beacons whose pleasures he dismissed as inferior, or not even that, did not enter them into his calculations.

He looked around him, wide-eyed, suddenly perplexed. Then he shook his head and knelt down on all fours.

The lamp, though trained in the wrong direction, would suffice.

Clearly, as though he was standing in the room beside her, Sophie saw Andrew, in his Hawaiian shirt, drifting on his raft. And on the shirt hibiscus bloomed. Blossoms burst out one by one. Blood flowed out through them, and stained the carpet red.

Looking after the Investment

Elise and Marshall dressed up to go to the bank, Marshall in one of his new suits. If you stood close to Marshall, you could still see the hole where his lip ring had been. Elise had suggested a moustache, had gone so far as to buy a fake one at the *Funny Shop*, and try it on him. Marshall had entered into the joke, and worn it for a day. Now, in a dark suit, with Elise very proper in a long skirt and jacket, they made a couple you would turn to look at in the street.

Marshall and Elise were going to the bank, and liked the bit of solemnity surrounding their visit. They didn't need Mrs B to take the cash up, not today thank you. They looked as though they were planning to take out a loan.

Marshall winked and said, 'You ladies behave yourselves till we get back. No sneaking in the rooms now, Mrs B.'

Sophie watched them go, conscious of being the one in the middle. She'd raised the building plan's problem with Elise, one time when they were alone together in the kitchen.

Elise had been quick to take offence. Did Sophie expect her and

Marshall to leave everything up to that architect? Did she think they were fools?

Sophie listened to the front door click behind them.

'Aren't they amazing?' she said, hugging herself and thinking how much of life, of promise, was in the kitchen, right here now. Almost the whole future could slip down into the crack between 'aren't they' and 'amazing', but not in this house, not yet.

'Bonnie and Clyde,' she said, laughing at her fears, putting on an air.

Mrs B and Marika watched the procession too, Marika looking down her nose at Sophie, Mrs B smiling a little apprehensively, as though the walls were listening.

Mysterious illnesses could strike a person. Think of Kirsten. Sophie hadn't visited her for quite a while. She felt guilty as she drove to Kirsten's flat. At the same time, she wasn't sure – never had been – whether Kirsten cared about her visits one way or the other.

Propped up in bed in her white room, the sounds of the street rising beneath her, Kirsten looked queenly in a dark, unsettling way. She was trying a new drug the specialist had recommended, and it made her drowsy. She lay against fat pillows, smiling the slow smile the drug lent her, amused by Sophie's description of Marshall and Elise dressing up to go to the bank.

'Bonnie and Clyde,' Sophie repeated, beginning to feel drowsy herself, thinking of the early days, an oven full of money, then of Marshall buying new suits for his appointments at the Legislative Assembly.

Kirsten shook her head. 'Don't jinx us, Soph. Not Bonnie and Clyde. Not yet.'

Shopping in Civic

So we've reached this point, Sophie thought. Tamsin glared at her parents as she got out of the car. Both of them knew better than to offer to help her with her bag. It had not got any lighter. She refused to leave anything behind, at her mother's, or her father's.

Sophie stood in the middle of the path, in front of her flat, while Tamsin saw her ritual through to its conclusion. She avoided taking even one step forward to meet her daughter. She lifted her head and studied Andrew, who had to wait as well. He could not get into his car, or wave, or speak, until the bag had been delivered across the threshold.

Andrew leant against his car, in order to appear relaxed, but Sophie knew he was as tense as she was. They were connected to each other through the small determined figure dragging luggage as though her life depended on it. Tamsin had refused when Sophie offered to buy her a new bag, one with wheels, and had reacted with disdain to any suggestion which might lessen her burden. Two people, who believed themselves to be doing their best in relation to their daughter, stared helplessly at one another.

They'd agreed that Tamsin's behaviour wasn't normal, but the agreement hadn't got them very far. Andrew was inclined to blame

Sophie. After all, he reasoned, she was the one who insisted on keeping up the split week arrangement, which was proving – just observe – too unsettling for a four-year-old.

Layers of deceit had a cushioning effect. Sophie knew she couldn't blame anybody but herself for the lies she'd told, but went on believing that she had the right to some form of indulgence. To put this into words would result in a swift rejection, swifter than the first. So she said nothing, or else made excuses for Tamsin, and hoped the situation would improve. It seemed incredible that three people, no longer a family, could be so finely-balanced, each against the other, that the slightest extra weight, or wilful push, could set the whole lot tumbling.

Sophie turned over in her mind the possibility of talking to Andrew about Ann, but felt that he should be the one to raise the subject, and, moreover, did not know what to say, though she hugged to herself the idea that Ann might have brushed him off.

Sophie and Tamsin went shopping for a winter coat. Sophie liked, and was relieved by, Civic's anonymity. She could practise breathing normally and regulate her step, not too long, but not so short that Tamsin, impatient, ran ahead. She could pull the curtain that sat ready to be closed behind her eyes, and, with the blankness back there, enjoy her daughter's company.

Tamsin had relaxed after a night in the flat. Her eyes were clear. She'd sat on Sophie's knee after dinner, watching television. They'd curled up close together. Tamsin had not once mentioned her father's house, her other life. Nor, if Andrew was to be believed, did she talk about her mother when she was with him.

Tamsin bobbed and ducked. 'Look, Mum!'

Here was the window of the pet shop, filled to bursting with a giant rabbit called Boris, underneath him smaller ones for sale. Here was the puppy Mrs B's garden would never welcome, but her father might be talked into one day.

They were on their way to Target. They would look in Target first.

Money was no object, but there was Andrew to consider. Having survived the near-disaster of the violin, Sophie must not be seen to be throwing cash around. A modest, careful purchase, and an opportunity to show him just what she could afford. If not the Taj Mahal – let him think this anyway – she'd found work at some other forgettable, unimportant eating place.

'Mum!' Tamsin crouched, puppy height, her back a warm and supple curve.

Bobbing towards them was a man with long denim legs and a bouncing walk, a red-haired man with a flat top to his head, who lifted himself out of his hips as though with each step he might take flight, as though hips, legs, feet and what they touched, were a source of immense, continuing frustration.

Jack stopped and stared at Sophie. His jeans and denim shirt were covered with fine dust. His shoulders curved inward to protect his chest. Pale lips moved below his ginger moustache, but no sound came out. Shoppers were giving him a wide berth. He swayed lightly on the balls of his feet, his eye catching Tamsin with her back turned, close enough to touch.

Sophie was horribly aware of her daughter's shape, a coiled spring at the window. Still, they went on staring at one another, open-mouthed. Then Jack swung quickly on his heels, and returned the way he'd come.

Sophie grabbed Tamsin and hugged her, squeezed her hard enough to crush the life out of a smaller creature.

Tamsin wriggled out of her mother's grip. 'Look!' she cried again, pointing at the rabbit, at 'BORIS' in huge letters, inscribed along the bottom of the hutch.

That charmed space of footpath, bound on one side by the shop window, framing an overgrown pet in need of a home, and on the other by the road with its customary traffic – Tamsin in the middle – was not immune, and they weren't either. One enchanted space might become another and another, till the city was dotted with them, as though it had contracted measles or the chicken pox.

Once Target's automatic doors had closed behind them, Sophie breathed again. Tamsin's face was pink, her vision back there, moving past a rabbit large enough to stare down a small dog, or squash it.

Mother and daughter chose a coat, to the cost, colour, size and cut of which neither paid attention. The shop assistant bundled it into a white plastic bag decorated with a huge red bullseye. Sophie shoved the receipt into a corner. 'Let's go home the back way,' she said.

That evening, Sophie wrestled with her reflection. She chased it through the kitchen window while she was washing up, and through the bathroom mirror when she straightened after running more hot water. Behind her in the bath, Tamsin floated straight and pale, a naked elf that, victim of one more false move by her mother, would find herself frozen, unable to grow.

Sophie's reflections did not return her ordinary form and visage, the motherly form she relaxed into in the garden flat. She stared at Tamsin in the bath, but Tamsin was not paying attention to her. She'd begun making a doll out of her fist covered with a pink washer, and was singing to it in a high-pitched, admonitory tone.

Sophie kept on pursuing her unfamiliar, unsettling reflection. She recognised neither herself as a mother, nor the Sophie of the Kingston house, loosening the knot of her blue and brown sarong or, naked as her daughter in the bath, adopting any of the positions she had learnt.

Tamsin climbed out and dried herself without Sophie's help. She decided she wanted to try on her new coat, and sat up in bed, wearing it over her pyjamas, to thumb through her favourite books.

This other person, this vagrant, freakish Sophie, who stared out of the small mirror on the back of her daughter's door, had lost, in the aftermath of bumping into Jack in Civic, some crucial stabilising element. If they'd met Jack once by chance, who was to say that chance might not bring him their way again?

Sophie kissed Tamsin goodnight, and would have run out of the flat, rather than face those dissolute reflections. She was frightened of what Tamsin might see when she opened her eyes next morning, the next time she looked at her mother with unguarded eyes.

There'd been that extra pocket of air between Jack and other shoppers, other passers-by. Perhaps they'd sensed his passionate, solitary focus that required a special space, in which he could succumb, while remaining in command. Certainly some of them would have noted his ungainly walk, his demeanour that, in the open air, was fixed, intent and strange.

When Jack turned up next time, she would tell him she had had enough.

Jack and Sophie faced one another in the side room. He was ready. All that remained was for her to play her part.

The fish moved on his shoulder, though he stood quite still.

Sophie felt a quiver underneath her nails, where traces of good earth from the garden lodged.

Jack watched her steadily, his expression calm. Her fingers opened, as the side room threatened to implode with the weight of irreconcilable desires and ambitions.

Still Jack stared at Sophie with resolute, pale eyes, testing her with the insistent bundle of his wishes, his preparedness, his nerve. He'd stopped in the middle of a footpath full of shoppers, right in front of Tamsin. The city had presented them one to another, then absorbed them once again, without either having to speak, or acknowledge the encounter.

Perversely, for a second, Sophie imagined that she and Jack might deliver each other into a world of ordinary things, but she knew that, were she to broach this possibility, attempt to speak of it, Jack would fix her with his heron's eyes, and the tension in his long, thin legs of a race about to start.

He lifted one foot, and with the other rubbed a wiry calf muscle. He held her spellbound while they took one another's measure.

The air thickened with the breath of all Sophie's past customers, accumulated bodies and their associations, men who'd been satisfied, or not, whose residue filled the cracks in walls.

Jack defied the shadows on the ceiling she'd made into floating panels for John the Cyclist. He'd cleared his own space, and had taught Sophie to respect his means of doing so. Hesitating, wanting to speak yet tongue-tied, Sophie became intensely aware of the weight of all her Johns, surrounding the bed and sticking to the walls, inhabiting its crevices and cracks, as cave-dwellers might, who had fled an abandoned city. Surely John the Cyclist, having found his own niche, shared their tenacity. She felt as though he was there, watching her, right now. Anger took her by the right arm and propelled her forward.

Movement unlocked her mind, and changed it. She arrived at the opposite decision to the one she'd made in her flat. She could, and would, keep her different lives apart. She resolved not to lose her nerve or turn back. She would not flee from this scene, as she had from others. Jack was necessary to her, part of a larger understanding she was groping towards, even if she couldn't put it into words.

Sophie began carefully, trusting her right hand and arm to seek out these colourless legs that disappeared before her, these upturned white feet. She raised her whip. Jack followed the trajectory that she could have traced blindfolded. He crouched low, circling the towel, rocking on his hands and knees.

In the small hours of the morning, Sophie lay on her back, in her bedroom, in the dark. She had avoided looking in the mirror as she brushed her teeth. The temperature outside was minus four. She lay with her arms behind her head, recalling John the Cyclist's pose, a bordello pose she'd thought it, picturing the man himself with a certain satisfaction, but without desire.

She dreamt of new and different ways of defeating her ex-husband, a means by which she could take away his power. On a cold, pure night, night of distilled emotion, she believed that she would have understood if Andrew had told her he'd fallen in love with someone else. It was his insistence on a future without even a pretence of commitment that she found so hard to understand, more degrading than her answer to it. To be replaced in Andrew's affections would have hurt, but by now, she told herself, she would almost be reconciled to the woman, whoever that woman had turned out to be.

She got up and stood looking out the window, seeing right through, no reflection of herself at all. Out of season blossoms shone. They exploded in the night, and filled the sky with red.

Colours in a Paintbox

Oblique sunlight poked its fingers into Number 10's neat, quiescent yard. Mrs B did the banking and filled in her time with errands. Though quizzed about it, Elise and Marshall would not divulge their reason for visiting the bank, all dressed up, with big smiles on their faces.

Sun tempted customers from their offices at lunchtime. Steam poured out of huge human sandwiches of buildings now the central heating had been turned on. Driving across Commonwealth Avenue Bridge on her way to work, Sophie watched it rising from the boilers of Parliament House, gushing into the still air, a winter fountain.

She acquired another regular, an artist who wore chartreuse underpants. He told her their colour, enunciating clearly, as though she'd never owned a paintbox. He told her how he liked to undress behind a Japanese screen, then paused, as though giving her the opportunity to apologise for not being able to provide one. Sophie imagined the artist undressing at home, the way the bright bluey-green material might be hung over the screen at a certain moment. How would it be hung, exactly? And who would be watching?

It was almost an occasion for applause when he removed his underpants. Sophie noticed how thin he was, and wondered about the scar that stretched from the bottom of his lowest rib to the top of his left thigh. He brought his new painting of the Yarralumla Brickworks to show her. It was a large canvas done in greys and blacks and browns. She thought how sad it was, knowing the brickworks were abandoned, a hole in the ground that was filling with water. She preferred his renditions of the lake and mountains – Black, Majura, Ainslie. It became the artist's habit, each time, to bring along a different one. He lined them up under the window of the side room.

Sophie admired the paintings. The artist accepted her praise. He was not much of a talker. She liked the way the landscapes made places for themselves under the window, with its drawn blinds and curtains, their way of altering perspective. She wondered if they were in any way a substitute for the Japanese screen, though of course a person could not undress behind them.

In the kitchen, Marika asked questions, and Sophie described the paintings in as few words as she could, careful to point out that the artist wasn't rich. He drove an older car than any of them, and paid only for the basic service. At the same time, she did not think she would mind all that much if she lost him to Marika.

Marika curled her top lip. Her expression said she would make her own decisions, thank you, about who was worth pursuing and who wasn't. She'd seen the skinny man arriving in his Kingswood, taking wrapped rectangles from the rusting, dented boot.

The landscapes made an emptiness in Sophie's stomach once she'd spoken of them in the kitchen. On her way to replace the towels in the side room, loud voices in the front room stopped her in her tracks. She stood in the corridor and listened, waiting for the pit-pat of feet, the reassuring murmur, but it was Marshall in there with Elise.

Sophie knew she should slip into the side room. Instead, she sank her face into her armload of towels. The towels were white, not soft, but stiff, and smelt of cheap soap powder. She was accustomed to loud voices, certain kinds, but not these two, who debated, expressed differences of opinion, but had never argued like they were doing now.

Why choose the front room, and what was Marshall doing there? Elise had been tidying up, as Sophie herself was about to do.

The door opened. Marshall came out first, walking quickly. Elise was a pace or two behind. As soon as they saw Sophie, they drew together, forearms, wrists and backs of hands almost, not quite touching. They looked at Sophie with her arms full and their expressions changed, Marshall's becoming graver, conciliatory, and Elise's superior.

'Soph,' said Marshall pleasantly. 'Hold the fort for a while, will you? Elise and I are just on our way out.'

Sophie nodded, watching them go, still close together, Marshall's shoulder higher than Elise's, the muscles packed and ready.

In the kitchen, Marika raised a dark, sarcastic eyebrow. 'What was that about?'

'I don't know,' Sophie said.

Marika smiled her disbelief. 'So they've gone then. Trusting pair, aren't they?'

'You could look at it like that.'

Marshall had a way, Sophie decided – thinking it over, after the bell had rung and she was alone in the kitchen – of not confronting opposition. Despite the raised voices, Marshall would not be caught with his hands up, backed against a fence, or marching out the front to meet his adversary head-on. When Marshall strode out front, it was to meet men who were on his side. He adapted to criticism. More than that, he incorporated those who set themselves up as his enemies.

But she wondered whether Marshall had misjudged the opposition this time, and if Elise knew this and was prepared.

Sophie rang Ann, who sounded busy. She asked if Ann knew whether Marshall and Elise had been to the building office to try and hurry things along.

Ann said impatiently, 'Surely they're not that dumb.'

Sophie heard the noise of something being dropped, followed by a man's voice in the background.

The next time she was alone with Elise in the kitchen, Sophie took her chance.

'I thought the plan was to rent a place in Fyshwick. That's what we'd discussed.'

Elise frowned, straightening from the fridge with the juice bottle in one hand.

'What's the money for, Elise?'

'What money?' Elise's voice was sharp.

'The money you and Marshall got from the bank.'

Elise put the juice down with a small, flat sound. She appeared suddenly much older, a woman on whom responsibilities weighed dear.

'What did Marshall tell you?' she asked.

'Nothing. But whatever he's planning, I'm sure it's a mistake.'

'You think I can stop him once he's got an idea in his head?'

Elise poured juice for herself, but offered none to Sophie. Pressed together round the glass of orange liquid, her lips became a barrier a person would think twice before attempting to cross.

'You can try,' said Sophie firmly.

She remembered arguments over photographers, and earlier, and more importantly, the kitchen.

'You're the only one who can.'

Jack on the Threshold

Jack stood in the kitchen doorway, balanced on one leg.

Sophie was sitting at the table, having just put down the phone.

'How did you get in?' she asked him.

'Through the front door. It was open.' He looked genial, benevolent.

'I'm sure the door was locked.'

Sophie checked it whenever she went past. Elise was careful too. She recalled Jack's head bobbing over the fence the time he'd brought her a present. For once she wished that Marshall was there.

'No, it wasn't.' Jack shook his head with simple but complete conviction. He took a step inside.

Away from the side room's atmosphere, he appeared pared back, as though several of his layers had been skilfully removed.

Sophie shepherded him along the corridor with a rigid arm.

Repetition was important, the routine that, on good days, made a pattern that might hold, might frame the energy of better times. Sophie sought courage, and some easing in herself, in the silences between the words she had been taught to say, and in the words themselves. *Move. Get over there.* How harsh and cold they were. But they did not feel cold, and were balanced now by Jack's unheralded appearance in the kitchen.

'Don't do that again,' she said.

Jack stared at her, and repeated his assertion that the front door had been open.

Sophie told Elise as soon as they were free.

'He was standing in the doorway on one leg.'

Elise frowned and said, 'We'd better get the locks changed.'

Without putting it into words, there was an assumption between them that they could deal with trouble on their own, that Marshall needn't be involved.

Sophie's muscles ached. A headache seemed about to push her over some physical boundary she hadn't known was there. She'd never talked to Elise about Jack. It seemed enough that Marshall had encouraged her to expand her clientele in his direction, and it had not worked out. She wasn't sure if he'd discussed this with Elise, or what her opinion had been.

Elise looked tired, a little sad. She said, in answer to Sophie's unspoken question, 'I think between us we can handle Jack okay.'

Sophie drove home with one eye behind her on the road, following the bridge that arched like a huge, upside-down smile. She stared at patterns made by headlights and the lights on water. She sighed with relief as she pulled into her driveway, as though a barrier had clicked into place behind her. There was no reason to suppose the part of Canberra where she lived was safer than any other, but she felt that it was.

Visiting Kirsten in her flat next day, Sophie told the story of Jack walking through a locked door, Jack standing on one leg on the threshold of the kitchen.

Kirsten nodded, looking sleepy.

It was difficult to recall the Kirsten of the summer, casual knot holding up her brown sarong, her way of laying claim to certain words, tossing her net wide, and then drawing it in.

Chronic fatigue syndrome, the new specialist had said, ordering more tests. There was still no sign of the killer virus. Kirsten said it was something to be thankful for. Doctors went up and down in her estimation. Sophie encouraged shopping. If one did not give satisfaction, try another. She wished she had better advice to offer.

Sun shone through high, wide windows onto a white bed. White curtains that Kirsten had bought at the beginning of her illness were pulled back. There was the matter of health benefits, possibly a pension. Sophie had brought forms for Kirsten to fill in. She tried to amuse with stories of her customers – the artist with his gift for colour, how she'd lost the big foot man to Marika.

Kirsten waved a hand at the form and said she would look later. She smiled slowly, her face half in and half out of the sun. Sophie noted, on the sunny side, her nicotine-stained teeth.

'Marshall's going to do something dumb. You need to warn Elise.'

Kirsten looked down at the bumps of her legs under the sheet. 'Take up thy bed and walk,' she said.

'Ring her and make her see that it's important,' Sophie insisted. 'Better still, ring Marshall.'

'And say what?'

'Not to be a fool.'

'Marshall put up with me because I was Elise's friend. He was happy to get rid of me.'

'Let him know he hasn't.'

Kirsten coughed. Sophie felt dizzy, as though she was about to fall.

Mysterious illnesses could strike a person. A person might strike back, flail and thrash about. But where would that get her?

Without a diagnosis, and less confident, as each week passed, of getting one, Kirsten hung suspended in her high, wide room, and Sophie understood that she would not let it go without a fight. Kirsten had refused to say how much the rent was, or whether she had savings, nor had she told Sophie what the flat meant to her. But Sophie saw how Kirsten, with a glance here and a touch there, reaffirmed possession.

She had not filled it with furniture. The space beneath the windows, which an armchair might have taken up – perhaps an old-fashioned model, covered with a tartan run, drinking in the light and within easy reach of a CD player – instead was left as open space. This was partly where Sophie's feeling of vertigo came from, that between the bed and window, there was nothing but clean air, promising serenity in spite of the coils that humans got themselves into, whispering that there was always a way out.

Kirsten hummed, reaching for her cigarettes, then thinking better of it, sitting on her hands. Her nightgown was thin and faded, just as her sarong at Number 10 had been. She hummed along with music recorded in her inner ear and her pride held up, in answer to Sophie's careful but insistent probing. She said that yes, she was managing, she could.

With one letter changed, 'mystery' became 'my story', thought Sophie on the way home from Kirsten's, reflecting that she continued to develop a taste for the former, while accumulating details for the latter.

She did some housework in a desultory fashion, waiting till it was time to drive to Kingston. She wanted the mystery of Kirsten's illness to be solved, and wished she knew more about medicine. But the mystery she'd cultivated for herself – what she was doing at Number 10, and why – this she spun out, rather than took steps to solve, or simply end.

As soon as a house had doors that opened on the inside to reveal, or not reveal, said Sophie to herself, then there you had a mystery, for you could never truly know what you would find on the other side. And, before this, there were doors that separated the outside from the inside – a red door, it might be, with ancient, peeling paint and a bell that had died from overuse, so that you had to raise your fist and knock. With that small action, unheralded and scarcely comprehended, an unsuspecting person shut another door, invisible, to going back.

Miniature Landscapes

A young cat had taken to hunting along Mrs B's back fence. Sophie watched him stalking small, swift birds at dusk, and wondered if he was a stray, or if dinner was waiting for him somewhere in the street. Tamsin had spotted him first. Sophie hoped he'd move on before her daughter decided they should offer him a home.

Mrs B would not be pleased, and Sophie did not want the responsibility. Yet the grace of the young animal stayed with her as they hunkered down to winter. Small deaths occurred, minute by minute, in the city's cracks. Arriving at work, Sophie stared at a sparrow in the gutter at the front of Number 10. It lay slantwise across the grating, colour of leaf mould, sodden, stuck.

She felt the rhythm of the cat hunting in herself, soft footfall after footfall, then the circling closer, the rush, an explosion in her diaphragm.

She took her turn in the armchair. A small graveyard of dead insects lay between the kitchen window and the flyscreen. She scooped up a handful of light, husky bodies, surprised that she hadn't she noticed them before. The colours that they might have had in life were gone – that green-blue-purple on a fly's wing. She recalled one summer evening, smell of a thunderstorm, bodies hitting the wire, wings invisible in the night outside. She had laughed at something Kirsten had said – she could not remember what – and then the bell had rung.

She let herself out the back door, and walked over to the shed. She stood for a few moments with both hands around the statue, breathing in the cold, strong smell of him.

The artist made himself at home in the side room, removing his colourful underpants and revealing his long, curved scar. He lined up a set of miniature landscapes underneath the window. Sophie said how nice they were. She performed her duties well.

Elise was in the front room. It was off-pay week, so Marika wasn't there. The house was as quiet as any in a Canberra suburb. This house, this suburb, the regularity of days are the best disguise, thought Sophie.

After she had said goodbye to her artist, she looked about her at the empty kitchen, taking in, through the open door, the supple spine of corridor and the three rooms leading off it, where the business of the house was done. If you listened hard, you could hear the shower dripping, harder, the whole house breathing in and out.

Sophie drank a glass of water, thinking of three suitcases, one each for Marshall, Kirsten and Elise. She imagined opening up the cases, in the boot of the car, on the highway bound for Canberra, noting the individuality inscribed there – Elise's tights, Marshall's hair gel, Kirsten's faded, comfortable sarong – how these objects were waiting for expression, and a place to settle down.

A thump on the far side of Kirsten's door caused Sophie a shiver of alarm. She rattled the knob and called, 'Hello! Kirsten?'

Another thump was followed by a curse, whose meaning Sophie made out, if not every word.

She said loudly, 'It's me, Sophie. What's wrong?'

The Kirsten who finally got the door open was so drunk she fell against Sophie, a can of beer in her hand.

Sophie put her arms out to steady Kirsten, her own feet planted solidly, aware of how much lighter and thinner her friend had become, how her frame of bones and muscles felt like kindling underneath her nightgown.

Kirsten dropped her beer can. 'Look at this,' she crowed.

On a table, a whisky bottle jumped as she banged her hand down on a sheaf of papers.

'Look at all these. Negative. Negative. Negative. Negative. You know what? I think I'd rather *have* the disease.'

Sophie pulled back. 'Don't say that.'

Kirsten laughed, and threatened to topple over again.

Sophie sat her down on a straight-backed chair, registering how bare the room was – a table and two chairs, an empty bottle, no sign of any food. She'd scarcely paid attention to the rest of Kirsten's flat since, all the other times she'd visited, Kirsten had entertained her in the bedroom.

'I'll make toast,' she said. 'Have you got any bread?'

'In the freezer-deezer,' Kirsten said.

Sophie boiled water, found some instant coffee so old it was welded to the bottom of the jar. The toaster smelt of ancient dust. The light in the room was so pure it made the most humble of amenities ashamed.

Kirsten was clutching her list of test results, and jabbing with an angry finger.

'Those bloody specialists and Capital Pathology. Have they got a racket going? Look at this. Legionnaire's disease. Now how the hell would I catch legionnaire's disease?'

'It spreads through building ventilation,' Sophie said. 'But I agree, it's unlikely.'

'Soph,' said Kirsten, sober suddenly and wide-eyed as Tamsin when faced with a problem that she couldn't solve. 'I just want to *know*.'

Sophie stayed later than she'd meant to, making Kirsten swallow toast and drink the coffee that she'd melted and disguised with sugar. Kirsten made a face and spat. Sophie hugged her quickly as she said goodbye.

She drove fast across the lake. The bridge's smile was long and muscular. The glare of the flat water teased her. Her car obeyed the movements of her hands and feet. She flew above the water, her mind with Kirsten in her flat, Kirsten drunk as Sophie had never seen her, drunk and left behind, high up off the ground.

She should not have left Kirsten by herself. She should have rung Elise. Did Elise know what was happening to Kirsten, shut up, alone? Did she care?

Without warning, the car in front was close enough to strike. Sophie braked with three centimetres to spare. She'd raced along behind it, seeing but not paying attention. Her foot on the brake, operating independently, had saved her.

Too shaken to continue, she pulled off into the next side street. The car in front – her eyes had registered it clearly – three children in the back seat, none wearing seatbelts, one with a small, pale face and long, dark hair, intent on what was about to overtake her.

Theft

With Marshall occupied elsewhere, Elise took on the job of adding up the takings.

It was the end of a long pay night. Elise and Sophie had each rung Kirsten to check up on her. Kirsten had been cheerfully abusive. She said she was going to bed, and not to bother her again. Sophie and Elise had agreed that this was a good sign.

Jack had turned up later than usual – no appointment, of course. Sophie had fitted him in, somewhat distractedly, between two newcomers flush with funds and ignorance, needing so many explanations that she became suspicious.

Elise said goodnight to her last client and opened the oven door. Where the pile of fifties, twenties, now and then a hundred, should have been, there was nothing. The tray was empty.

Marika had already left. Sophie was about to.

Elise made Sophie open her bag and empty the contents on to the kitchen table. Furious, she made Sophie take off the jeans and jumper she had dressed in for driving home through the freezing streets.

Just one night's takings, but pay night and a good one.

White with anger, at herself as much as anyone, Elise insisted that they turn each of the rooms upside down. She glared at the front door's new lock as though it had deliberately let her down. She dialled Marika's number. The fruitless search, late hour and fatigue made her angrier than she might have been. Marika denied, accusing Mrs B, who'd left the house at dusk.

Elise's shoulders sagged as she put down the phone. 'I guess *she* won't be coming back.'

Sophie was tempted to say good riddance.

'When did Jack leave?' Elise asked her.

'It would have been two hours ago.'

'The money was still there then. It must have been Marika.'

There was doubt in Elise's voice, the echo of Marika's hot denial in her ears, the memory of Jack walking through a locked door.

'I'm sorry,' Sophie said. 'We'll make it up somehow.'

Busted

A good day to be outside, unseasonably warm. They should make the most of it, said Mrs B. Elise was expected soon. The three of them could give the yard a last good digging over.

Sophie was subdued, thinking of the stolen money, and of Kirsten, who had not answered the phone. Sophie had dithered over going round there, then decided she would be better to let Kirsten sleep it off. She did not feel like talking. She wondered if Elise was late because of having to tell Marshall, or perhaps she'd gone to Kirsten's. Perhaps she'd taken her to see yet another doctor.

Mrs B was inclined to blame Jack, rather than Marika. In either case, she considered it futile to cry over money they would never see again.

Sophie almost didn't hear the bell.

Two policemen stood there. The older one had rung the bell, while the second looked down at his feet. Everything about him said that this was his first brothel raid, and, please God, his last. The older one had a walleye, and looked sad rather than embarrassed.

Neither man looked fully at Sophie. The younger went on studying his feet. The other's short grey hair stood up as though full of electricity. His left eye wandered, though his pressure on the bell had been direct.

Sophie craned her neck, looking for a squad car, backup support guarding the driveway, in case she decided that her best chance was to run.

Mrs B pushed her aside and asked, 'What is going on?'

The older man looked at her as steadily as he was able to and said he was charging the occupants of 10 Andover Street with conducting an illegal business. It seemed to Sophie, standing back and biting her lip, that he was reaching for a dignified approach.

'Officer,' said Mrs B respectfully, 'we are here to work in the garden. This is my assistant.'

She held an earth-stained gardening glove in one hand. She introduced herself and Sophie, not going so far as to put it into words, but her manner suggesting family. She elbowed Sophie, who held up her own hands so the police could see the deep half-moons of dirt under her nails.

Sophie backed up Mrs B with as much force as she could, exposed at the front door in her wellingtons, in her clothes of an apprentice gardener. She watched the senior policeman's expression change to puzzled. She watched him thinking that it could just be true, exercising the tact that went with having a walleye, turning over options in his mind. She knew that it was best, now Mrs B had made her pitch, to say nothing further, but she kept her hands extended slightly, their dark nails proof of her veracity, if he liked to take them that way – proof enough.

His manner remained courteous and solemn. 'With your leave, ladies, we'll need to search the premises.'

Mrs B led the way, and everyone else followed in a clump. She stood aside, pulling Sophie with her, while the two men examined each of the rooms. The young one made notes, the older lifted items from the tables and replaced them.

In the side room next to the vacant block, the officer in charge rocked the bed. The wedge of newspaper Sophie had shoved under its short leg finally came loose. There they were, the lamp, tissues, condoms, towels, baby oil, the place under the window where the artist would lean his painting of the day – all to be taken in and noted down. There was the floral carpet, with its numbered stains. Watermarks were tremulous and stark. The officer replaced Sophie's paper wedge.

The kitchen stood ahead of them, where Sophie's whip shared wall space with Elise's mat. Would the police consider an inspection of the kitchen necessary? Would they give it more than a once-over glance, cursory at best? When they got to the whip, would one of them say, 'Who does this belong to'?

Mrs B led them down the back steps, and briefly described her plans for the garden. Smell it, Sophie felt like saying. Smell the dirt on my hands, here.

Mrs B moved briskly. The phone rang behind them. Sophie held her breath. It stopped after the fourth ring.

There was the fountain in his shed, in the middle of the well-turned earth.

'Jesus,' the young policeman said, stepping back and bumping into Sophie.

'Not quite,' replied the older man.

In the shed's close dimness, their cupid with his quiver and bow looked almost menacing. His snub features gained an edge, their own authority. Here I am, he seemed to be saying, right where you did not expect me.

Hoses coiled in corners, and from hooks which Mrs B had fixed to walls. On other hooks hung secateurs of different sizes. Two rakes, one black-handled, another green, leant against each other in the corner furthest from the door.

The policemen looked around, though the younger one's eyes never strayed far from the cupid's smile, his plump raised arm.

Sophie stood back, rubbing her foot where he'd trodden on it, wondering what seedlings would be planted now, what leaves would fall, to be raked and stacked in piles. The shed and its contents felt like a child's grave come upon by accident.

Mrs B was explaining the one fact that surely did not need explanation, that these were the tools of her trade, and her assistant, Sophia's.

The officers remained aloof. Yet neither had laughed, or laughed now, at their claims. The young one went on writing in his book.

Sun shone through the kitchen window. It was early in the afternoon. No customers had turned up yet, but could any minute. Elise, who might be quarrelling with Marshall, could turn up any minute too.

They sat around the table and discussed the house's other employees, or occupants. The older man, who did all the talking, didn't seem able to settle on a word. Mrs B and Sophie affected to know nothing of these others, claiming to keep to the back of the house, outside.

'Though we are allowed to use facilities,' Mrs B said firmly, her resolution having grown throughout the tour. She seemed bigger, taller, to have filled out altogether.

They knew no names, addresses, phone numbers.

'Sorry, officer,' they said.

Sun shone through spotless windows, picking out the policeman's bad eye, which flickered to the stove and over items leaning on a wall. Yet he did not ask, Who does this belong to, and who that?

He took all of it in, with his one good, one vagrant eye – what the rooms stood for, and how a temporary emptiness, absence of business, might be noted, along with the time of day. His blue eyes drew conclusions with a certain satisfaction now. The younger officer's eyes were blue as well, but lacked cloudiness, or signs of wear. They were framed by pink, elastic skin. He removed a tape recorder from his jacket pocket, placed it in the middle of the table, and continued taking notes. Absent voices could not be recorded. Still so early, hardly one o'clock. The telephone, mercifully, did not ring.

Both men had their share of tact, and a plan worked out in advance. How could it be otherwise? The rooms and their contents were recorded, yet certain distinctions blurred, were allowed to blur, and Sophie's place in any one not yet defined.

The senior man spread out the authorisation to close them down. He said he'd leave a copy with them, implying that, no matter what they said, what answers were given or withheld, he knew where to take, and where to leave, his other copies. He knew who had bought the house, whose name it was in.

Tact held. A peculiar courtesy, plucked out of the clear winter air, held in earthy-coloured hands. It had got the two women through the search, and now this next part, which might prove to be more difficult. Sophie felt it palpably, this courtesy, this tact, a bubble that she clutched at, Mrs B's hand a warning pressure on her wrist. They asked no questions, kept 'Why now?' to themselves, but did not pretend ignorance of what was at issue.

Sophie did mention, in a small voice, that the law was about to be changed.

'That's true,' the senior policeman said, as he would of a relevant point that required consideration, perhaps even one that summarised all that could be questioned, still, between them.

'But in the meantime,' he continued reasonably, 'the business is illegal and zoning regulations' – here he stopped and looked straight at Sophie, as straight as he could muster – 'when zoning regulations are drawn up, assuming ladies,' he nodded deferentially towards Mrs B, 'assuming our politicians vote to change the law, zoning regulations will not allow brothels to operate in residential areas.'

'But – ' said Sophie.

Mrs B put her hand over the top of Sophie's and squeezed hard. 'Thank you officer,' she said, 'for your information.'

Could a walleye be said to wink? Could the policeman possibly have winked in response to Mrs B's interruption, her reigning in of her young assistant's indiscretion?

Mrs B smiled and nodded at both men, warming her thanks and making it appealing, warming it with the pressure she was still applying to Sophie's hand underneath hers on the wooden table. She smiled and nodded her acknowledgment of the deep water they were all treading. Sophie saw her small gap of escape widening, and also how she might close it, swiftly, with a word. She bit her tongue, and allowed Mrs B's thanks to cover hers as well.

The policeman blinked, an onion skin of movement. One corner of the sheet of paper, the authority to close them down, lifted in the beginning of a wind.

Sophie showed the police to the front door. They left through it, disappearing down the path of what was suddenly an ordinary suburban house, a little the worse for wear. No sign of anything or anyone suspicious.

Back in the kitchen, Sophie said, 'They didn't want to arrest anyone. They didn't *want* to charge me. Otherwise they would have come at night. They *wanted* to let me off the hook.'

They laughed, and Sophie spread her hands, palms downwards, on the table. There were her nails with their saving bands of soil.

'Did you see how relieved they were, to be given an excuse?'

Mrs B said, 'We must leave now. We must get out of here.'

The doorbell rang. They're playing with us, Sophie thought. That was the rehearsal.

Jack stood on the porch, lifting himself out of his hips.

'The police have been here,' Sophie said.

'Are you okay?'

Sophie nodded. 'Yes. We're locking up.'

Mrs B pushed past her for the second time. She waved her arms and shouted. Jack looked startled, but he stood his ground, sticking out his chest, pulling his stomach in. Mrs B flailed at him with both arms. It didn't take much to tower over Mrs B, but Jack held his arms up in self-protection.

'I'm sorry,' Sophie said.

'Sorry!' cried Mrs B, and chased Jack down the path.

Returning, puffed, she was all industry. She made sure the back door and windows were locked. She removed her tools from the shed, and secured them in the Datsun's boot.

'Did you have to do that?' Sophie asked her.

'Did I *have* to, Sophia? Did I have to save your skin? Did I have to lie? And what if I have to stand up in a court? What then?'

'What if I hadn't run him off?' cried Mrs B. 'What if the police are watching from down there?' She flung an arm towards the city end of Andover Street. 'And I am standing in the doorway with a thousand lies to tell, and I smile at your Jack the Ripper and tell him, "Come on in!"'

'All right, all right,' said Sophie. 'There's just one thing. It will only take a minute.'

Convalescence and a Missing Fountain

Sophie told Kirsten how two policemen, one young and one with a walleye, had stood at Number 10's front door. The younger one had blinked and looked down at his feet, while the older one held Sophie with his good eye. With a few quiet words, a flourish of authority, the police had closed them down.

Sophie told Kirsten the story of all that had taken place that day, while Kirsten sat up in her white bed, with her curtains open to the evening cold, to snatches of other tenants' conversation from below. All that had happened – Jack running, ginger tom, chased by an old woman brandishing her threats like fire, and before that, Mrs B's quick thinking. *We are the gardeners, officer.* The embarrassed young policeman, and the older one, both with a job to do. Mrs B's quick wit, Sophie's dirty fingernails, her whip in a corner of the kitchen.

Kirsten smiled at Sophie's picture of Jack making tracks, Mrs B with her look of *take that, and that!*

Kirsten looked pale and thinner than ever after her drunken rave, but with a more lively, wide-awake expression. Sophie noticed that the cigarettes were gone from her bedside table.

They turned on the TV for the evening news.

'Marshall Matt!' she said.

There was Marshall in a three-piece suit, white shirt and matching tie, his black hair trimmed close about the ears, his expression the most persuasive of accessories.

The interviewer wasn't in the frame. Her voice was young and clear. Was it true that Marshall had offered bribes to politicians?

'Campaign donations,' Marshall said, facing the camera with steady eyes, no air of defeat about him.

'Who to?' the reporter asked.

'The Liberal and Labor parties.'

'And?'

'Several Independents.'

'How much?'

'It's common for interest groups to offer political parties campaign donations,' Marshall said with a smile. 'Everybody does it.'

'Which interest group do you represent?'

'The sex industry.'

'The Magistrate's Court in two days' time,' the interviewer prompted. 'What plea will you be entering?'

'Not guilty.'

'What about Elise?' Sophie asked Kirsten.

'If she's got any brains, she'll deny it all.'

'Where's Elise now?'

'I don't know.'

'You never rang to talk him out of it.'

'I tried to,' Kirsten said.

Marshall faced the camera squarely, the charge of bribery fresh on him. Another man so charged might cower, or appear aggressive, or defiant. Marshall spoke about campaign donations in a voice that combined his youth and optimism.

Sophie and Kirsten listened, waiting for the interviewer and the law to spike, waiting for Elise's name.

When it didn't come, when the next item appeared, Sophie said, 'Let's phone her.'

There was no answer, neither on Elise's number, nor at the Kingston house.

Kirsten sat in her high white bed, eyes focused on the television at its foot.

Impatient, Sophie said, 'You know what? It's time to get up. Half an hour. First sitting in your armchair, then moving around the room.'

Kirsten blinked and turned to face her.

'You're done with being tested,' Sophie said. 'Whatever it is, you're going to get better.' She paused and added, 'Think of it like training.' She leant forward and repeated her instructions. 'Just think of it as one step after another.'

Next morning, Sophie woke to the memory of Mrs B chasing Jack down the driveway, more confused than when she went to bed. She hadn't been startled awake during the night by the sound of the phone. She checked for messages as soon as she got up. The silence that was Elise not ringing, not explaining, was blacker now than it had been at midnight.

There was a picture in the *Canberra Times* – debonair Marshall in front of the Magistrate's Court, Marshall with his winning smile. But still no mention of Elise, or any of them.

Sophie phoned Ann, got her machine, hung up.

Elise's voice rang clearly down the path. 'Where is he?'

Sophie watched Elise and Kirsten walk towards her. It had rained during the night, and the ground on either side of the path was sticky. She'd already made the mistake of stepping across it, and her good new boots, that she'd put on that morning with a sense of finality, had mud up to the instep.

She'd come back for her whip, and, lacking a key, had stood hesitating, thinking of ways she might break into the kitchen. She'd opened the shed door to stare at the space where the fountain had been when she heard voices.

Kirsten was making her way slowly along the path behind Elise, dressed in a woollen beanie and a long black coat Sophie had never seen before.

Elise marched ahead, repeating her question.

'Who, Marshall?' Sophie asked.

'My fountain.'

'I don't know,' said Sophie. 'What's going on?'

Kirsten offered her a colourless, but steady smile.

Sophie smiled back and said, 'It's great to see you up.'

'Come inside,' Elise told them. 'We shouldn't be standing here like monkeys in a zoo.'

Sophie's whip still leant in its corner of the kitchen, but Elise's mat was rolled up by the door, and there was a pile of smaller items on the table.

Kirsten shoved her hands deep into the pockets of her coat and sat down in the armchair. The dampness of the day outside had crept into the kitchen. Sophie recalled one long afternoon when business had been slack, making up a game, peopling the cracks in the plaster, joining them into imaginary countries, the bounty of an ark.

Had Elise gone round to Kirsten's after she had left the night before? And where was Marshall?

'What happened?' she asked.

'Marshall fucked up.' Elise looked at Kirsten as she spoke, not Sophie. 'He said they were a bunch of squabbling old women and he could wind them round his finger.'

'The politicians?'

'And those idiots in the building office.'

'He tried to bribe them too?'

'He would have, but he never got around to it.'

Kirsten absorbed this conversation silently, her hands holding tightly to the chair's thick arms. She was shivering, but did not pull her coat tight, and it was too thin anyway, made of some flimsy, decorative material, not at all the kind of coat you'd expect Kirsten to be wearing.

'Marshall never had any common sense,' Elise said, with another glance in Kirsten's direction. 'Anyway, they weren't bribes.'

'The correct answer is no,' Kirsten replied without turning around. '"No, officer. I know nothing, heard nothing, saw no money changing hands."'

'It didn't. Nobody took it. The idea was to offer it to all of them at once, Labor, the Liberals and the Independents. Campaign donations. Everybody does it.'

'Marshall wasn't everybody,' Sophie said.

'He was lobbying. What do you think those church groups do, and all the others, do you think they've never offered anybody a campaign donation?'

Kirsten was a magnet in the huge, ungainly chair. Elise's mat was waiting. A cardboard box held crockery and glasses. The stove's black door stood open.

'Did you know the police would be here yesterday?' asked Sophie.

'I was out when they arrived. They took him to the station. Do you think they took my statue – the police?'

'They might have,' Sophie said. 'I don't know what they were expecting to find in the shed, but it certainly surprised them, the younger one at least.'

'Maybe Marika took him. If she took that money.'

The three women were silent for a moment, staring out across the backyard to the garden shed, its flimsy door unlocked and hanging open.

Sophie told Elise, briefly, what the police had said and done, how Mrs B had thought and acted quickly, how luck had been on their side.

'We ought to leave, in case they come back,' she said.

Kirsten stood up unsteadily, leaning with one hand on the armchair.

Sophie offered to take her home, but Elise said sharply, 'I'll do that.'

Elise and Sophie carried boxes of CDs and kitchen utensils out to Elise's car.

Kirsten hoisted Elise's yoga mat onto a black shoulder.

'Don't worry. It won't break me,' she said.

Sophie tossed the whip into the back of her car and said goodbye, feeling shy all of a sudden, oddly formal. She gave Kirsten a hug, and shook Elise's hand.

On the way home, she took a detour to the lake. The winter sun picked out shadows with a sharp, uncompromising eye. For the last time, she pictured Marshall, Kirsten and Elise driving down the highway with Canberra still ahead of them, the two women in the front seat, Marshall in the back, changes in the air around them, loss of the sea and smoke haze – the subtle changes, but precise and complete, of inland. And at last the bush capital with its trio of mountains, parliamentary flagmast. The approach was wavering, mirage-like, but at the same time prosperous and solid, marbled through with European gardens, the closer that they came.

Three cases in the boot, three people in the car, smiling at each other, making plans. How rich and ripe the small, neat city, ready to be plucked.

'Fourteen politicians!' Marshall would have said this with a laugh, leaning his chin on the back of Elise's seat, rubbing the back of her neck affectionately. He'd done his homework. Fourteen new politicians in a town that had just attained self-government, puffed up with self-importance, full of men with money asking to be lifted from their pockets.

Sophie pulled up at a part of the lake where the land sloped downwards to soft, welcoming brown water. She stood on a small raised lip of land, holding her whip high in the air, then throwing it forward with all the strength of her strong right arm.

The whip arched and bucked, as though a wind out there, not felt on land, gathered under it to make it fly. For a long time, she watched the whoop and spring and long feathered resistance of the instrument, wind making play with it before it dived into the water, elegant and straight, handle first and leather fronds descending.

She drove back past Tamsin's preschool, through daylight as clear and clean as any she remembered. Tamsin would be there, taking the nap the teacher had at last trained her into. She would be fresh and full of energy when Andrew picked her up. Sophie had sometimes thought, when she did not have Tamsin, before Number 10 had started opening in the daytime and long, soft afternoons had been hers to fill, of walking into the preschool unannounced, upsetting the schedule.

Ann's car was missing from her steep driveway, which was covered at the bottom with dead leaves. Sophie recalled visits when Tamsin's stubby toddler's legs had ached and protested at the climb, occasions when, proud of walking, yet wanting to be carried, Tamsin had held up her arms and cried, 'Too far!' Sophie had bent down and laughed, making a game of it. 'The *grand* old Duke of York! He *had* ten-thousand men!'

She knocked on the door, and listened to the echo of her knock inside. She waited and knocked again, then walked around the back.

Ann's house was built into a curl of hill, a fold of mountain, small, domestic-sized. There was a terraced vegetable garden, which Ann, initially enthusiastic, had lost interest in. There was the tree Tamsin had fallen asleep under in the summer, a scrap of lawn, garden chairs covered with dry leaves.

Sophie thought of leaving Ann a note. It dawned on her that it would be very strange if Ann had not seen, or heard the news.

Instead, she rang Ann's number from her flat and left a message, the bare bones of the story. Ann must be out of town. Sometimes her work took her to Goulburn, or Cooma, or even further afield, and she stayed away overnight.

Tamsin came to spend four days with her mother.

Mrs B made pizza as a peace offering, though she didn't, and would never, apologise for chasing Jack away. They circled each other with Tamsin in the middle, smiled falsely over pizza. One of the good things about Mrs B was that she didn't expect Tamsin *not* to make a mess. But Tamsin took care now, with everything she did. If there were no napkins out ready for her to wipe her hands on, she didn't ask, she fetched them herself.

The small girl knew that something was the matter, or rather that trouble, already giant-sized, had grown even larger. This knowledge translated itself first into reproach, then silence. She no longer asked questions, and replied to them with monosyllables.

Sophie waited for a knock on the door announcing the police, or worse, a clutch of journalists. While Tamsin was at preschool, she lay in bed with the curtains open, letting in the sun. She read, and dozed, and puzzled over where Ann was, and why she hadn't rung. She thought of the model room shut up in a cupboard and switched on the TV for the news, paying fitful attention to three international, and one local item.

Cameras caught Marshall leaving the Magistrate's Court, flanked by his barrister, a dark-haired young man who looked remarkably like him. True to his word, Marshall had entered a plea of not guilty to the charge of attempted bribery.

Microphones made a frame around two men in identical dark suits, white shirts straight off the hanger. Marshall's hair was trimmed, his dark eyes unwavering. Sophie waited again for Elise's name, spoken out with harsh intent, or dropped softly into reporters' waiting ears. She held her breath for the pushing off, the balancing of responsibility that might come, not from Marshall, but his lawyer, that well-timed disclosure, accompanied by the jutting of a padded shoulder, that revealed 'my client's partner', and named their 'working girls'.

The Letter

Sophie turned the letter over in her hands, unable to make sense of it, or to put it down. She paid attention to the whiteness of the paper and the letterhead, which seemed, with its sprung thistles of names, to stand for solicitors' letterheads everywhere. Smith-Morton, Holmes, Chan and O'Farrell. All there, thought Sophie. A person need go no further.

What was down the page must surely be a joke, a trick, yet such a bad one, so nasty, in its intent and its effects, that no gang of lawyers could have dreamt it up.

After a long time, she returned to the breakfast alcove, to a table decorated with the makings of her brunch. She'd slept late, her first morning without Tamsin, then prepared a meal she'd been about to start eating when she'd heard the chug of the postman's motor-bike.

The curtains at the house were still drawn, front and back, and Sophie had been wondering, as she lifted the lid of the mailbox, whether Mrs B had slept in too. There'd been a phone bill, and this good quality envelope with her printed name, no window. Another bill, she'd thought.

Sophie felt the teapot with the back of her hand, then realised she hadn't made the tea. She'd decided to fetch the mail first. This sequence of events seemed important, as though, if she could go back and re-order them, the result would turn out differently. At the same time, such a consideration seemed so trivial and beside the point that to be entertaining it, even for a second, brought tears of anger and frustration to her eyes. She picked up the empty teapot and banged it on the table.

So much had happened in the last week that this letter must surely be a continuation of it, its officialdom that of the police with *their* letter of authority.

Sophie stared at the premature ruin of her breakfast, and then, as though it must now be protected from any damage she might inflict on it, before she ripped it up or spat on it, or spilt tea all over it, she picked up the letter again and forced herself to read.

It was from a firm of solicitors, from one of the partners. There was the signature at the bottom, James O'Farrell, and the name printed underneath. There was Monday's date. The body of the letter referred to 'my client, Mr Andrew Harper', to 'family court proceedings', to 'application for sole custody of Tamsin Harper'.

Sophie scrabbled for clues between the phrases 'relevant matters', 'grave concern', and 'documentary evidence'. She realised she was again half standing, her hands pressed on the letter, carefully but hard, as though, if only she pushed hard enough, it would sink through solid matter. Nowhere were the words 'prostitute' or 'sex worker' to be found, though 10 Andover Street, Kingston appeared as if in bold type. The worst sentence was in the middle of the page. It said, 'Photographs have been obtained'.

Sophie knocked loudly on Mrs B's back door. It wasn't until she shouted that a white face appeared at a window, curtain pulled aside.

Mrs B unlocked the door and let Sophie in. She wore a dressing-gown of deep red velvet. Her hair stood out around her head in stiff grey configurations. Red velvet seemed so out of the character she'd created for herself that for a second Sophie simply stood and stared.

'What is it? What's the matter?'

Sophie waved the letter. 'It's Andrew. He's taking Tamsin.'

Together, they studied words and clauses as though, by picking individual threats out of a maze, they could dismantle them.

Sophie wanted to storm Andrew in his office, beat with both fists on the door.

Mrs B said, 'Wait.'

'These photographs,' Mrs B said quietly.

Andrew might have hired a private detective. On the other hand, he might have done the sneaky work himself. Sophie recalled a day of hoarded fistfuls of sunlight, working in the garden in a borrowed pair of gumboots.

'The afternoon Jack came round the back,' she said.

'Jack!' cried Mrs B, as though all she needed was the name.

Sophie said, 'I took him to the front room. I left the curtains open.'

She relived the sense of occasion, the way the sun had moved across the carpet, a grateful warmth afterwards, sitting on the bed.

A telephoto lens from Number 13 would have been more than adequate. Oh, a good view there! Bare street and nothing blocking. Any number of places, really, to take shots, for someone with experience.

Sophie stood in Ann's workroom and said, 'You were sleeping with him.'

AnnAndrew, AndrewAnn. Their names ran together, fitted. Foolish not to have paid attention to what this might mean.

Ann said, 'No I wasn't.'

'But you told me.'

'There was just the once. It never happened again.'

'He must have asked. You must have said something.'

'Soph, listen. I had no idea. What's important now is to get you a decent lawyer.'

Ann telephoned from another room. She came back and said, 'I explained that it was urgent. Pat Holmes, I went to school with her. She's a top divorce lawyer. She'll see you at one-thirty.'

'Where have you been?' asked Sophie.

'In Sydney, at a conference. I'm sorry about Andover Street, but it was a gamble from the start.' Ann stared at Sophie unapologetically. 'What are these photos, anyway?'

'I'm not sure, but I can guess.' In as few words as possible, Sophie told Ann about Jack.

Ann swallowed hard. 'Leave it to Pat. She'll know what to do.'

The solicitor's office was all veneer, dark wood veneer arranged to resemble walnut. Veneer leather, building even, in the middle of Civic, looking down on traffic. The office was on the eleventh floor. Windows offered a view of the university. A great park it looked like, full of plastic trees.

The lawyer was well-dressed, with dark red lipstick and nail polish, thick hair. She regarded Mrs B and Sophie with the confidence of a busy schedule that had nevertheless made room for them.

Sophie introduced herself, holding the letter tightly, as she had done all the way there.

She glanced at Mrs B, sitting with her knees together on the edge of her chair. The chairs were so close that their legs were almost touching. Sophie felt tension flair between their two pairs of knees, then circle the office, inserting fingers under the veneer. She handed over the letter, not trusting herself to speak again, dreading the moment when the lawyer finished reading.

She thought of Mrs B's velvet dressing gown and how it matched this woman's lipstick. She wished she'd taken more care with her own appearance, then reminded herself that the solicitor faced angry, distraught women every day. She knew something about professional demeanour, could try to let herself sink under it, and use its threads to anchor her.

Mrs B had pinned up her hair in a hurry, and it had released most of itself from its pins already. She'd brought nothing with her, not even a handbag.

The solicitor looked up. 'Where's your daughter now?'

'With her father,' Sophie said, and explained about their split week arrangement, worked out without the family court, arrived at without rancour.

'Neither of you has applied for custody?'

'Not till now.'

'You've been separated for how long?'

'Nearly nine months.'

'And you'd no idea your husband was intending this?'

'No idea at all.'

'Have you spoken to your husband since he sent the letter?'

'The last time I spoke to him was when we swapped Tamsin over.'

'Did he raise the issue of your ability to care for Tamsin?'

'No.'

'These photographs that he refers to – what are they?'

'I don't know for sure, but – ' Sophie told her about Andover Street. She listened without comment, then explained that before they went any further, she needed to see the photographs, establish proof of their existence. Andrew could be lying, bluffing. Custody battles brought out the worst in people, too often were decided on lies, on the whims of one partner or the other.

Sophie said, 'We weren't having a custody battle.'

'Well, now you are. You didn't tell your ex-husband where you were working. You must have expected a negative reaction.'

Sophie said, 'Even in my nightmares, I never expected this.'

The solicitor rang Andrew's lawyer, said 'Yes,' and 'Yes, I see.'

She put down the phone and told Sophie, 'They're sending over copies. It might be half an hour.'

She asked them to wait outside, not looking at Sophie, or at Mrs B, but at a spot on the wall between them, behind Sophie's right shoulder and Mrs B's left, her favourite spot, Sophie guessed, when not wishing to look directly at a person.

Pat Holmes passed across half-a-dozen photographs of Sophie and Jack. There was the front room, in the early afternoon, with the curtains pulled right back. Sophie held the whip above her head, right arm tense and ready. Jack crouched in a corner with his teeth bared, scrabbled on all fours, knelt on the towel with his right hand raised.

That same arm of hers – Sophie glanced down at it with surprise – had pulled the curtains back, to let in what might turn out to be the last warmth of the season.

Where was Jack now? Sophie pictured him walking with his bouncing gait up to a stranger's door, introducing himself to the girl who opened it, and responding to the words, 'I don't do bondage,' with 'You can learn.' She heard Jack's voice as though he was sitting next to her, that tone which was entirely his, which brought the possibility of learning up so close. It made a person's hackles rise, so that a person stood aside and said, 'Come in.'

'I take it this is authentic,' the solicitor was saying. 'It is you, and you were whipping this man?'

'Yes,' Sophie said.

The sun made shimmering balls of light across the carpet in the front room. Jack's towel was almost hidden under them. Blood might have spurted out onto the towel, but had not.

Sophie swallowed, and asked about legal precedent. The lawyer said that she was not aware of one. Sophie asked if the pictures could be used to prove she was a bad mother, unfit to care for her own child.

Custody was usually determined, the solicitor explained, according to criteria like income, who *had* been looking after the child, and so on. A criminal record, especially one involving violence, would be considered relevant.

'I don't have a criminal record.'

'That's something, then.'

The court appearances, the publicity Andrew would make sure she was subjected to, the hatred between them – once it began, or, since Andrew had started it, once she joined in battle – at the end of all this Tamsin would be the loser, must be. Yet Andrew must have doubts. He must have hung onto the photographs for weeks before deciding what to do with them.

The solicitor spoke again to Andrew's on the phone. She would draft a letter for Sophie to sign. She called this step one. There was no need for Sophie to confront her ex-husband. The lawyer used the word with great precision. Sophie was to stay right away, was not to phone or attempt to see him.

But she could not sit in her flat and watch the walls. She phoned Andover Street to find the number had been disconnected. She tried Ann, got her machine, hung up. The walls went round and round. She looked up the solicitor's name in the phone book. Holmes, P.L. When she came on the line there might be music in the background, the sounds of dinner being served. All very well, Sophie might say, to order me to stay away from Andrew. When a truck comes hurtling through your house, can you sit there and wait?

Mrs B offered to cook a meal, but Sophie said that she would go to bed. Mrs B did not try to hide her relief. Sophie vacuumed Tamsin's room and tidied her daughter's already neat belongings. She rang Ann's number again, and this time left a message. She sat by the phone, waiting to pick up the receiver and hear Ann's voice.

She recalled sitting in the lawyer's office on fake leather chairs. Why was she trying to convince herself that they were fake? Why had she fixed on this? Because of the photographs, which she *so much wished to disprove*. The solicitor could afford real leather, the leather in that office had been real. The photos were indelible, branded on her forehead, on her arms and legs.

Sophie pictured Mrs B in her large house, sitting over a solitary meal in her red dressing-gown with her hair down. Her kindness, her willingness to be of use, had its limits. Nothing unreasonable in that. Mrs B would open one of her albums and sit there looking at it till she felt tired enough to sleep.

Andrew would be boasting, gloating, popping bubbles at his ex-wife's expense, saying to the aunty of the moment, *I fixed her*, while his daughter slept with one ear open in the next room.

The town swallowed and made way for the people who trundled through Sophie's tired, unresting mind. There was Ann, who was avoiding her. There were Marshall and Elise, whose phone was disconnected and business plans in ruins. But Sophie guessed that Elise had planned what would happen if circumstances rose up to slap them, as circumstances had, planned that Marshall would take the rap, when raps were given out. Good luck to her, she thought.

Sophie hated Andrew for his clear-cut and decisive ways, his brandishing – it seemed a sword, pulled out of burning water – of the law against her. She hated him for all his decisions, the one he'd made to leave her, and those that flowed from that. She hated him for writing to her through a solicitor. They might have talked, might have teased out some sort of compromise, might even have reached the point of admitting their rafts had not been floating so very far apart. But then she admitted to herself that Andrew *had* tried to talk. She'd refused to answer his questions. She'd reacted angrily, telling him he had no right. She pictured herself and Andrew weighing up issues of morality under the crab-apple tree, discussing shades of right and wrong, a luxury it was too late for now.

The question Sophie kept coming back to was, Where will I go from here? The whole of Canberra seemed dangerous – not just Kingston, with its new apartments round the shopping centre, couples young and rising in the world, Andover Street with its abandoned house, its backyard ready to be planted out for spring. Fyshwick and Mitchell, where the business future lay, seemed just as treacherous, as did the central triangle of parliament, family court and government offices, so clean and straight they might have passed from a design board to the air between kept trees – might have done this, been erected, without human intervention.

She'd almost asked, back in the solicitor's office, if she could keep one of the photographs. Evidence was suspect, wasn't it? Even the most concrete. But those particular documents could not have been faked. She tried to think of facts that might condemn her ex-husband, and how they might be won. She pictured herself lurking under bedroom windows in what used to be her house, clicking shutters, carrying her prizes away. There would be no whip for her to capture, in black and white or colour, but she might freeze positions, movements and contortions, crouching in bushes by the master bedroom. Mentally, she measured the distance between this and proof that Andrew ought not to be allowed to care for Tamsin.

She came back to the whip, Jack on his hands and knees, picked out and cast forever, moulded by the winter sun. Ambushed by the camera, Jack had looked pale and thin, but strong, panting, as an athlete might, at the end of a well-run race.

All her ideas, the images that walked into her mind and out again, were useless. She could mull over how Andrew had found out, but that was useless too. If there *had* been doubt, if doubt was what had kept him waiting, it might provide a chance, but she could not think how. She recalled the times she might have told him, when courage had slipped out of her grip, or when she'd dropped it. Or when greed, the desire to buy pretty things and go on buying them, had been stronger than the impulse to confess.

The Family Court

Sophie stood on the Family Court steps and looked straight ahead into the building. She remembered the news reports after one of the judges had been shot, blood draining off the concrete, on the television. The underground car park was supposed to be the safe way for staff and judges to enter the building, to avoid enraged and maddened husbands – it seemed always to be husbands – waiting at the front with guns. Car to lift, two steps, guards on either side to block the bullets.

Sophie studied the building and watched well-dressed people come and go. Try as she might, she could not see herself and Andrew there, being counselled, making cases, while another, supposedly well-meaning counsellor questioned Tamsin, wrote her answers down.

Her mind went blank at the prospect of living without Tamsin. But surely she would be allowed to visit. There would be weekends later on, after Andrew had got over his anger. Mrs B would not pester her for rent, but there would be rent to think of, when the money from Andover Street ran out, if Mrs B allowed her to stay in the flat.

The clear, thick lines of the Family Court were repeated everywhere that Sophie looked, clean lines with the confidence of sun on them. Sophie realised she hadn't, until that moment, believed in the permanence of buildings. She'd seen Canberra's architecture rather through

Ann's eyes, Ann who'd fashioned a moon path for a single woman, floating, shell-shaped ceilings for a bunch of whores.

Though Ann's designs might seem fragile, over-decorative – Sophie remembered Kirsten's mocking laugh – they gave a person something to put her shoulder to, to live for. If this was a contradiction, it was a necessary one. Sophie thought of the model in Ann's cupboard, a rejected sleeping beauty. But there remained what Ann had taught her about visions, what Ann herself claimed to have been taught, about the grasp and falling back, failure to measure up, and then the glimpse of grace.

On the eleventh floor of the legal building, P.L. Holmes sat upright and solemn at her desk. She seemed to be wearing exactly the same clothes, same make-up as the time before. Her movements and voice seemed speeded up, like in the nature programs Sophie and Tamsin sometimes watched with Mrs B, marvelling at what a camera could do. 'Look at that, Sophia!' Mrs B had exclaimed at a blackberry vine scuttling across the screen, rewarded by Tamsin's high, delighted laughter.

Mrs B was working in her garden now, while Sophie sat listening to the lawyer.

'I've talked it through, not with your husband directly, but with O'Farrell's office. People get mad, they thrash about, make threats. Dangerous, but it passes. Then you can negotiate.' She paused for a second. 'Others plan.'

Sophie nodded. 'Andrew's a planner,' she said.

The solicitor pursed her red lips. 'I'll contest your husband's claim, if you want me to. I'll fight your case. But it will be a fight. Have you got anything on him?'

Veneer lifted from the corners of the desk, the chairs. The fine, dark red leather must be vinyl underneath. The photographs of Jack and Sophie turned the paper they were printed on into large, misshapen questions. Jack and Sophie. Sophie. Jack. Everything was out of place, thin where it ought to have been solid, and solid where it should be paper-thin, to be ripped up, once used, and thrown away.

Events needed only the littlest change, really, using a fast frame camera. Out the window and across Marcus Clarke Street, the Family Court was as close as the crow flew, or a stone. Visitors to the legal building, finding that they had no business there, might fly down the lift and out. Men shot their wives at the entrance. Judges had body-guards. In the underground car park, blood flowed over concrete, its smell mingling with car exhausts. It was fascinating, the way the city lived in layers, the way these layers might choose, or not choose, to reveal themselves.

Sophie swallowed hard and said, 'Nothing that would show he's a bad father. In any case, I've decided not to challenge his claim.'

The solicitor did not try to hide her relief. 'Well,' she said, 'if that's really your decision.'

'I do have one request,' said Sophie.

'Yes?'

'Tomorrow's the day for me to pick Tamsin up from preschool, my turn to have her for three days. I'd like – I don't know how much her father will have told her, but I'd like to have her with me, one last time. I'd like to prepare her for the changes in my own way.'

'I'll ask,' the lawyer said, 'but I think the answer will be no.'

Sophie took this for the dismissal it was intended to be, and left.

She waited all that afternoon for the phone to ring and, when she could no longer bear the waiting, got into her car and drove to Civic.

She crossed the street near the corner of the pet shop, bearing in mind that Jack, being a creature of habit, might well pass that way. It might be one of his tracks across the city. Each time she'd been out with Tamsin, she'd pushed this consideration down, but now she wanted to find Jack again.

She bumped into a woman in a hurry, with a baby and a toddler. The toddler made a dash for the shop window. His mother glared at Sophie and yanked him by the arm.

She walked – suddenly, it didn't matter where – but found herself at her car again, and drove to Fyshwick, to the brothels and their discreet dispersal among used car yards and shops selling computers. She cruised up and down, looking for red hair almost curly, denim shirt undone one button too many.

She parked and sat in the car for a long time. Business was brisk. She remembered it was payday. One man emerged doing up his fly. He disappeared quickly. She thought, Oh my paws and whiskers, the duchess, and then, Did I really see that? Was he really in so much of a hurry?

Sophie leant her arms on the steering wheel and decided, I will not cry now, not here. She thought of Mrs B, her kindness and her way with alibis, her contempt for self-pity, her patience at an end. She conjured Jack from between squat buildings with no tickets on themselves. She thought of whistling, and of Jack's response from way across the city. If he appeared, she would thank him for helping that day with the client who was causing trouble. She would not blame him for the photographs. She would say goodbye. The twin possibilities, of greeting and farewell, were more shocking to her just then than the whip, the towel.

A raw pine smell hung about the street. Soft winter undulations of light turned hard and cracked. The street buckled underneath them. Pale blue curves could crush a person. That could happen quickly!

Sophie got out of the car and stood on a corner. She moved towards a tree. It stretched its thin and faithless branches out to meet her. She looked back at the corner. Was it safer there? The curb swayed, then the gutter. The line of the curb was a long, soft arc, though underneath it must be sharp, a right angle, first this way and then that. In just this way the square, the rectangle, the sharp and hidden corner.

'Look out!' she called.

Leaves from recent rains, left over from autumn, crowded at a grating that led underground. They held each other up, brown with a pink stain, as though blood had been mixed with them as compost. The tree on the corner was a prunus plum. Its twigs, even its larger branches, were covered in spikes. Sophie held the trunk. Behind her cars, trucks, semitrailers massed, it seemed without a destination. They all appeared to be driving in circles, so that, a few minutes after seeing one lot pass, she saw the same again.

If they were travelling in circles, on endless roundabouts, they did not seem to know it. There was no push up and out, over the hurdle of the gutter and across the curb, though Sophie kept hold of her tree trunk as a small precaution, watching drivers who looked identical inside their vehicles. And over all the blue waves continued and were broken up, as though blue was the colour of geometry, and – they were intimately connected – the colour of boundaries, and judgment.

'Jack! Jack!' she called, as though he were a dog and she had lost him.

She imagined herself driving to Andrew's house, pulling up outside, walking to the front door, knocking. She pictured Andrew coming to the door in his pyjamas. Blood would flow down the porch steps as she backed away, not slowly, not fast. There were places in Fyshwick where she might buy a weapon, or, if not here, across the border, in New South Wales.

Blood would flow down the steps of her old house, in the light of the clear winter night she had chosen for revenge. The phrase 'family home' seemed pregnant with just this possibility. Sophie thought of other weapons, of her whip drowned in the lake. She smiled to herself as she pictured fish swimming in and out between the leather fronds. Her mind lay open, waiting for details to slot into place.

Driving back across the lake, straddling the long arc over Burley Griffin, she thought once more of the Andover Street house, suspended between illegal and legal, and of how it might remain there, just as she might remain forever on the bridge, while beneath her dark, unnatural water beckoned. The arc pleased her, and water that would take the offer of a body, swallowing it whole.

There was a message on her answering machine from Pat Holmes, saying that Andrew had agreed to her having Tamsin one last time. Sophie could pick up her daughter from preschool the next day.

She rose bright and early. There was so much to do. She cleaned the flat more thoroughly than she had since moving in, finding small objects that had been given up as lost – a pink plastic ring one of Tamsin's preschool friends had given her, two fifty dollar notes that had fallen from the back of the drawer where she had stuffed her earnings before opening a bank account.

She kept expecting Mrs B to call in, and was grateful when she didn't. She had not worked out what explanation she would offer her landlady, or if she would offer one at all.

She called by the grocer's, not to shop, but to pick up a bootload of cardboard boxes.

Methodically and calmly, she began to pack. Into cardboard boxes, cushioned in newspaper, went her yellow cups and saucers, and a few more fine things she had bought. Clothes fitted into cases. She wasted long moments staring at the Yamaha. Perhaps she would leave her note for Andrew on its keyboard, the note that would enrage him further. But she and Tamsin would be gone by then.

Tamsin was tired and disinclined to talk. In the car on the way home she leant against the window frame and closed her eyes. Sophie had to coax her out, and it was easy, for once, to leave her bag on the back seat.

Inside the flat, Tamsin blinked and rubbed her eyes, then walked slowly over to the Yamaha, by some instinct homing in on one item that would not be moved.

She climbed onto the piano stool, but sat facing her mother and the room.

'We're going on a trip,' said Sophie.

'Where to?' Tamsin blinked again.

'To a nice beach,' Sophie said, improvising rapidly.

Tamsin's small, alert, upturned face searched for understanding.

'It'll be fun. We'll walk along the beach and find beautiful shells.'

'What about my things?'

'We'll take them with us. I'd like you to help me pack. Will you do that?'

'What about my piano?'

'It's too big, sweetheart.'

'Dad will be cross if I don't practise.'

'Then we'll find a way for you to practise when we get there.'

Tamsin let herself slide off the stool. But when, a few minutes later, Sophie poked her head around the doorway of her daughter's tiny room, Tamsin was lying on her side on the bed.

'Hey there,' Sophie said.

Tamsin's eyes were open, but she didn't move.

Sophie sat down and stroked the fair hair off her forehead, which was hot.

'I've got a heagate,' Tamsin said. She had not muddled up the word since she was two years old.

'Did you feel sick at preschool?'

'No. Will Mrs B be coming to the beach with us?'

'Not straight away,' said Sophie. 'Are you thirsty? What about a glass of juice?'

Tamsin sat up to drink, and some colour came back to her face.

Sophie planned to leave soon after nightfall. Easier to get away in the dark. If Mrs B heard the car, she might think they were going up to Ann's. She hoped, though, that Mrs B had not seen Tamsin. On the other hand, if Tamsin really was coming down with something, perhaps they ought to wait till morning, get a good night's sleep.

She went on with her packing in the other rooms, an ear open for her daughter, who, she discovered when she next poked her head around the door, was sitting propped against the edge of her bed sorting through her books, placing each one fastidiously in a cardboard box.

Sophie sighed and wondered how she'd ever thought that she might hurry Tamsin along. She continued with her own packing, calculating how much the car would hold, deciding that their bikes would definitely have to stay behind. That line about the beach and shells had popped into her head when she'd needed an activity that might appeal to Tamsin. But there was nothing wrong with the idea, she decided, conscious that before long she would need to write notes to Mrs B and Andrew, or Mrs B at least. She couldn't leave that till the morning.

A beach somewhere on the south coast, not a resort popular with Canberra residents – further south perhaps. And not a hamlet either, but a town big enough for one woman and her child to lose themselves in. She must husband her savings, spend them wisely, and she would have to get a job. She would change her name, and Tamsin's. Perhaps her lie to Andrew about waitressing would turn out to be true.

They'd be off at first light, or even before. Once Tamsin was asleep, Sophie would steal into her daughter's room and finish off her packing, in the dark if necessary.

She prepared a simple meal, which Tamsin nibbled at. She made tea and sat with her hands around the pot. She looked down at her red hands, and was grateful for the sharp and painful heat.

She listened nervously for Mrs B's knock on the door, pictured Tamsin running to her in greeting, grabbing her around the thighs, Mrs B pretending to be winded, Tamsin's high voice fluting, 'We're going to the beach!'

But the short evening passed without incident, or interruption, and Tamsin was content to go to bed early.

Now, thought Sophie, I'll really have to get a move on. She'd filled the car with petrol. At least that much was done. For the next two hours she sweated, lugging boxes, fretting over space. Tamsin's essential belongings went first into the boot. They took up more room than Sophie would have liked. She squashed her own things in around them, then began filling the back seat. Tamsin would have to sit with her legs stretched out horizontally.

She couldn't help making some noise, heaving back and forth. There were lights on at the front of the house. She hoped that Mrs B was occupied, and had her windows closed. She sat down, in the small breakfast alcove, to write the notes that she'd been putting off. She held a pen above a sheet of paper, but words refused to come. A single lamp magnified the piano's shadow, and cast its light on bare walls. The room seemed foreign. She and Tamsin had used the flat without paying attention to its origins. She had never thought, in all the times she could have, to ask Mrs B who'd lived in it before.

She heard a soft knock, tentative at first, then a little louder.

She stood just inside the door. 'Who's there?'

'It's me, Soph. Open up.'

Ann grabbed Sophie by the shoulders, her face excited, flushed. She took in the dismantled flat.

'What's going on?'

'Shh. Keep your voice down. We're leaving first thing in the morning.'

Sophie's legs crumbled. She sat down on the chair she'd left only seconds before, and pushed the sheet of paper to one side. She *would* carry out her plan, even though the remaining boxes by the door threatened to topple, their insides dissolving like her legs. She opened her mouth to tell Ann that it was too late to stop her.

But Ann was grasping Sophie's hands, face pink, hair wet as though it had been raining.

'Listen, Soph! It might just work. It's not an honourable deal. But it is a deal and I think he'll stick to it.'

Bewildered, Sophie shook her head. 'What deal?'

But Ann did not want questions. Ann was like spun sugar, she who had been opaque, swarthy with her own ambitions. She'd spun out through the night to Sophie's flat.

'I couldn't stand it, so I went round there.'

'You went to Andrew's?'

'To his office. I met him after work. I argued with him. I said there were other ways of getting at you, getting back at you. He didn't have to use Tamsin. He shouted at me, said you weren't a fit mother. I thought, Good, let him get it off his chest. He said I should have told him what was going on, I should have stopped you. You were supposed to be my friend. You were stupid. The whole thing was unbelievably dangerous and stupid.'

Ann paused to take a breath.

Sophie said, 'I still don't understand.'

'I grovelled, Soph. It worked. You couldn't have, it was too late for that. But I could, so I did. It's a breathing space,' Ann went on cheerfully. 'He'll talk to his solicitor in the morning and I'll talk to Pat Holmes.'

'I told her I was giving in.'

'I'll deal with Pat. Leave her to me.'

For a moment, she was the old Ann, quick at grasping a construction problem. Her cheeks were red, her eyes wide and bright as a child's announcing Christmas.

'He wants me, Soph. That's what made the difference.'

Sophie pictured Andrew waking up in Ann's bed, the breathing space that Ann had made for her.

'I love you for this,' she said.

Ann looked around the room, but did not say a word about the boxes stacked and ready, never alluded to them, either that night, or in the weeks that followed, though there was a question at the back of her eyes sometimes, surprise that, whatever else she had expected Sophie to be doing, it was not running away.

In the morning, Sophie was sitting in the breakfast alcove, spooning sugar into grapefruit.

In her room, Tamsin sat up in bed, and blinked. The room was back to normal, her books lined up on the shelf below her soft toys. The box had gone from beside the door.

She'd slept in. The sun was bright underneath the curtains. She jumped up and ran to find her mother.

Sophie smiled and asked, 'Are you feeling better?'

Tamsin nodded, though she'd forgotten yesterday's fatigue, and sick had been her mother's word, not hers.

Sophie smiled again, and patted the seat next to her, but Tamsin stood looking up at her mother, frowning and uncertain.

'I decided we wouldn't take our trip to the beach just yet.'

'Why not?'

'Well, I got to thinking – you know how you asked if Mrs B could come?'

Tamsin nodded.

'What I thought was, it would be mean not to ask her. So let's put it off until summer, when it's warm enough to swim.'

Tamsin went on staring, and seemed about to challenge this version of events.

Then suddenly she wheeled and ran over to the Yamaha, raised the lid, careful not to let it thump, and climbed onto the stool.

Soft notes and chords, then louder, more aggressive ones, filled the garden flat.

Luck

An opportunity might arise, one day, for Sophie to tell Ann the whole story of her time at Number 10. For the present Sophie faced, at night in the dark, the path along which her grasp at independence and her will towards revenge had led her, and the reprieve Ann had devised. With luck and in good time, a lightness might develop from the inside, be felt, first of all, as a softening at the core of malevolent intent.

Sophie thought of Tamsin's ways of coping, and how miserable she'd been. She hadn't allowed her daughter's rules and rituals to worry her too much, preferring to ignore them in the hope that they would go away. She had refused to pay attention to Tamsin's unhappiness. She might have registered it, but she hadn't *seen*.

She woke before dawn, her body caught in a photographer's flash, and lay sweating and afraid of what Andrew knew about her – the unhusbandly knowledge that he'd stolen and might still use. He might seek, in anger or in self-defence, to steal Tamsin again. For the rest of her life, she would have to consider this, that there were many ways to turn a daughter's mind and her affections.

Sophie thought of Ann, who'd compromised herself for friendship. She understood, as she suspected Ann didn't, or not yet, how a compromised self might turn in the middle of the night and bare its yellow teeth. The self, or part of the self, that Ann had conceded in the interests and the name of friendship, was her will to choose, to say yes to this man if she fancied him, and no to that. Sophie had no doubt that Ann would stick to her side of the bargain, would say yes to Andrew as often as it took, and for as long. Practical and careful in her own way, Ann had cast off on a raft not of her own making. She would laugh if she saw another woman setting out on such a leaky vessel. For Ann, who had seemed to Sophie to be effortlessly independent, to have done this for *her*, made her wondering and grateful.

She asked herself how she would feel if Ann grew tired of Andrew, yet kept on seeing him, and how she could possibly repay her friend. The thought of Ann trapped, unhappy, not shrugging off her burden, made Sophie feel hot with anxiety and guilt. Perhaps Andrew would lose interest first, releasing Ann from her promise. But what if she'd grown fond of him by then?

She compared the contract Ann had entered into with her own trade-offs and negotiations, now sealed up forever in the side room, along with the carpet roses and the bed that rocked, John the Cyclist with the jacket of his suit pulled over his head, and Jack's ghostly outline on the wall. Lines blurred and reformed around what ought to be simple, but never was – a man and a woman together in a bedroom, by mutual consent.

In the afternoon, Sophie and Mrs B stood on the very edge of the lake, and stared at the water lapping at their feet. Another step, thought Sophie, and we'll be out of our depth.

'When was it flooded?' she asked.

'1963,' said Mrs B. 'But Sophia, it wasn't an Old Testament occasion. This lake took months to fill.'

Slow-lapping water was brown and cold, quiescent. The earth around it, that had not been flooded yet, was brown.

Mrs B told Sophie the story of how the valley floor had been turned into an artificial lake, burying a farm and racetrack. Sophie pictured her whip, then jockeys' silks fluttering in the breeze, glaring colours of the horses and their riders. Underneath the water's glaze, the excitement of a race about to start.

She imagined lying down at the new lake's edge, waiting for the water to move forward slowly, slowly, the way Mrs B had captured the event in the old photographs she kept in her album. Sophie studied her landlady with a new respect. Had Mrs B contemplated drowning, not as Sophie's whip had drowned, but inch by inch?

She felt for Mrs B as they stood there in silence, and sent her heart out towards her friend, through years back to the raw time when her son was killed. Her own threatened loss was shallow by comparison. She reached across and took Mrs B's hand, guessing why Mrs B had brought her there, what she'd wanted her to see.

Mrs B returned the pressure of Sophie's hand, but kept her eyes fixed on a point over the water. 'Running away, Sophia,' she said, with a slight shake of her head.

'You knew.'

'I saw you taking boxes.'

'You didn't try and stop me.'

'No. I'm sorry for that.'

'Don't be. It's okay.' Sophie went on after a moment. 'You came down here, when your son died.'

'Every day I came.'

'What stopped you?'

'I think it was this lake itself, so flat and grey and shallow. And so slow, like a tortoise. I would have to wade far out, just to find a place.'

Sophie let go of Mrs B's hand, and put an arm around her shoulders, feeling thin, strong bones.

She said, 'Just think what you would have missed.'

'Yes.'

Sophie was adding up and counting. 'You'd have missed Tamsin,' she said.

The cycle that had begun with Andrew leaving her was ending now.

Sophie watched it move, while Mrs B went on staring out across the lake.

Tamsin was with her father again, with Andrew gracious in his moral victory. But there was the weekend to look forward to. No need for a public brawl, Andrew had told his solicitor. The lawyers were drawing up an agreement. Sophie and Andrew would share custody. It would be written down.

The circle of water where the whip had sunk was there, across from the gentle shore where they were standing. Sophie looked over at the place where she'd flung her weapon on a clear winter morning, while sun warmed the grass, and each blade held one precise, commanding shadow. She flexed the muscles of her right hand, picturing the whip embedded, handle down in mud, how the mud contained and might even preserve it. But what of the racetrack then, the farm? She thought of the leather fronds, those split ends of floating, underwater hair, moving back and forth, numbly, it might be, hypnotically, waiting for a natural tide, a tide that might once have been whispered about in promises, but would never arrive in the artificial lake.

Added to these memories now would be one of Mrs B lying down at the very edge, the boundary of the water, then losing patience, getting up, waving her long skirt so it would dry in the wind.

There was Tamsin to watch growing, Tamsin's fifth birthday party to plan, a party in the garden, a table covered with a linen cloth and piled with good things to eat. The earliest of the acacias would be in flower. Sophie was drawing up a list. The children who'd asked her daughter to parties, the friends she'd made at preschool, must be invited in return. John Trickett's name – though Tamsin had confessed to Sophie that she did not like him – was at the top of the list. Sophie hoped Tamsin's solemn approach to her obligations might slide, slip off her shoulders a little now. Ann would come to the party. Ann was making Tamsin a surprise present, and would not even throw out a hint, a crumb of a clue, as to what it might be.

The Gardening
Business

That night they made plans in Mrs B's kitchen, sitting at a wooden table cleared of the remains of a meal. The photograph albums with their red and yellow covers occupied a shelf under the window, not quite out of sight.

Mrs B said, 'We could make gardens for people.'

Sophie stared at her, then smiled. 'Why not?'

'We could start a gardening business,' they told one another.

Mrs B redistributed her weight, as though her body had been considering the proposal for a long time, and now had to deal with it. She smiled at Sophie, a slow smile, beginning with her mouth and moving up to her electric hair. She rubbed her hands together, but spoke with deliberation, as though her thoughts, if rushed out, might evaporate.

'Do you know, Sophia, I have a diploma from the Institute? In horticulture,' Mrs B said proudly, 'specialising in the landscape side.'

They laughed, exclaiming, 'Landscape designs! A big board at the front!'

They described for one another what it would be like, how they'd feel answering the doorbell, showing customers into a bedroom that would, by then, have been turned into an office. They glanced at one another sideways, surprised and delighted to catch, under the irony, a steely, professional intent. They would know what to do. They saw this instantly, and wondered why they had not taken stock of it before.

Mrs B fetched her diploma from the box where it had been packed along with other keepsakes. She unfolded it with careful fingers and examined it with her mouth closed tight, as though she expected it to crumble at the touch of her breath.

Smiling, she asked, 'Who will be our customers? Why will they choose *us*?'

They exchanged another wicked, calculating look. Sophie said, 'We'll advertise in all the right places. We'll be brilliant, you'll see.'

They began to speak again, in low tones this time, using words that asked for a different kind of attention than either had been used to giving or receiving – words like investment, profit and cash flow.

They would not need much capital, Mrs B said softly, testing the word against the roof of her mouth. Indeed, pooling their savings – 'My husband left me quite well off, Sophia' – she thought that they would have enough.

They would be selling ideas first of all. This they agreed on with a quick, assessing glance. Sophie said that she wouldn't mind the physical work. She would enjoy it. Ann would help them to find customers, would perhaps be able to pass her own clients on to them. They made a list of what equipment they would need, and mapped out a budget. It occurred to Sophie that her clerical skills, once dusted off, would stand her in good stead. She would teach Mrs B to use a computer, and teach herself to use programs that would model the designs.

Sophie stared into the darkness through the kitchen window, at a garden waiting for nothing more exceptional than the return of daylight. She looked back at Mrs B and sighed, as a great and singular weight was lifted from her.

Responsibility for Tamsin, facing clearly what it meant to be bringing up a daughter and providing for her, felt like getting out of bed after a long illness.

A few days later Sophie sat at her window in the breakfast alcove, waiting for Andrew to deliver Tamsin. She thought of Mrs B pursuing Jack along the driveway of the Andover Street house, recalling how she'd watched Jack running, and afterwards gone looking for him. This might be different slightly, or a large amount, in the re-telling, were she ever to tell the whole story of herself and Jack – to aim at truth, even if she could not reach it. She might stop with Jack outside a pet shop window, or walking through a locked door. She might end with waving a white handkerchief, or calling out goodbye. She might picture a red-haired man forever running down a driveway, forever escaping, he from her, and she from him.

Sophie sat at the window of her flat and stared out at the garden, rejoicing at the places the story had not stopped – how it included Ann tapping at her front door, flushed, exuberant.

There was a smell to the garden, of what was almost ready. Sophie nodded good morning to the fountain at his post, and thought how he might charm potential customers, so that they exclaimed, 'That's it! That's what I want exactly!'

'Where does the water come from?' a woman might ask. 'Where's the pump?'

Her voice would be curious and slightly puzzled. She would not expect a fountain under the crab-apple tree, and having found one there, would not know what to make of him.

Another customer might laugh, if either Mrs B or Sophie happened to mention his name, embarrassed at the oddness of it. Two eccentric women. Your own garden god, one versed in mythology might add. Their boy might turn out to be worth his weight in gold.

The city had lent Jack to her, and then taken him again. It was right and fitting that it should, just as it was right and fitting that the stolen statue should be named after him. Mrs B had wanted to call him Marshall, but Sophie had put her foot down. After all, it had been her idea to take him, a last minute idea when the house was already locked, and hoses filled the Datsun's boot.

The city had lent a living, breathing Jack to Sophie, then reclaimed him. He'd fallen back between its strong, straight lines. Sophie sat at the window, staring out, feeling relief and incompleteness, escaping, minute by minute, the consequences of her will towards revenge. She recalled her whip alighting centimetres from Jack's back. His impatience and his patience. The mistakes she'd made, her clumsiness, before her hand and right arm had become secure. She tasted what was left over from desires which must remain closed up now, in the house at Number 10.

Even Kirsten had turned away from examining this closely, the day Sophie had broached it on the way to the doctor's, in the car. It had been Sophie's way to bring up things that mattered at the wrong time, when the other couldn't possibly, and then to say, Oh well.

It was Mrs B who'd chased Jack away, in the shadow of two policemen, the fear of their immediate return, one young, embarrassed, one older, with a blue walleye.

Jack, Jack, Sophie whispered, waiting for the return whisper of her breath on glass. Your back – let me run my fingers over it, let me kiss your fish tattoo. But there was no answer, and she could not go on sitting at a window, staring out at one tree, or many through a glass. No more than she could say, and mean it, now I can forget.

The morning, this morning, was well underway. In an hour or less, Tamsin would arrive.

Sophie walked outside. The garden wore its layers of cultivation lightly. Perhaps this would draw customers, without their knowing why. She passed the rhododendrons, the daphne and camellias. Jack seemed to smile in greeting as she moved towards him. He seemed to lift his head and say, 'Here I am, right where you did not expect to find me.'

It was good to have him there, stone statue, satyr in disguise. The moss and lichen were coming along nicely. It was good for Mrs B to share this secret. Sophie recalled her drawer full of money, in the days before she got around to banking it, the way the notes had fluffed and preened. It would not be unreasonable if she should be charged with theft.

She rested her hands on Jack's stone temples. She only had to look at him to be reminded of a truth that seemed a long way from what he *ought* to represent, a truth which declared that the bottom could fall out of houses, and what people sought to make in them, whether marriage, or a place of work. Roofs could lift, without warning, off the shelter families sought. Decay could rend and tear all in a moment, or creep dankly from unnatural water. Or there could be a narrowing, to the point where destruction waited at the centre of a flower.

Sophie stroked Jack's head. Soon water would flow out of the bag of arrows on his back, into a small oblong pool, where lilies and other plants would become established. Goldfish would be tickled by the stream of water. The roughness of the stone against her fingers gave her pleasure. She pressed down, as though she could make indentations in it.

A pair of wings were small, folded and symmetrical, simply stylised and almost without artistry. They brought home to Sophie, standing in the quiet garden, the idea that crimes might be added on top of one another. Theft might be added to deceit, or the other way around. The list, once begun, might grow. Prostitution might be counted a beginning. Lies might build, gradually, or suddenly. The line between deceiving someone – deceiving an ex-husband, say, because he'd wronged you, and deceiving him out of the pleasure of it, out of lust – might turn out to be no line at all.

For a fountain designed to remain in one spot, where water ran, Sophie reflected that this one had already moved about quite a bit. She ran the pads of her fingers over his head once more, then along his arrow pouch and raised right arm, admiring the design and contours, tilt of curls, weapon at the ready, arm of an exacting fleshiness, dimple in the elbow there. Sophie pinched it, in the clear wintry light. She relived the simple crime, lugging him into Mrs B's car, then driving off as though their hands were clean. How good taking him had made her feel. And how fitting afterwards to settle him under the crab-apple tree.

She thought of the mystery that could accrue around a person or a thing. A thing couldn't answer back, couldn't say, Oh no, it was *this* way, not *that*. Jack seemed to smile, in a sly and knowing way, while Sophie stood there, while memories descended on her from the bare tree, and nobody appeared to rake them up. His plump thighs ensured a kind of modesty, one arm forever fixed in the act of releasing an arrow. Who was to judge which attitudes, which gestures, would be the ones to define a person – which invited wickedness, which might turn out to be good?

Jack might stay till Mrs B died and Sophie left, not wanting to remain without her friend. The young couple who bought the house might decide he wasn't to their taste. Or it might be something other than taste, or in addition to it, the sense of mystery surrounding an object that, with its owners gone, could never be enlarged on or elucidated. This feeling might be irritating. It might produce a sudden need to scratch.

When an object is lost, the mystery surrounding it becomes distorted, growing into weirder shapes, strengthening with loss or unexplained removal, growing more potent over time. Visitors approaching the statue in the future, after Sophie was buried in the earth, might feel unsettled without knowing why, and decide they did not like this feeling, would prefer to live without it.

Sophie gave thanks for what she had been allowed to borrow, as well as what she'd taken without leave. She said thank you for the uses to which, in this breathing space she had been granted, her lessons might be put.

Tamsin stood on the doorstep, at her feet a heavy, well-used bag. There was a line of perspiration at her hairline, and her face was pale.

Sophie bent down. Tamsin raised her face to accept her mother's kiss. Sophie saw that she was curled tight as the tautest spring.

'I'll take that,' she said gently, reaching for the bag.

Tamsin did not speak. Instead, she stared at her mother out of huge brown eyes, Andrew's eyes. Sophie had not admitted to herself, until that moment, how physically alike her daughter and ex-husband were.

With slow, deliberate movements, Sophie picked up the bag and took it to her daughter's room, while Tamsin looked around her with quick glances, alive to the smallest change.

'Come here,' Sophie said.

Tamsin lifted one foot, then the other.

'See,' said Sophie, when her daughter was sitting on her knee in the breakfast alcove. 'What if we set up the birthday table out there?'

'What's that?' asked Tamsin, pointing.

'That's Jack. He's a fountain, or he soon will be.'

'How?'

Sophie began explaining about a pump, and pipes laid underneath the earth.

Tamsin frowned. Sophie said, 'Let's go out and see.'

They walked hand in hand, Tamsin stepping carefully, as though the path, the grass, the apple tree, the fountain, all might break beneath her.

She put out her other hand and ran her fingers lightly over Jack's stone head, then turned to stare once more at her mother, with wide eyes that the sun caught, young face with its mask of careful dignity, its premature reserve.

Light footsteps on the path announced Mrs B carrying a tray, three glasses, lemonade. Sugar crusted a glass jug. Pale yellow liquid washed from side to side.

Tamsin ran forward with a cry of joy.

Sophie smiled, standing back and picturing a garden full of children, sausage rolls on paper plates, and chocolate cake, some squashed in the grass, that they would pick up later. A birthday hat would perch on Jack's stone curls.

Tamsin ran back, laughing. 'Will Dad be coming to my party?'

Sophie hesitated, then she said, 'I'll ask him.'

Tamsin knelt to brush a few dead leaves off the wooden table. 'Here,' she said, and then, to Mrs B. 'Can I sit on your knee?'

A New Place

'What do you think ladies?' Kirsten asked.

Sophie looked around and said, 'There's no room for a garden.'

Elise, Sophie and Kirsten were examining the back of the premises. It was a concrete square. You could sweep and keep it tidy. There were no weeds even in the cracks. It was worse than the backyard of Number 10 in the dog days of the summer.

Elise said. 'We could manage something.'

'A courtyard?' suggested Kirsten.

Having been absent for the making over of Number 10's backyard, Kirsten was not as sensitive about it as she might have been.

'Fuck a courtyard,' Elise said.

Sophie thought of the ground bush she had liked the best, with its small blue pointed flowers, that day at the garden centre. She thought of the business she and Mrs B were launched on, how Kirsten had given it her blessing, when she'd rung to ask if Sophie wanted to look at a new place in Fyshwick, and said they'd value her opinion.

The rent was what you'd expect, Elise said, unlocking a blue door. There was the option of buying, but not immediately. She'd want to see how things panned out first. There was the sale of the Kingston house to organise, she added, with the confidence of a woman who had money in the bank, in her own name.

Elise had lost her effervescence, and there was no doubt that she was in charge. She was sharing Kirsten's flat for the time being. Watching them together, Sophie saw how thoroughly Marshall had been left behind.

Elise was still going to the gym every other day, and keeping up her yoga. She held this over Kirsten as a routine that should not be allowed to slip. Of course, Kirsten needed to get completely better first. At least she'd quit smoking, Elise said, while Kirsten smiled and shoved her hands in the pockets of her coat.

The rooms were poky little boxes, hardly wide enough to hold a bed. But they would, each one of the three would, just.

'No room to swing a cat,' Elise said.

They were silent for a moment, recalling other rooms and the plans that had been made for them.

The house at 10 Andover Street felt like a drop of rainwater to Sophie then, a single drop of water, disappearing between foundations all the more solid for having absorbed it. She licked her lips, as though to catch the taste of something that had already evaporated. The trade she'd shared with Elise and Kirsten would continue to grow here, now that it was legal, where it had never left off growing, where the politicians, for good and practical reasons, had voted to keep it under their control. For who *did* want a brothel on their street, worst of all opposite, or right next door? Not the residents, and not the girls either, in the long run. It was too much trouble.

Sophie felt herself begin to sway, unbalanced, as though one hip, one knee, stood higher than the other. She put out a hand to steady herself, and looked down at her legs. Kirsten leant forward. For a second, they balanced one against the other, Kirsten holding Sophie by the hand.

She smiled again and said, 'At least the rooms are airconditioned.'

Sophie waited for the sarcasm, the tail with its sting. But it was Elise who said, 'Airconditioning's not healthy. Maybe airconditioning's what made you sick.' She took note of Kirsten's expression and went on, 'I'm serious. Haven't you ever heard of a sick building? There's heaps of them in this town. It's a growing concern. And there's legionnaire's disease.'

'I got tested for legionnaire's disease.'

'Well you *could* get it. So could I.'

'I thought you liked airconditioning,' said Kirsten.

'I never did. Airconditioning was Marshall's idea.'

'Where is Marshall?' Sophie asked.

'I don't know,' Elise said, her tone warning Sophie against asking any more about him.

Sophie held her tongue, but pictured Marshall one last time, not the Marshall of the TV interviews and charges of attempted bribery, but Marshall holding up the fence at Number 10, back to the setting sun, Marshall the good husbandman, checking that all was well, all would be well, till morning. This other Marshall, Marshall with his sting removed, made Sophie smile. She was tempted to tell Elise and Kirsten about the fountain, where he was, what had become of him.

She didn't though, and Elise said nothing further by way of explanation. The trial date had been set, but neither Elise nor Kirsten mentioned it.

What if Marshall was convicted, Sophie wondered, had to pay a hefty fine, what if he was sent to jail as an example? Would Elise care? Might she be glad? Of course, it could be that Elise simply had no wish to explain how matters stood between them. Let Sophie think whatever she wanted, let her make what she would of the fact that Elise and Kirsten were together again, would be working together again soon.

Kirsten was to start off as the receptionist. Later on, with the return of warmer weather, who could tell?

'We'll see what happens,' Elise said in a more friendly voice, conceding Sophie's presence at the inspection, if not entirely happy with it.

For the time being then, a pale yet cheerful Kirsten, much stronger than when Sophie had last seen her, would earn her honest dollar by answering the phone, taking down appointments, chatting to and chatting up the regulars. She would sit at a small shapely desk and be responsible for front of house, although the premises was not a house, and never could be, such a house as the three of them had known.

Elise would hire two new girls, and here Kirsten would prove useful as well, keeping them in line.

All of this made sense to Sophie, as Kirsten and Elise went over it between them, Kirsten frowning lightly. Receptionist was all very well, Kirsten's frown said. Receptionist would do for the time being, but it lacked an edge, both the word and occupation, the edge Kirsten had come to expect as part of her idea of herself, a necessary ingredient in the making up of who she was.

'We'll have to advertise,' Elise said.

'The downside,' Kirsten made a face, 'will be increased competition.'

'Oh downside upside. We'll get off to a good start.'

Kirsten and Elise laughed with their arms around each other. They laughed at the idea of making history, being pioneers, how the *Canberra Times* had referred to the legislation that had finally been passed as 'pioneering', and how Kirsten did not like this word, and mocked it, along with 'potential', and 'sex worker'. And Elise called her a twit, indulgently, and said what was 'pioneer' if not an old word, an ancient, if not honourable one? And Kirsten said that if Elise was a pioneer, then she, Kirsten, was a granny pioneer, being a career path whore, having already decided on this path while Elise was learning her times tables, getting her pigtails pulled. Elise said twit. Elise said rubbish, you're not *that* old, poor dear.

Sophie thought she could leave the two of them just like this, think of them always like this, sparring. If they did not have an object to hand for disagreement, they would find one. Whoosh! There it would be. She thought they were a couple, more than colleagues, less than married, who'd lost each other for a time, but that no longer seemed to matter so much now.

Marshall might reappear, in spite of Elise's determination to separate herself from him, in this time before the trial. He might turn out better in court than anyone predicted. The courtroom, evidence given under oath, might be the place where Marshall named his business partner and his girls. Such naming, now that Andrew knew her secret, had lost much of its power.

Or there might be another Marshall. Elise might fall for him, or use him and discard him. So many young men waiting in the wings, for a cue or opportunity. Competition might spur this or that one to gain a leading edge.

Sophie recalled Mrs B's presence in the Andover Street house, her refusal, in advance, to have anything to do with this new one, which was not a house, but a concrete block containing three rooms that would fit a bed in, just. There could be no kitchen, but nobody had mentioned that.

Ann insisted that she and Andrew were getting along fine. She looked well and prosperous. Her model had been bought by a naturopathic clinic. People who came to the clinic for a massage, or to discuss vitamin therapy or the use of aromatic oils, would find themselves inside purple rooms, with ceilings shaped like fans or shells. Clients who paid for acupuncture would lie on their backs, looking up. They might lie behind a screen. There might be music playing. Their vision would be filled by overlapping panels and colours of the sea at night. They would go home dazed and wondering. Custom would increase, and the clinic prosper.

Describing the sale to Sophie, Ann had been flushed and pleased. She had another house to build. The satisfied lawyer had spread the word around.

'Better than to have it gathering dust,' Ann had said, then, seeing Sophie's expression, 'Isn't it?'

'Gathering dust,' Sophie had repeated, and then, 'Yes, oh yes.'

Sophie would have liked to see the model once again, but did not know how to ask, or how it would affect her.

Elise and Kirsten stood with their arms around each other, sufficient for now, a pair, laughing because they recognised something of themselves in Sophie, that they had put behind them.

And Sophie realised that she preferred, if she must be on the move, if she must carry her mark with her, at least to leave it here and there, in passing. Of all the people she'd met and got to know at Number 10, Jack had answered this desire in her, accepting that the mark might – it was a chance you took – draw blood. Sophie should have thanked him for that much at least. Jack would have liked the gardening business. He would have understood that, too.

Mrs B was brave, and Sophie hoped to make a new and brave beginning with her. Ann would design whole houses, and make the most of the raft she'd chosen for her friend's sake. Kirsten was getting better. Elise would work the legal system, and the business, to her own advantage. Marshall waited in the wings.

But most of all there still was Tamsin, whom Andrew had not stolen after all. Love could be square cut, fitting in between all these acute and definite angles, or else sliding past, a curve in the darkness, then a glimpse of grace.

Arms around each other, Elise and Kirsten gave the new place a last look over. Then they closed the dark blue door and returned the key.

Acknowledgments

I'd like to thank my editor, Lois Murphy, for her unfailing good sense and good ideas, my agents, Jenny Darling in Australia and Michele Rubin in the United States, for their enthusiasm and support, and my publishers at Wakefield Press, Michael Bollen and Stephanie Johnston, for continuing to have faith in me. Thanks, too, to friends and readers who gave their time generously and helped this book along the way, including Ivor Indyk, Margaret Barbalet, Suzanne Edgar, Marion Halligan, Dorothy Horsfield, Lesley Fowler and Barbara Holloway.

One For The Master

Dorothy Johnston

When Helen Plathe sets out along the Barwon River path for her first day at Highlands woollen mill, she is following in the footsteps of her mother, her uncle and her grandfather. Inside Highlands' tall black gates, Helen is initiated into an extraordinary world and discovers its secret history.

Like a medieval castle, the bluestone tower of Highlands casts a long shadow over those who work there – the maverick Queenie Bisset, railing against a world of men who 'liked neat ideas, and liked their women to be neat as well'; Helen's uncle, Lennie Pritchard, tragically thwarted in his bid to make a new life outside the mill; young Wally Sullivan, torn between his family and his struggle to keep the mill afloat; and the mysterious Miss Foot, silent witness to the decline of an industry that has ruled the lives of the people along the river from generation to generation.

One For The Master was short-listed for the Miles Franklin Award.

For more information visit www.wakefieldpress.com.au

The Trojan Dog

Dorothy Johnston

'I should ask your department's accountant whether he's missing nine hundred thousand bucks.' This is the anonymous message that will change Sandra Mahoney's life.

When a powerful but unpopular bureaucrat is accused of theft and computer fraud, Sandra is convinced that the charge is false. But how to track down the culprit when almost anyone could be an enemy? In her search for the truth, Sandra finds herself in a battle of wits against an elusive and unscrupulous opponent, a battle in which no one's allegiance can be taken for granted.

The Trojan Dog is a compelling story of computer crime, loyalty and betrayal against the backdrop of a city – and a country – on the cusp of political change.

For more information visit www.wakefieldpress.com.au

The White Tower

Dorothy Johnston

'Here is the big major talent that publishers tell us no longer exists. If you combined the two strands of Ruth Rendell and her alter writing ego, Barbara Vine, you'd come close to Dorothy Johnston's talent.'

Ken Bruen

'Jumpers,' McCallum was saying. 'Jumpers are – well, in my experience jumpers are always badly disturbed. They choose to jump because it's so violent.'

A mild young man's addiction to a role-playing internet game has led to his death. Disturbingly, his suicide is a bizarre echo of his chilling execution in the game; his only note a digital mirror image of his own death.

But where do blame and responsibility lie, in a world where powerful men are as seductive as they are unscrupulous? Sandra Mahoney finds that the threads of truth and illusion can easily wind into a choking scarf of manipulation and deceit.

For more information visit www.wakefieldpress.com.au

Wakefield Press is an independent publishing and
distribution company based in Adelaide, South Australia.
We love good stories and publish beautiful books.
To see our full range of titles, please visit our website at
www.wakefieldpress.com.au.

 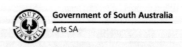

Wakefield Press thanks Fox Creek Wines
and Arts South Australia for their support.